RECKLESS goals

KATIE RAE

Reckless Goals

Nothing is more reckless than falling in love.....

<u>Rhys</u>

Despite being in my mid thirties and one of the world's best soccer players, I had never reached my main goals in life—to be a husband and a father.

But after being left heartbroken and alone on the night I planned to propose to my girlfriend, I realized how reckless that goal was.

Love, in general, was reckless....

In order to keep from self-destructing, I'm forced to train with college soccer star, Ashlynn Keller. She was young and naive, too caught up in her own life goals to focus on her game.

We were on very different paths in life, but we found common ground on the playing field. It may have been wrong, but sparks started flying between us. And when we finally gave in to each other, we realized that being a little reckless was exactly what we needed.

That is, until my ex showed up....

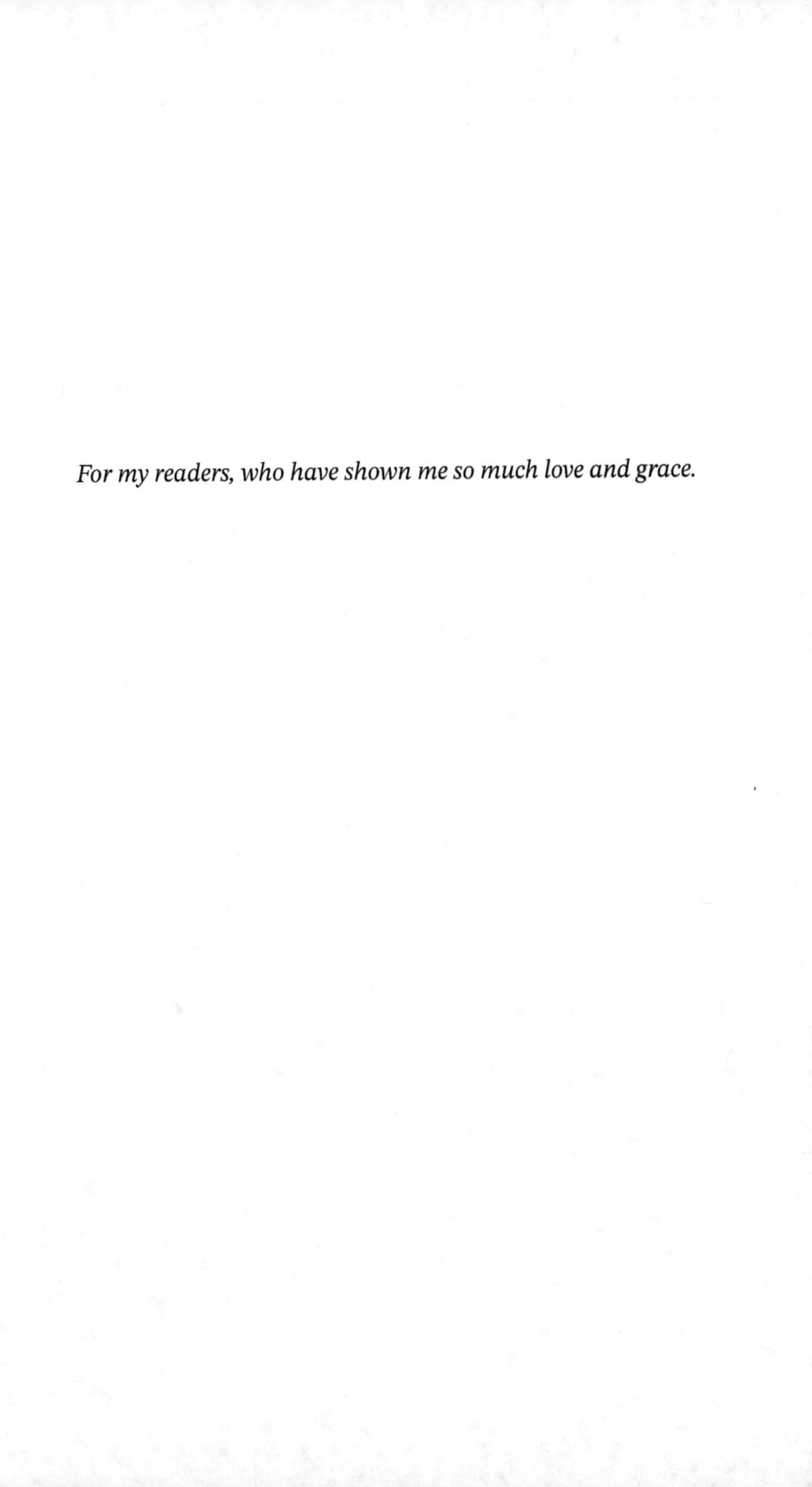

For my readers, who have shown me so much love and grace.

Prologue

Rhys

My head throbbed.

My body was wracked with pain.

My heart was broken.

Every night since Mel left, I had been living the same miserable existence. My very own *Groundhog Day* script. A loop of soccer practice, games, pushing myself to pain, and then falling into my bed at night, hoping sleep made me forget.

This wasn't supposed to be how the story ended.

I was miserable, intolerable.

"Back, back, back," my teammate, Cruz, yelled from his position in the goal. The entire team shifted at his command as the other team pushed down the field. When they took a shot on the goal, Cruz caught the ball, and punted it toward me.

The crowd was excited and started chanting my name. Despite the aches and pains in my body, I wanted to drive the ball all the way to the goal, but I was double teamed and would never make it. Choosing to pass it to Tripp instead, I let him drive up while I set up for another pass.

When Tripp kicked the ball back toward me, I didn't give my

opponents time to crowd me again. I took a long shot on the goal, aiming toward the left corner of the net. It flew past the reach of their keeper and in, making the home crowd scream even louder. *Let's Get Loud,* by Jennifer Lopez, played in the stadium while my teammates tried to congratulate me on the score.

I accepted their pats on my back and words of praise, but I stayed quiet, walking back to my position as the ball was brought to the center of the field. But my eyes scanned the crowd, just like they did every night for the last few weeks, always looking for the same thing.

Bright green eyes.

Always looking, but never finding them.

"*Que te folle un pez.*" A guy from the other team ran past me as we reset the field. I had no idea what he said to me, but it didn't sound like 'good job.' I guess he had no way of knowing how short my fuse was, so he didn't count on me turning toward him and approaching.

"Excuse me?" I realized the player was Hugo Garcia, a big name from Spain who was a renowned competitor, and spoke very little English. That meant whatever I said back to him, he may not interpret correctly. So to make sure he understood how I felt, I chose the universal language of throwing my fist.

Knocking him in the side of the face with a sucker punch, he fell, and I pounced on top of him trying to get another jab in. My teammates started pulling me away as his teammates did the same for him. The referees were blowing their whistles and the crowd was going wild.

I could hear my coach yelling from the sidelines for me to hit the showers, while Cruz had run all the way from the goal and was telling me to cool down. When I was sure I wouldn't get any more hits on Hugo, I turned toward the bench and marched off the field, assuming the referee had already flashed the red card, indicating my night was over.

As I walked, I glanced up one last time in the crowd, looking for green eyes.

"Do I need to bench you?" My coach asked when I passed him. But I kept walking, shrugging and letting him do whatever the hell he wanted to do. He couldn't afford to bench me, because despite how I reacted to Hugo, I was the leading scorer in the league.

When I got to my locker, I sat down and flexed my hand, looking at the blood that covered my knuckles. It had been a while since I'd thrown a barehanded punch, and it felt fucking good. Those days of boxing with gloves on to relieve stress may have to be a thing of the past. I wanted to feel more pain, see more bruises.

My phone started ringing, and I knew before looking that it was my brother. The game was being broadcasted on TV and he watched me play, when he could, from his place in Atlanta.

"What?" I answered.

"Do I need to fly down there and beat your ass?" He yelled. Levi was my favorite boxing partner, but living so far away from one another meant we didn't get much sparring in.

"Don't bring any gloves," I snapped back at him.

"Get your head together, little brother. Focus on what's important."

Levi, always the coach, always spewing advice. He was the dad I never had when I was younger, and the best friend I needed when I was down. I knew he was already calling for a flight to Miami and would be at my place by the time I showered and talked to my coach.

"It's hard to remember what's important."

"Focus on the good. Remember your goals."

I scoffed and shook my head, even though he couldn't see me. The blood on my knuckles started to drip, and I flexed them a little more to feel the pain. In the past few weeks, I had learned one thing I knew was certain, and one thing I don't think Levi yet realized.

"Goals are reckless."

Chapter One

Rhys

"Not interested," I mumbled, kicking a ball directly to the corner of the net. Colin was catching on that I was too fucked up to be of any help to him.

"There's no one better," Colin urged. "Plus, I could use the help, and you could use the distraction."

"I spend ninety percent of my life on a soccer field. What makes you think I want more right now?"

"Because ever since Mel disappeared from your life, you've been a dick." *Ouch*, he came right out and said it. Poked the bear. Hit me while I was down.

But that wasn't going to work.

"No," I said again, stoically, kicking another ball as hard as I could. That time, I lacked my usual precision and finesse, and the ball flew past the net into Row Z. "Godammit."

Colin Mestick was an ex-player, the captain of my first ever Major League Soccer team. Once upon a time, I looked up to him, idolized him. Now I was having trouble tolerating him. Yet, there he still stood, watching me lose my cool.

"I need you."

"You don't need me." I walked closer to him as I wiped the

sweat from my brow with my forearm and then crossed my arms over my chest. "So what gives?"

"Sandy," his breath came out quickly, a hint of exasperation in his tone—along with a hint of truth. "He came to me and asked me to find you something to do."

That actually made more sense. Sandy was my head coach and since *that day*, he'd been questioning my sanity almost daily.

But still.

"No."

"Can't you just make this easier on both of us and show up for me? It won't even be the whole team, just one girl that needs extra work. Ashlynn Keller, maybe you've heard her name?"

How the fuck would I know her name?

"You've never minded the extra work," I reminded him. He would sleep in his office if he could. He'd spent years helping players at the college level. Most of them were now pros.

"Justine minds the extra work," he pointed out. "See where I'm going with this? Sandy? My wife? Hello? Between the two of them, I practically sprinted out here to find you, and ask you to help me. Justine wants me home more, and Sandy needs you out of your sad, depressed era. He even threatened to bench you." He paused for a moment and then added. "Plus, Ash really does need help focusing on the game. I'm not making up busy work."

"For the record," I bit out. "I'm neither sad, nor depressed. I'm pissed. And Coach won't bench me."

"As you should be. I never even met the girl but I know how much she meant to you. She put you through hell, and you've played the last two months without her like a man possessed. If I were Sandy, I would let you just keep tearing everyone apart on the field. But he thinks you are one game away from self-destructing. He *will* bench you if it helps the rest of the team. Just like I'll have to do to Keller if she can't remember why she's on the team in the first place."

"Sandy isn't my dad." I practically growled, glossing over everything else he said, and knowing damn well I sounded like a pissy teenager.

Fuck, maybe I did need something else in my life.

Levi was in Atlanta so he wasn't around as much as I wished. Mom still lived in California, where we grew up, spending all her time doing volunteer work. And Mel disappeared from my life just like my father had, leaving me too pissed off to be around anyone else.

Colin must have sensed my internal debate starting to shift in his favor because he was no longer asking me to do it—he was already assuming I would.

"I'm going to have Ash stay after practice tomorrow. Show up at seven. You know where—across from the stadium. I'll introduce you to the team, and then you can run drills with her. She's distracted, and needs the extra work. Just see how it goes." He babbled on while he backed up toward the exit. Not waiting for an official answer, he turned and walked off the field toward the benches.

What the hell?

The stadium *was* dimly lit, most everyone else had left for the night. I was always the last to leave. It was part of my post-relationship personality, to work myself until I could no longer stand, and then go straight to bed when I got home. It kept me from wallowing in anger at my ex—or being tempted to call her.

I guessed if I helped Colin, the outcome would be the same. Instead of working out at the stadium, I would be working out at the University. Sandy would be off my back for a while, that would be nice. Plus, Justine would be happier–I liked Justine.

When all the balls were kicked into the net, I pulled my shirt off and used it to wipe the sweat from my face and neck. I took a minute to look up and look around me. Trying to remember who I was before everything inside of me broke.

There I was, in the middle of a professional soccer stadium, team captain for the hottest city in the country, and with enough money to do whatever the fuck I wanted. I had dedicated my life to getting where I was, and while I took a shot at love, it backfired, but I still had a life most people would kill to have.

It was time I attempted to get my head out of my own ass. I almost felt sorry for poor Ash Keller. She had no idea what she was in for. But fuck, neither did I.

Practice ran longer than usual, but Sandy told me to hit the showers early and head out. In fact, he insisted, like I had been summoned by God himself. It left me with little doubt that he and Colin had been conspiring together.

The college was only twenty minutes from the stadium, and I somehow managed to avoid the infamous Miami traffic jams getting there, so I was actually a few minutes early. It gave me time to check things out.

With my hair slicked back from my shower, and sunglasses shading my eyes from the early evening sun, I looked out onto the field to soak in whatever hell I had gotten myself into. Colin was standing with his hands on his hips, and had a whistle in his mouth, while his assistant coach was waving his arms. They were telling the girls what drill to run, and the girls all followed the directions like a dance.

When the whistle blew again, the girls took off running around the length of the field–a clear sign practice was almost over.

"Rhys," Colin yelled, waving me toward the center of the field.

Slowly, and cautiously, I started walking as I watched the girls running from behind my sunglasses. All of them kept the same pace, and kept themselves poised like professional athletes usually did. It was clear they were well coached and a force to be reckoned with in their division. I had already started to admire them, as it reminded me of my own college days in Sacramento.

Eyeing each of them more closely, I was curious as to which one was Ash. The blonde in the front? The one with all the tattoos? Maybe the short one in the middle of the pack? Or damn, the one whose eyes had found me, and was curiously watching me back, probably wondering what I was doing there? She had a scowl on her face, and despite keeping her pace, it was clear she was distracted.

Or didn't want to be there.

Or both.

Yeah, that had to be Ashlynn Keller, because I would have felt the same way if it were me. Hell, I was pissed off on her behalf.

I lifted my sunglasses into my hair and tilted my head a little, letting her know I saw her. When she rolled her eyes, I smirked before she turned back to her task, and started another lap around the field.

"This should be fun," I groaned to myself.

"Glad you made it," Colin rumbled as he reached his hand out for me to shake. I took it, and then tried to shake the hand of his assistant coach, "This is Hunter Ward."

"Nice to meet you." My hand was still in the air, but Hunter left me hangin'.

"Yeah," Hunter grunted, his arms crossing over his chest instead, keeping his attention on the girls.

In a way, he looked like a drill sergeant, statuesque and ready to yell, *"Drop down and give me twenty,"* if one of the ladies so much as sneezed during their run. He didn't appear to like me much, turning his back on me immediately following our introduction, but I tried not to take that personally. After a few awkward minutes of silence, he quietly walked off and headed to where the girls were gathering, making me sigh.

"Don't mind Hunter," Colin laughed. "He's a former player here at Miami. He came back thinking he would take over because he was so revered as a player. He's not exactly happy, nor proud to be a part of this team."

"Then why's he here?" I scoffed, watching the way he walked around the women while they stretched.

"Boosters," Colin said plainly. That was all he had to say. Just like in every operation, the people who fronted the money were the ones who got the say so, regardless of whether it was good for the team.

Especially in colleges.

"He must be pissed I'm here," I mused.

"He'll get over it. Probably just jealous, seeing that he knows exactly who you are. His goal was to go pro when he graduated."

"If he's so good, why was that goal unattainable?"

"As far as I can tell, he just couldn't cut it with a pro team. He doesn't talk about it much, and we get along better when I don't ask questions. Let's go meet the girls."

A small huff of acknowledgement came from my chest as Colin started walking toward the team. I followed behind him, still keeping my eye on Hunter. Something about him made me uneasy, though to be fair, I barely knew him. Still, I was going to watch him closely.

Chapter Two

Ash

The second I saw Rhys Peyton, I knew exactly why he was there. Well, my first thought was, *"Oh my God, that's Rhys Peyton."* But my second thought was that he was there for me.

My new babysitter.

Coach had told me he wanted me more focused, and I needed to stay for extra practice. It pissed me off, because it was time being taken away from my studies. At the same time, I knew I had been a mess, and if I wanted to honor my scholarship, I had to play better than I had been.

Especially since it was my senior year. The first three years flew by, and keeping my focus on soccer was easier because there was no light at the end of the tunnel. Now that light was all I saw, and I kept trying to skip past it, and reach out for what I really wanted.

To be independent. Stable. Safe.

Soccer wasn't the end game for me. It never had been. But for a few more weeks, I knew Coach wanted me working on my game, and depended on me to focus. I had been mentally preparing myself for the extra work and for Coach to create something that left me no choice but to work on soccer.

But of all people, why Rhys-freaking-Peyton? He once set the internet on fire just from a picture of him biting his fingernail. The comments consisted of, "Lucky finger," and "Look! No ring!" That was years ago, and from what I could tell, he only got sexier with age. I mean, I may, or may not, have kept a game program from a couple of months ago with him on the cover just because I was afraid it would set my trash can on fire.

Then there was that added fact that he was a soccer God. He had won a World Cup, and had been awarded the Golden Ball. Not to mention he was named the MLS player of the year the last two years in a row.

Geez Coach. Brought out the big guns.

Rhys ran his hands through his light brown hair while his dark eyes darted around the team. He seemed uncomfortable, out of place, and it made me wonder what kind of strings Coach had to pull to get the best player in the entire country to babysit me every night.

Be thankful he didn't ask Hunter, I thought to myself. That man had issues, and calling him 'Coach' made me want to vomit. Rhys appeared to sense that in Hunter as well, because his eyes got even darker for a few moments while he eyed Hunter one more time.

Then like a switch, he refocused and turned toward the team, looking at everyone individually. He intimidated me when our eyes connected. He was much closer than he was when I was running my laps, and it was hard to remember that I was mad he was there. His stare held mine for a moment longer than it did everyone else's, and a shiver ran through me.

Just like before.

It was all sinking in. Rhys Peyton was there to help me, and even though I didn't even want to be there, I was semi-impressed with the fact that Coach brought in soccer royalty just for me.

"As you know, Rhys plays for the Inferno here in Miami. He's the best there is, since *I* retired of course," Coach joked, getting a laugh from the team. "He's a friend of mine, and has agreed to help out around here for a bit. With the Women's College Cup coming up, we need everyone in peak playing condition."

"Wow," Rachel, the team Captain, said in awe. "*The* Rhys Peyton. It's a pleasure." She reached her hand out to shake his, her blond ponytail flopping on top of her head in a flirty way.

Rhys smirked again, something that looked natural on his face, making me think he did it a lot. As if words were sometimes unnecessary when he could just present that lopsided smile to someone.

"Nice to meet you..."

"Rachel. Team Captain. You can come to me for *anything* you need. I'm at your service."

I cringed, third party embarrassed for how Rachel was cooing and acting. I sent a quick side-eye to my friend Erin, only to see her face covered by her hand. I wasn't the only one that saw Rachel's personality change from badass captain to perky fangirl. Erin couldn't bear to watch the trainwreck any more than I could.

"Thanks," Rhys replied with a tight smile, giving her hand a professional shake.

"Okay ladies, to the showers." My eyes caught Coach's and his brows raised. That one look told me I was *not* hitting the showers, so I kicked a ball around while everyone else got their stuff and left.

"Ash?" Coach called me over. "Again, this is Rhys Peyton. I've filled him in, and he knows what you need to work on. Give him the same respect you do me."

Coach's voice was demanding, like he was putting on a show

of power for Rhys. Not that Coach wasn't respected, but his tone was more like he wanted *Rhys* to know he was respected.

A straight smile and small nod was all I could manage in return. I definitely couldn't roll my eyes the way I started to, or I'd be doing laps for days. He accepted my nod, though, and left the field, leaving me alone with Rhys.

Without a word, Rhys and I kicked a few balls around by ourselves, neither of us trying to speak to the other. But eventually, it got too awkward for me, and I stopped, resting my hands on my hips, waiting for his attention.

"What first, Coach Peyton?" I asked, when he finally looked my way.

Rhys shrugged and looked around, unsure what to do. For as formidable as he was walking in, he looked lost in that moment. The sun had just about disappeared and his sunglasses were now hanging on the collar of his shirt. His hands were on his hips, and he pursed his lips as he thought it over.

The stubble on his jaw, and the way his hair seemed to be messy, but perfect, made me zone out for a minute. I had been to an Inferno game, seen him on TV as well, but being ten feet away from him was something I could barely handle. If I was being honest, I could see why Rachel lost her cool when she spoke to him.

It was still inexcusable, but I understood.

The night was quiet, no threat of a warm Miami rainstorm, and with Rhys looking as lost as I felt, a calmness came over me. He was just as nervous as I was, and it made him seem more human, and less hero. It was somehow giving me a little comfort.

Closing my eyes, I took a deep breath and rolled my neck, giving him time to figure out where we were going to start. Little did I know, that would be the last normal breath I took around Rhys.

A gasp escaped my chest and throat, pain in my stomach

seeming to come from nowhere. I doubled over, grabbing my midsection, and tried to get the breath back into my lungs.

Glancing up, I saw Rhys with his hands on his hips as he watched me, and then I looked down at the ball lying next to my feet. The same ball he had just been kicking.

"Did you just kick that at me?" I yelled, my anger bubbling over, and still in pain from the slap the ball made against my thin shirt.

"Coach said you need to work on paying attention," Rhys shrugged. "You didn't even see that coming."

"You son of a bitch!" I screamed back, fully aware that I was closing the book on my college career. There was no way Coach would let me keep playing if I couldn't cut it with Rhys' help.

"You can talk about me," he smiled. "even talk about my brother if you need to–hell, I will give you insults to use and we can both giggle at him. But let's leave my mom out of this." His voice was even and unbothered, not matching the words coming out of his mouth. He made me want to laugh and cry, all at the same time—a feeling that I hadn't yet realized he would be giving me a lot.

Whiplash.

"What the hell did you do that for?"

"You weren't paying attention."

"I was waiting for you to 'coach me' you piece of shit."

"You're a senior player at a division one college. You wouldn't be here if you needed to be told, or coached, on what to do."

"I'm sorry, then why are you here again? Help me out, because I've never had a sexy pro athlete show up to 'teach' me. I was unaware of where we were going with all this." Dammit, that was the second time in a row I used air quotes with my fingers, and I already hated myself for it. But then it got worse as realization set in, and the actual words I'd spoken made my air quotes look like chump change.

The good news was, I no longer felt the pain in my stomach, just the knot in my chest as embarrassment made its way through me. Did I just call him *sexy* to his face? Even if he knew it, had heard it a million times, and was not bothered by it, I was mortified.

He acted like it was just another random Tuesday night. Relaxed and chill. Waiting on me to be over my meltdown. "You done?"

"Done what?" I yelled again, unable to control my anger–mostly at myself that time.

"Whatever it is you're doing."

"I'm not sure my scholarship is worth this." I started toward the gate to the field, deciding to walk home and shower.

Five minutes of extra practice, and I was already turning into someone I wasn't. I needed to get home, crunch numbers, and do equations. Something with correct answers to the questions being asked. I didn't have room for confusion and doubt.

With what little self-preservation I had, I aborted the entire mission, and made peace with my decision. I would talk to Coach, tell him it didn't work out. Maybe if I told him about being kicked with a ball, he'd understand.

No, Ash, he wouldn't understand a soccer player complaining about being hit with a ball.

"It is," I heard him say from behind me, making me filter back to what the hell we were even talking about. *What did I say?*

"Dammit!" I yelled again, as another ball hit me right in my ass. It hurt way less than the one to my stomach, but I spun around and charged back toward him, stopping only when I saw his smile widen across his face. His shoulders were shaking, laughter taking over his body. "What is your problem?"

"Nothing," he said as he lifted his hands in surrender. "The first kick was to make you pay attention. That one was just for fun."

"I'm not a target, asshole."

"The first time a coach changed my life was after he kicked me in the gut with the ball, and told me to pay attention."

"And you're going to change my life?" I laughed humorlessly, shaking my head in disbelief.

"Starting now." His eyes looked into mine and he got closer to my face, remnants of his laughter lingering in his eyes. He was a lot taller than I was, and he bent down so that our noses were a foot apart from each other. He repeated himself with a sincerity that made me want to stay put. Words that sounded like a gift. "Starting now."

Chapter Three

Rhys

There was no denying I shouldn't have kicked the ball into her stomach. But Colin told me she had been distracted, not playing to the best of her abilities because she couldn't focus. And before we could even get started, she made herself an easy target by drifting.

"I'm not a coach," I said as I backed away and pulled another ball underneath my feet. "I don't know how to coach someone. I only know how I was taught, and what I was taught. A lot of it came from Colin. He knows what players need."

"I'm a lost cause." Ash wasn't fishing for pity, or acting sad. She looked strong, riled up, and ready to kick my ass. But her words were matter of fact.

"Why is that?"

"Because I don't want to be here. I got a scholarship because I'm good. But my main goal in life is to use that scholarship to get an education, and be able to take care of myself. Soccer is not what drives me, it just pays the bills until I graduate. And graduation is close. Soccer feels less and less important by the day."

"Well so much for me changing your life." The sarcasm was

meant to be funny. Maybe telling her I would change her life was a tad narcissistic, but the second she started talking to me, it felt like both of us were going to somehow change forever. I had never coached, or helped anyone else in that capacity, surely it was an experience I would always hold close to my chest.

The smile that almost crested her face was the first sign that Ash wasn't made of bricks and ammo. That underneath her tough attitude was a woman just trying to get through the motions. Something else I could understand completely.

"Look. You may not want my help, and I may not even want to be here. But let's make it work for a few weeks. Colin will get off my back, and yours, for that matter." I left my own reasons for being there vague. She didn't need to know how close I was to riding the bench, nor did she need to know the reasons why. As far as Ash was concerned, I was pushed to help her as a favor to a friend.

Her smirk mirrored my own, and the way her eyes rounded, created a glint in them that I hadn't noticed until that moment. She seemed satisfied, and for a moment, I was glad I'd knocked the wind out of her. It was payback, because she was doing the same to me without even meaning to.

"No more balls to my stomach." She meant that as a warning, but immediately turned red when she realized the innuendo those words took on.

I gave her a wink and licked my lips, not cutting her any slack. "Then you better stop calling me sexy, as well, or no promises."

Her face somehow got redder, and I bit my lip to suppress my laugh. The small woman was every bit the fireball I didn't need in my life, but I embraced the light energy I had since she started yelling at me.

Using my toes, I popped the ball lying next to my feet, in the air, then bounced it on my knee. I volleyed it to her, and expected her to catch it with her hands, but to my surprise, she caught the ball with her foot and balanced it before kicking it to her other foot. Then she used her knee to pop it back in the air, turned quickly, and kicked the ball hard past my head into the goal net behind me.

I wasn't surprised, but I was impressed. Maybe even a little turned on. Not from the kick alone, but from that look in her eyes. As if she was telling me to take that ball and shove it up my ass.

"Let's do this." I kicked another ball her way, gently that time. She stopped it before kicking it to the side to try to get around me. She was doing exactly what I wanted her to do in the first place—owning the field.

For the next few hours, we quietly scrimmaged one on one, and it gave me a chance to see her style and her work. There was no way I was going to be able to do Colin's bidding in a day. It was important that I saw for myself what the problems were. But as far as I could tell, she didn't have any.

She didn't get past me very often, but I was bigger than her.

Older than her.

A professional.

She knew there was no way to beat me in every attempt, but when she did, her eyes widened, and her face flushed that pretty shade of pink. A smile would try crossing over her face before she suppressed it, and kicked another ball my way.

There wasn't much I could see that Ash needed help with, other than focusing. With me, she was focused just fine, and her game was impressive.

"I lost track of time," I admitted, stopping her from kicking another ball my way. "I have practice tomorrow morning."

Her game face fell and she looked around as if she was coming out of a trance. "Oh shit, I have early classes. What time is it?"

"Almost ten o'clock."

She walked slowly toward the middle of the field, pulling her shirt up and away from her stomach, using it to wipe her brow. Then she pulled it all the way up and off, showing off her body in her tiny practice shorts and sports bra.

Fuck, Ash was hot. I had been attracted to her from the moment she started stomping off the field in anger, but seeing her body covered in sweat, huffing as she tried to catch her breath, was making my dick twitch. She had dark, silky hair, smooth skin, and her lips plumped every time she licked them.

"You must be hard up," I groaned under my own breath, speaking primarily to my dick. Ash was not the kind of person I needed to find myself attracted to. But she was the first woman I had spent any time with since Mel left, and it was safe to assume I was feeling drawn to her because I was fucking lonely.

If my dick suddenly wanted some attention, there were a million no-strings attached women in Miami that could fill that need. Not a young, college girl, who Colin had entrusted me with to help.

Too risky.

Too reckless.

"You can take off," she yawned as she got closer to me. "I'll take the balls to the storage room and clean up."

"Hell no, I can..." I trailed off when my eyes caught the redness of her skin. Her stomach was almost blistered with a round area where the ball had hit her earlier. "Oh shit."

Without thinking, I closed the distance between us, and took my hand to her stomach, gently running the tips of my fingers over the edges of her sore. She stiffened, but didn't stop me, watching as I tested the pain she was feeling. Goosebumps rose on her skin and her breathing started to get ragged.

"Oh fuck," I whispered, anger starting to stir up in me. I have kicked soccer balls at a million people and never left a mark. Not like the one on Ash's stomach. Regret was seeping into me, and I started to shake my head as I backed away.

"I had no idea it was even there. It doesn't hurt anymore."

I could hear the desperation in her voice, wanting to save me from the anger that had undoubtedly started to surface.

"Fuck." It was the only word I could say, and I was repeating it over and over again as I began to pace in front of her.

"Rhys," she tried getting my attention, but I was now the one that couldn't focus. All I could think of were ways to make it better. An apology wasn't enough. The only thing that came to mind was to buy her a car, add an apology note, and maybe a red bow.

"I didn't think I kicked it that hard," I tried explaining, a grimace on my face as I squinted toward her stomach again.

Finally, her laughter stirred me from my self-loathing, and my eyes found hers. "We are a mess. We need to decide who's going to be the crazy one. It can't be both of us."

"Do you need a car?" I was serious, but her laughter got louder.

"No," she waved me off, shaking her head. Her attention had turned toward the slew of balls in the middle of the field and she started putting them in the netted storage bag. "It was an accident, go home."

My face scrunched up and my lips curled in confusion. "That wasn't an accident."

"Luck, then."

"Not luck."

She stopped loading balls into the bag and looked at me like I had lost my mind. "Whatever you want to call it, it's fine. And I think it's safe to say that you've been nominated as the crazy one."

I nodded, agreeing with her—I was losing my shit. But it wasn't because I kicked her so hard, it was because of how much I cared. I started backing away, knowing I needed to get out of there. The whole night had been nothing like I expected it to be.

When I got to my car, I realized my fingers were still tingling from touching her, and my head was still spinning with anger at myself for hurting her.

What the fuck, Rhys?

Chapter Four

Ash

Rhys Peyton was nothing like I imagined him being when I first realized he was there to run drills with me. I imagined a cocky playboy with a little swagger, and very self-absorbed. Some of that peeked through, but ultimately, he was just a guy that loved the game.

When we finally started kicking the ball around and playing one-on-one, the awkwardness and anger I had felt, drifted away. We both focused on what we loved and how we knew to play.

Most plays, Rhys bested me, but I expected that–he wasn't a world champion because he was just so-so. But those few times I got past him made my own swagger soar a little. I hadn't felt like that after practice in a long time.

Thoughts that always weighed on me seemed to be suppressed. The pain of losing my grandparents, and the fact that they never got to see me play at the college level. Guilt that they had to sacrifice so much for me always lingered. Grandpa used to sell his model cars just to pay for my cleats, and grandma canned jellies to pay for the uniforms. It should have made me want to play harder, but it usually made me shut down. I never knew if I would be able to play the next season of soccer so I never made it my dream, or part of my goals.

The only thing I knew for sure was that I never wanted to be like my mother. She had a child she didn't want and couldn't take care of. She prioritized herself over my needs, and was too selfish to even worry about how hard my grandparents struggled to raise me. It had been almost a year since I had heard from her, but I knew she kept tabs on me in case she ever needed something. Not that I had much to give, but that didn't discount me as a tool she could use, if necessary. If I thought about her too much, I usually panicked, so having those worries shoved to the side for the night felt good.

No panic, no pain.

There was even a smile on my face as I hopped into my shower and then climbed into bed. I pulled my laptop up to get some work done on a paper that was due soon, about the concepts around the Dirichlet–Jordan test. But as much as math fascinated me, it seemed to pale in comparison to spending the evening yelling at Rhys Peyton. It was hard to get my mind off of everything that had happened, how crazy the whole night was. Eventually, I scrubbed the paper, and found my way to YouTube, typing in Rhys' name.

I wanted to see more of him. Watching him play might even help me to beat him on the field the next time we practice together.

For almost an hour, I watched videos of his best plays, his leadership at the FIFA cup, and his interviews from years past. There was a lot I had already known about him, such as his older brother being a football coach in Atlanta, and the fact that he'd played for Seattle before signing with Miami. He had been in Miami a while now, making it his home, and making it clear he had no desire to leave for another team.

The only new information the videos gave me was that he

smiled a lot, was carefree, and seemed to draw people to him wherever he went. But the more recent videos showed him surly and grumpy, almost sad. I wondered what had changed, or if it was just a coincidence. Rhys showed me glimpses of both sides of himself, so maybe that was just who he was. We all had a grumpy side, his just seemed to be shining more than normal in the more recent interviews.

Right before I was going to click off for the night, I saw one more video labeled 'Rhys Peyton–Precision.' I clicked the link and saw what seemed to be an amateur video taken from a phone. Whoever was filming was laughing, and Rhys was shaking his head at him, with his hands on his waist. The smile Rhys sported showed no signs of being annoyed, but he was refusing to do whatever had prompted the cameraman to start recording.

"Come on, one more time for the camera."

"No," Rhys laughed. "Put that shit down."

"Not until you do your party trick for me."

Rhys blushed a little, making me glance down at the date the video was posted–one year ago. Back when he'd seemed to be more carefree.

"One more time," Rhys agreed. "Then you are buying me a drink."

"Deal," the cameraman said before losing focus and showing mostly grass. They were doing something, setting something up, as they said things like, *Right there, over to the side, and perfect.*"

When the camera showed Rhys again, he was angled away from it. I could see ahead of him and realized they were in a park somewhere in Miami. The camera zoomed in on a water bottle that sat on top of a sign pole before panning out to show Rhys again. The bottle seemed to be fifty yards away, and Rhys had started tilting his head back and forth looking at it. There was a ball at his feet, and he took a stance like he was going to strike.

After the cameraman counted to three, Rhys pulled back and

kicked, hitting the water bottle with precision I had never seen from a soccer ball. My eyes widened and I watched as Rhys walked away like it was just another day in his world. The other guy was laughing and running with the camera, wanting to show everyone that Rhys hit the bottle.

"What the...," I mumbled to myself. Soccer players had impeccable aim, no doubt about that, but the shot Rhys had done, with the distance and the small target, was incredible. It was either a camera trick, or luck.

Luck?

"Not luck."

I closed my laptop and started looking around my room, as if someone was watching me. A replay of Rhys' words to me on the field flashed back into my mind. He said it wasn't luck. That he meant to kick the ball into my stomach, and apparently he wasn't joking.

That bastard did it on purpose.

"How was practice with Rhys?" Erin asked as we made our way to the only class we shared.

Confusing?

Awkward?

Fun?

Crazy?

"Fine," I shrugged. "Just scrimmaged."

"Just fine?" She sighed. "Ash, at the risk of sounding like Rachel, that was Rhys Peyton you were hanging with, ya know?"

"Yeah," I nodded, squeezing the book I was carrying to my

chest. "But all I care about is him helping me stay on the field until this season is over and I fulfill my scholarship obligation."

"You're almost there," Erin nudged my shoulder in encouragement. She was the only one that knew who I was, and why I did the things I did. She supported my goals and never tried to persuade me to try going pro with her when we graduated. She knew I needed something stable, even if it wasn't millions of dollars in MLS contracts.

Her life was soccer, my life was anything that freed me from the chains I felt tethered to my ankles since my grandparents passed away. They had raised me, nurtured me, and–given me more love than most kids got from their parents.

But they passed away, one right after the other, during my senior year in high school. They lived a meager life, providing for me with what little they had.

I loved them more than anything.

Losing them changed me.

Soccer helped me.

Right before they passed, I was able to secure a scholarship with the University of Miami. There was no way I could be anything more than the hand I was dealt, unless I found a way to get an education. It became my only focus.

The problem was, the closer I got to graduating, the less I wanted to play soccer. My mind kept thinking of jobs that involved my passion for facts. Like math. Equations weren't subjective.

Coach was right, I wasn't focused on soccer.

The game felt irrelevant.

A means to an end.

At least it had until Rhys showed up.

Chapter Five

Rhys

The girl was good.

Colin had given me game footage, per my request, and I spent every spare moment I had watching Ash play. I could see why he wanted her head back in the game, because when it was, she was unstoppable.

The volume on my phone was down as I watched a few more plays from the front seat of my car. Colin was still practicing with the team, and I had no intention of joining them until Ash was ready. I didn't have it in me to face Rachel, or Hunter, head on again.

When I heard the whistle sound for the end of practice, I climbed from my car and leaned against it as I watched the team walk toward the locker room. Colin gave me a quick nod, a silent thank you for showing up again, and Hunter took a long hard stare at me, like I had punched his puppy or something.

Fucking tool.

On the field, Ash stood alone, twisting her body in stretches, getting ready for more work. Inadvertently, I bit my lip when I started walking toward her as I watched her move. My cock twitched a little, remembering how attractive she was, but I immediately reminded myself that she was too young to be fucking around. Even if her eyes had been calling to me like a siren.

Ash saw me in her periphery, and stopped, turning to place her hands on her hips, watching me as I approached her. My sunglasses were still on so she couldn't see the way I was running my eyes over every inch of her, getting one last fill before I had to let reality set back in.

Practice was going to be different now that she was no longer angry, no longer pissed. We worked well together, and she knew that now.

But when I took my eyes from her body and got close enough to see her eyes, I stopped walking, and tilted my head at her in question. *What the hell?* She looked ready to pounce, her green eyes beaded, and a small snarl on her lips.

She actually looked incredible, all fired up and pissy. *Damn I really was crazy.*

"What did I do?" I finally asked, breaking our intense stare down.

"You kicked me on purpose," she seethed.

"I know," I nodded, as if to say 'duh.'

"I thought you kicked it at me and got lucky."

The smirk on my face made her nose scrunch up, but she stayed still, waiting for my response.

"I meant to hit your ass too. That wasn't luck either."

She let out a sigh of frustration, and fisted her hands at her sides. "You piece of shit. I tried making you feel better, and less guilty. But you were so guilty!"

There was no way I could hold in my laughter. I wasn't sure what made her realize the truth in what I had already told her, but it was cute watching her trying to be indignant about it.

There was a ball near where I was standing, and I popped it into the air with my foot the way I always did. Once it came back down, I lined myself up and aimed for her shins, being mindful not to kick it as hard as I did before. No way was I leaving any more marks on her body.

At least not with a soccer ball.

She stood there, unmoving, even after she saw what I was doing and took the hit, trusting that I was not going to hurt her, or aim for her face. Her gaze stayed locked on me, quietly watching as I took two steps toward another ball. This time, she held out her right hand offering me a challenge to hit it.

Popping the ball in the air, I did the same movements as before and hit her hand, right in the palm. The anger on her face was waning and she was looking more intrigued than before. "Can you do that every time?"

"I fuck up every once in a while," I shrugged.

"How?"

"Sweetheart, I have been playing soccer since before you were born, it is literally the only thing I know how to do."

"You aren't that much older than I am," she scoffed, pointing out the obvious instead of focusing on the endearment I accidentally used. Not that I meant it to be an endearment, but I certainly wasn't trying to be condescending either.

"I came out of the womb playing this game."

"It's impressive."

"Sometimes I even impress myself," I teased, kicking another ball and aiming for her hand again, although it was on her hip instead of being held up. The soft kick got her attention though, and she caught the ball in the air before it hit. "Let's do this."

Dropping the ball, she kicked it back to me and nodded, "Okay, Coach."

"Don't call me that."

She laughed as we both took off running. I dribbled the ball to get past her and she screamed in frustration. But there was a hint of laughter in that scream, and I reveled in making her feel so much at one time.

For almost two hours, we barely spoke, kicking the ball around, and moving the way it came naturally to us. There wasn't much I could 'coach' her on. Like the night before, as long as she stayed focused, she was dominant and trusted her instincts. She moved how I would have moved, and made the same decisions with the ball that I would have.

By the time we finished, I fell down onto the grass and looked up at the sky, catching my breath. I thought she would gather the balls and leave me there, but instead, she fell down next to me.

"So what's wrong?" I asked her, hoping she knew I wasn't talking about soccer.

"Ready to be done," she admitted.

"Pro?"

"I told you I just use soccer to pay for college."

"If not soccer, what are you wanting to do? Settle down? Have kids?" I cringed to myself a little, hoping she didn't assume I thought of that because she was a woman. Those were just my own goals, and it always popped in my mind as a logical question to ask.

She sat up, placing her hands on her knees and pushing them into a butterfly stretch. She didn't seem fazed by my question, and my head had turned in the grass to watch her as she spoke.

"My degree is in finance. I love math more than anything. I would love to be a CPA, or CFO one day. I don't know, just something with money and math. Stable. Self-sustaining. I want to be settled, but definitely no kids."

"You know what pays well? Pro soccer."

"Not as much for women," she eyed me. "But making it isn't the point. Managing it, saving it, and spending it appropriately, is my goal."

"That sounds boring."

"I'm good at math. Good at figures. I love things that are reliable."

I didn't say it, but I thought that her goals for independence and no kids was a good one if she wanted something reliable. Trying to have that dream was unsafe, and risky to one's mental health.

"Then you can be my CPA when you graduate. Manage my money."

"Are you a reckless spender?"

I sat up so I could look into her eyes, getting lost in familiarity and feelings of ease. Something about that girl felt comfortable, simple. She wasn't a fan, or a threat, just another person to talk about life with, play soccer with, and enjoy being around.

Everything I had been missing, and pushing away since Mel left.

"I've been known to be reckless."

Without meaning to, I licked my lips and zeroed in on her eyes. We stayed locked like that while she processed the meaning behind my words. I kept telling myself not to flirt, not to charm, and not to engage with her beyond kicking the ball around. But like I had just said, I was occasionally pretty reckless, and she was making me fight that urge every second we sat there together.

Her green eyes contrasted with her dark hair, making her unique, and so fucking beautiful. A woman's eyes had always been my weakness, and I could count on one finger the number of times I got lost staring into them the way I was with Ash in that moment. Her eyes were phenomenal.

She was staring back at me, holding me in her gaze, but she seemed to be asking questions without saying anything. Did she want to know more about me? Did she read some shit on the internet and wonder if it was true?

"I have a game tomorrow," I said abruptly, making us both

shake from our heads, the lust that had settled in during our quiet stare.

"Yeah, I know," she nodded. "I have one the day after that."

"So then, see you Friday?"

"Don't ask me," she scoffed. "I'm here when Coach tells me to be."

"Then be here Friday."

"Thought you weren't my coach," she teased.

"I'm not." I stood unable to help her clean the balls up again. I had to get out of there, get myself away from the temptation burrowing inside of me. I started walking backward toward my car, so clearly running away that it was almost embarrassing. "But be here anyway."

Chapter Six

Ash

Two goals and an assist by the sixty-minute mark, and I looked up to see Coach calling me to the side of the field.

"Sub," he yelled at the sideline referee, getting his attention to pull me from the game. Erin gave me a high five on my way off the field, and Rachel did a dainty clap, as if I was a princess in a parade.

"Good job, Keller," Coach said when I got to the bench. "Glad to have you back."

Hunter was sitting on the end of the bench, his eyes on me. Instead of saying something uplifting, he looked at me with haughtiness, and stayed silent. He was starting to scare me a little.

What happened? I wondered to myself. A week or so ago, Hunter was nicer, happier. Yeah, we all knew he wished he had gone pro, and was disappointed he was an assistant coach for the women's team, but he wasn't normally scary. Just moody.

Bringing my focus back to the game, I watched as we scored two more times, beating North Carolina by six goals. The win was huge, and everyone was giddy as we celebrated in our locker room.

Coach gave us a quick speech before leaving us alone to change. Home games were the best, because I got to walk back to my apartment and crash the rest of the day. After the long week, being alone sounded like Utopia.

"Coach wants to see you," Rachel said, quickly brushing past me on her way to her locker. I had already changed, but she was still in her uniform, having to do the post-game wrap up duty that came along with being the captain.

I figured Coach wanted to make sure I was still planning on meeting with Rhys. It shouldn't take long to tell him I'd be there and keep working on whatever it was he thought I was getting out of it.

"Come in," Coach mumbled after I knocked gently on his ajar door.

"Hey, Coach. Got your message to come see you."

His eyes shot up, and he seemed to be distracted by whatever was sitting in front of him. He took a minute to look around and clear his head before standing and waving the sheet of paper at me.

"Good game."

"Thanks." I took the paper and looked at the numbers written haphazardly in his messy script. "What's this?"

"Rhys Peyton's cell phone number."

Had I been anyone else, I may have passed out from holding those numbers in my hand. Women would sell their soul for those ten digits. As for me, I was more concerned than excited.

"What for?"

"I asked him to keep working with you. But um, also..." He trailed off and looked around again, making me uneasy. Something was wrong.

"I was already planning on practicing tomorrow," I assured him. "Whatever keeps me on the field, Coach."

"Yeah, I just..." he cleared his throat and then coughed into his fist before looking back up at me. "Hunter is taking over the team for a couple of weeks. There has been a family emergency and I need to tend to it."

"Oh shit, is your wife okay? Anything I can do?" I realized his inability to talk had been coming from his will to keep from crying. Coach wasn't a crier. Whatever had happened, it must have been new information and he was still processing everything.

"Yes actually," his answer surprised me. "Justine is fine. It's my sister. She was in an accident and I am her only living relative. I know it's crunch time with the team, and I've been asking a lot from y'all. Leaving is not what I want to do, I promise. But she cannot make her own medical decisions right now and—"

"Family first. Always." I assured him. "We got this, Coach. We will stay steady here so you have nothing to worry about."

"Thank you." His lips thinned out and he tried smiling, but I could see the pain in his eyes. "I will address the team before I leave, but I wanted to talk to you personally since I have been asking more from you. Keep in touch with Rhys, please. He needs these practices just as much as I think you need them, and I want them to continue until I get back."

"Yes sir. No reason they wouldn't."

"Hunter may tell you it's not necessary, but it is. Keep Rhys busy, and use him to help you focus on the game."

I nodded, staying silent when he mentioned Hunter. Even Coach could see how Hunter was acting, and I bet it bothered him that he was leaving us in his hands. Hunter was in no shape to be making decisions about the team. But that decision was out of Coach's hands. It was up to the university.

"Rachel will help Hunter unless the athletic director sends him an aide."

"Yes, Coach." I glanced down at the numbers again and then

back to him. His eyes were on me, but I could tell his head was with his sister. "Rhys okay that you gave me his number?"

"Yeah I just got off the phone with him. I told him I would ask you if I could send him your number as well."

"Of course." I tried to placate him, even though inside all I could think of was, *Rhys Peyton is about to have my phone number.* "Take care Coach. You have my number, too, if you need anything."

"Stay focused. That's all I need."

I nodded with a sad smile and turned to walk out the door. The entire walk home, all I could think about was Rhys, and the words that Coach said about him.

"He needs these practices just as much."

Why?

Was that how this all came about? Coach was trying to fix both of us? Two birds with one stone?

It didn't matter, something was working. Even if it was just the thought of Rhys watching my game and judging me, it kept me focused and playing the way I used to. That was all Coach wanted from me.

What did he want from Rhys?

By the time I got home, had another shower, and slipped into my comfortable clothes, I could barely keep my eyes open. All I had to sit on in my studio apartment was a bed, but I feared once I sat on it, I would be asleep before I could feed myself, and do a little school work. Grabbing a banana, I slid down against my wall to settle on my floor.

For a few minutes, I mindlessly flipped through my phone, checking social media. Rachel had a post from the day before that bragged about how she had met Rhys Peyton. In fact, it was an entire dossier on what good friends they now were.

Lord, Rachel. Have some dignity.

I read a few more posts from girls on the team, a couple of classmates, and checked in with my favorite celebrities.

I started to set my phone down and open my computer when a new text came through from an unknown number.

Guess it's just me and you.

Um, who is this?

My mind immediately went to Hunter. I wouldn't put it past his ego to start boasting about being the new head coach, even if it was temporary.

Your new coach.

See? What an idiot.

What do you want?

He shouldn't have been texting me. The coaches had our numbers but social calls were not usually part of the agreement. We saw them enough, anything they needed to tell us could wait until we were on their time, or was sent through our team message boards.

Ouch. Are we not friends anymore?

We were never friends. You're my coach. My assistant coach. If you need me, use the team message boards, Hunter.

I tossed my phone away from me and stood, agitated and antsy. What the hell had gotten into him? He was taking his mood swings too far.

I was two steps away from my phone and it lit up with an incoming Facetime call.

UNKNOWN.

Decline.

Answer the phone Ash. It's Rhys!

I grabbed the phone and sat on my bed, straightening my shoulders and readying myself to send him a rant about how inappropriate it was to act like Rhys.

Answer the phone so you can see it's me!

The incoming call started again and I stared harder at the number on the phone. Like a light bulb turning on, I remembered that Coach asked me if he could give Rhys my number. There was a chance it could very well be Rhys.

Oh no.

Swiping, I answered the call and covered my face, letting the video start while peeking through my fingers. It was like watching a scary movie, and I could barely bring myself to look.

Chapter Seven

Rhys

I was lying in bed when Colin sent Ash's number to me. I didn't need to actually text her, but my fingers just did it anyway. Teasing her about being her coach sounded fun, and I figured I would tell her good game. I even thought about seeing if she wanted to meet earlier than we normally did since she didn't have practice the next day.

No part of me thought she would think it was Hunter, and when I realized how upset she was, I panicked.

The Facetime call was instinct. It was the only way I knew to prove to her it wasn't Hunter and I hoped it calmed her down. The second time I tried calling, she answered, and I sat up as the video connected.

"Hey," I breathed a sigh of relief.

She had one hand holding her phone and the other covering her face. Her fingers were spread open and one eye was peeking through. "Hey."

"Not Hunter, just Rhys." I tried assuring her.

"Yeah, I see that. My bad." She dropped her hand from her face and I could see a faint pink in her cheeks. The lighting was dim but the angle of whatever light she had was reflecting perfectly in her eyes.

"Did something happen?"

"No. But with Coach leaving, I figured Hunter was overstepping."

My jaw ticked, wondering if Hunter was going to take advantage of the girls being at his mercy. When Colin called to tell me he was leaving, he asked me to keep practicing with Ash and keep an eye on her. I hope that meant I was given a green light to kick Hunter's ass if I deemed it necessary. Not that I ever needed permission to use my fists.

I started flexing my free hand that still ached from the last punches I threw. I wanted to promise her Hunter wouldn't be a problem, but then maybe I would be the one overstepping. I wasn't anything to her, much less her hero. She didn't seem like the kind of girl that needed a hero, anyways.

"Good game today." The pink that had started fading from her cheeks came back and a sweet smile crested her lips.

"Thanks, Rhys. Felt good to be focused. Playing with you the last couple of nights reminded me how much I love the game."

"I'll take credit for that."

She shook her head slowly and looked around her room before finding me on the screen of her phone again. I had laid back against my pillows, propped my head up with my free arm, and couldn't help smiling as I watched the look on her face change a million different times.

"Are you in bed?"

"Yeah I didn't exactly plan on this being a Facetime call until I realized you thought I was Hunter. I guess that was my bad since I called myself your new coach."

"Exactly. We had already established that you're not my coach, you're...you're... I don't know what you are. Somebody I play with."

Her eyes widened as my smile got bigger. She brought out the kid in me. The one that immediately took his mind to the gutter. I waffled my eyes at her to tease her, but I didn't want to risk her hanging up on me.

"So what's Hunter's deal?"

"Geez," she rolled her eyes at me bringing him back into the conversation. I couldn't help it, I wanted to know what she knew. How she felt. "Hunter has been acting weird for a few weeks now, and I honestly don't know why. The way he eyed me when I got to the bench today made my skin crawl."

"No one should make you feel like that, Ash. You may need to mention it to Colin."

"If it keeps up, I will. But not until he gets back. He has enough to deal with right now. Plus, this is a new development. Hunter was fine a few weeks ago. Maybe not a normal human, but not creepy, either. I'm sure whatever it is, it's personal, and he needs to work through that."

"I'll be around," I reminded her, making a point to be around even more if I needed to be. Not just for Ash, but for Colin. So he could take care of his sister and not worry about the team.

Yeah, for Colin.

"He's probably just pissy because Coach brought you in to help me. Speaking of which..."

She started biting her lip, chewing on the words she wanted to say. I was curious, and I liked watching her flustered, so I sat back and waited patiently for her to finish her thought.

"Um...so... Coach told me you needed these practices as much as I did. Why is that?"

That was not what I expected her to say, and I sat back up in the bed, barely able to keep my phone held up. "The fuck?"

Without looking at me, she shrugged and started picking at a string on the quilt that covered her bed. "I was just curious."

"Well don't be," I sighed, keeping my frustration down. The

idea that Colin and Coach were worried about me was one thing. The fact that he mentioned something to Ash bothered me.

"Sorry." I could barely hear her because she spoke so low, almost regretful. I wanted to fix that, tell her it was okay and that it wasn't even her I was frustrated with, it was Colin.

"I'll see you tomorrow." I didn't wait for an answer, just hit *end* and tossed my phone across the bed, feeling like an asshole for cutting our conversation short like that. I just couldn't risk over-sharing with her in an attempt to make her understand.

Not very many people knew about Mel. We kept our relationship a secret from the media and out of the public eye. That meant, when she left me, no one knew. I used to want to shout her name from the rooftops and tell the world how in love I was with Dr. Melanie Simpson. But it wasn't in our best interest to be open about it. As time went on, Mel wanted to remain out of the spotlight that tended to follow me around.

I respected that, but nothing made me happier than the day she told me she wanted to marry me. That she was ready for the world to see us and couldn't wait to show our relationship off.

Apart from my brother, Colin and Sandy were the first two to know about Mel. We had been invited to a party hosted by the City of Miami and even though Mel couldn't attend with me, I told them that night that I was in love.

They knew, though. The happiness I felt was contagious and they had long suspected I had found 'the one.'

Cruz Martin, our goalie and a close friend of mine, wasn't shocked either when I told him about Mel. He just laughed and told me that he figured I was in love by the way I had been acting. I guess when it came down to it, my relationship wasn't much of a secret after all. At least not to those who knew me.

But the public never knew. Especially about my plans to propose and the fact that I was left heartbroken. I wanted to keep it that way.

Reaching over, I pulled a black box from the top drawer of my nightstand and flipped it open. Four-carats, princess cut, and all white gold stared back at me. It was exactly what she said she wanted.

Colin was holding it for me that night, and when it all blew up in my face, he was the last person I saw as he quietly handed me the ring back, repeating over and over again how sorry he was.

Colin carried the responsibility for me on his shoulders, but I had been nothing but hateful and petulant toward him since that day. Now he thought he had found a way to fix it, to heal me. But that couldn't happen if he started telling my secrets.

I came close to sending a text and telling Colin I was done, that I was no longer going to help him because I didn't trust him. But I stopped short of hitting send because it didn't feel like it would be Colin that I would be letting down.

It would be Ash.

And despite how much I didn't want to be there in the beginning, Ash quickly grew on me. She made me feel like I had a purpose again and I enjoyed being around her. It wasn't because she was gorgeous, it was because she didn't treat me like some fangirl. She didn't try impressing me or being someone she wasn't just because of who I was.

It was refreshing.

And I wanted more.

Chapter Eight

Ash

It was glaringly obvious that asking Rhys about what Coach had said was a bad idea. He hung up on me and I tossed and turned all night worried I had made a fool of myself by being too curious.

Or worse, hurt him.

My afternoon class the next day seemed to drag on, and I fought every minute to stay awake. I was thankful I had time for a nap before meeting with Rhys again, but the knot in my stomach still kept me from fully resting.

He was the first one to the field for practice that night, and I watched him kicking a few balls around as I walked into the gate. Bouncing the ball skillfully between his head, knees, and ankles was making me forget that he was upset, and made a warmth pool in my stomach.

Dammit he was hot.

I remembered the first time I ever saw him on TV. Grandpa was watching the sports network and they had his stats up on a graphic along with a picture of his face. Soccer was already a part of my life, but at the time, I was only fourteen years old and couldn't completely comprehend what I had been seeing.

Later, as his career blossomed in front of the world, I thought about those stats and was awestruck. It was like watching Tom Brady become the G.O.A.T. in football. Rhys was soccer's Tom Brady, and the way his career had evolved was nothing less than impressive to anyone who played and followed the sport.

Now he was on my field, there to see me, and I had to take a moment to remind myself that I refused to fangirl. It was easier to remember that the night I met him, when I was angry, that he kept kicking balls at me. It made me feel like a joke to him, until I realized he was right.

I had been distracted, uncaring. I had just wanted to go home and get lost in my school work, maybe read, and be alone. In just one short week, that changed, and I pinched myself to stay grounded before walking up behind him.

"Hey," I breathed quietly, not wanting to startle him.

The ball was in the air when he turned around to see me standing ten feet away, but he still caught it without looking. With his hands, but no less impressive.

"You're early," I joked, holding my phone up to show him the time. "I was going to get here and get the balls out."

"Beat ya to it," he winked, then kicked a ball slowly toward me. I stopped it and dribbled it to the side of the field where I sat my bag down and started stretching. Rhys was watching me intently, not moving or kicking around another ball the way he normally did.

"Sorry about last night," I mumbled, wanting to get that off my chest and out of the way. "Curiosity killed the cat. And I'm the cat."

His smile was sweet and easy. "No, I'm sorry."

I wasn't expecting an apology from him. I was the one that snooped and upset him, he had no reason to be sorry. "For what?"

"Hanging up on you, for one."

"I shouldn't have asked, I just—"

"It's fine," he laughed and got closer to me. "I wasn't upset with you, I was upset with Colin. The man takes his mentorship too far sometimes."

"Coach is your mentor?"

"Sorta. We played together a long time ago. He was close to retiring and I was just starting out. He was someone to look up to. I wanted to emulate him in a way."

"Why do I get the feeling that it didn't turn out well?"

His arms spread wide and his smile grew impossibly big, making his dimples peek out from under the scruff on his face. "I turned out okay."

For some reason, I wanted to close the few steps between us and walk into his open arms. I wanted to pretend that he had opened them just for me, to make me feel better about our little mishap. Thankfully, he dropped them back to his sides before I did something stupid.

"Let's play."

I nodded and kicked the ball that was still laying near my feet. "Let's do it."

Faking to the left, and then faking to the right, I kicked the ball back to the left and passed him, heading toward the goal at the end of the huge field. Behind me, he gave chase and I could hear him laughing as he got closer. Right before he caught up, I kicked the ball hard and right into the goal.

"You cheated, you didn't tell me we were starting," he huffed as he caught his breath.

"I said 'let's do it.' What more did you need?"

"I thought you meant something else. Like the other 'do it.' Damn, how misleading."

My laughter echoed in the evening air and I shook my head. "Sorry to lead you astray."

"Don't get a guy's hopes up like that, and then take him to the goal. It's mean."

My stomach was hurting from laughing, tears had sprung into my eyes. He was playing with me, joking, and trying to feed off how bad I just beat him. It was endearing, the way he made me laugh, made me forget.

Made me have fun.

We lined up face to face, with a ball between us. I had barely stopped laughing, but was ready for his turn with control as we stood in a ready position at the center of the field.

"I'm gonna go between your legs," he growled, making me flush and stand up straight.

With my legs spread open a little, he had enough room to kick the ball softly between my feet. He rounded me on the left side, taking control of the ball again before I could make sense of his words. I didn't even try to chase him, just turned and watched as he took the ball to the goal.

When he turned back around, he ran a hand absentmindedly through his hair and winked. I knew he was toying with me, but his words made me feel something that I wasn't sure my expression could hide.

"Your turn."

Covering my face with my hands, I had to get a grip before he got closer and could see my eyes. I knew my eyes would tell him that between my legs was exactly where he needed to be, and he would never let me live that down. If I stood a chance of sleeping that night, I had to save face, and not let him see me turning into Rachel right before his eyes.

When I tried to hide behind my hands too long, his fingers wrapped around my wrist and pulled it down. "I said it was your turn."

"Yeah, but let's not play *that* game anymore," I confessed, because hiding was useless.

"Just playing soccer," he shrugged.

"Yeah right."

The rest of the night was easier, and we scrimmaged like we always did, making my normal vibe around him return. We were still having fun, still laughing, and I could feel everything I had weighing on my shoulders dissipating as the night went on.

I didn't want it to end.

"One last time," he said, tossing the ball at me. "This time, use your control. I can outrun you, I can overpower you, but if you can handle the ball with precision, I can't stop you."

I nodded and wiped the sweat from my face with my shirt. Rhys lined a new ball up in position while I planned my attack in my head. *Pull-back, sweep left, roll on my heel, and sweep back.*

Those were my best moves and with one last shot for the night, I wanted to beat him. I wanted him at home thinking about how he got bested by the little college girl he had to babysit.

"Ready?"

I nodded and attacked the ball, pulling it back to get control and then sweeping it to the side and out of his reach. Before he caught up to me, I rolled the ball under my heel to change its direction with my intention being to sweep it around him in the other direction.

But something in the way I rolled the ball made my ankle twist and I fell to the grass in pain. "Fuck!" I yelled, loud enough for anyone walking past the field to know someone was hurting.

It was late, though, and only Rhys and I were there. He fell to his knees next to me, stopping me from moving, and grabbed my leg to keep me still. "What happened?"

"I twisted my ankle," I cried, the pain not yet subsiding to a manageable throb.

"Fuck, let me get you to the hospital."

"No!" I yelled, not wanting to be anywhere near the hospital. I would rather live the rest of my life in pain than I would go to a damn hospital.

"What if it's broken?"

"It's not," I breathed, trying to get a grip. "I promise."

He ran an agitated hand through his hair again while he looked down at me. A few minutes passed while he let me calm down, and when the tears finally stopped, he moved to a squat and scooped me into his arms.

Chapter Nine

Rhys

"Let me take you home," I whispered as I set Ash down on the bench near the sidelines.

"Just not a hospital," she begged.

I knelt in front of her, making sure not to touch her where she hurt and steadied myself. "You think Colin is a pain in my ass now? Wait till he hears I broke his favorite player."

She smiled softly at my words but then turned her face to stone and shook her head. "Don't tell Coach. He has enough to worry about."

"I think when you end up in a cast, he'll notice."

"It's a sprain. I promise. If I can fool Hunter over the weekend, I'll be good as new by the game next Tuesday." She moved her ankle a little to prove her point.

My teeth clenched when she mentioned Hunter. I didn't particularly like Hunter to begin with, but ever since Ash panicked at the thought of him texting her, I downright hated him. He made her uncomfortable, and probably the rest of the team as well. There was no place for that shit on a team.

"Let me handle Hunter."

A scoff, or an eye roll, seemed more likely than the laughter that my words created. Ash found me funny, but I was serious. It may have not been one of my best ideas, but it came to me instantly, and I planned to follow through.

Pulling my phone from a bag I had tossed to the bench when I arrived, I pulled Colin's name up in a text message.

> Hope all is going okay. Just sending a quick note to see if you can let Hunter know that Ash won't be at practice this weekend. I have off and gonna have her practice at the complex.

Ash read my screen, and I hit send before she could protest. "It'll be okay," I promised.

"Coach is going to freak out."

"Nah. He knows how much I live for this game. He'll just assume I have you as obsessed as I am. Stay put while I get the field cleaned up."

She was scrolling her own phone when I got back and held it up as I got closer.

"Coach posted in the team forum that I wouldn't be at practice this weekend."

"Told you he would be fine."

I threw both of our bags over my shoulders before I reached down and cradled her in my arms without warning. A squeal escaped as she held on tightly to my neck in an attempt to hang on.

"I can walk, Rhys."

"Why bother if you don't have to," I nudged her.

She felt like nothing in my arms, our size differences glaringly obvious. I easily made my way to my car and set her down by the passenger door. It was a 1967 Chevy Camaro, flat black, with a new engine and interior that would make most men piss themselves with envy. A gift to myself.

"Is this a 1968?" Ash asked, barely paying me any attention while I threw the bags in my trunk.

"Close. 1967." I slammed the trunk closed and crossed my arms, eyeing her with a little bit of fascination, and a whole lot of concupiscence. Soccer was the first love of my life, but cars came in a close second. The fact that she was even within range made me swallow down the same feelings I got the other day when she got all angry and fired up.

"My grandpa loved cars," she explained. "He had collectables and models. When I got old enough, putting models together was how we spent time with one another."

She was quiet after that, seemingly reflecting on memories she didn't want to actually talk about out loud. Not until we were both in the car, and headed to the main road, did either of us speak again.

"I guess I should ask you where you live."

"Maybe a mile away. I seriously could have walked."

"And I seriously wouldn't have let that happen. Tell me which way."

It was two turns, and I never actually got to get above thirty miles an hour before we were in a small parking lot. I jumped out quickly from the car and made my way to her side, letting her stand out of the car before I lifted her into my arms again.

"Which one?" I asked, nodding toward the row of doors that looked like an old hotel set up. I imagined they were small apartments, but with how close they were to the campus, what more did you need?

"The first one, but Rhys, I got this." She tried wiggling from my arms, making me tighten my hold on her.

"I'm not putting you down, Ash." My voice was low, a deep declaration that gave away how much I needed to take care of her. Even if I couldn't explain why.

When we approached her door, she pulled a key out from her

bag and dangled it in front of my face mockingly. If she thought I was going to put her down to open the door, she was wrong.

"You're ridiculous," she muttered, giving up.

"That is one of the nicer adjectives used to describe me."

She managed to get the key in the door and pushed it open for me to turn and get her inside safely.

The room was no larger than the size of a hotel room with the added bonus of a small kitchen to the side and a partition that created a small separation between the kitchen and the bed.

Gently, I set her on the edge of her bed, and made my way to her freezer, hoping she had something we could use on her ankle. There was no food or ice, but she had frozen cold packs lined up like that athlete she was.

"You are more than prepared," I laughed. I knelt down in front of her and carefully pulled her foot to rest on my thigh. I pulled her long sock down and unstrapped the tight fitting shin guard. The shape of the shin guard was embossed into her skin, and without thinking, I started rubbing the image.

"Rhys," Ash moaned, her eyes rolling to the back of her head and her body swaying with the pleasure she felt. My dick instantly hardened, not the least bit concerned that I had decided Ash was off limits.

I pulled off her cleat and the rest of the sock, exposing her entire leg before placing the cold pack in place on her ankle. She jumped at the sudden change, then moaned again when I ran my thumb across her shin before grabbing her other leg and repeating the process.

"You need new shin guards." I wasn't even sure if that was true, or if she had even heard me. I just needed to say something that excused the fact that I was still rubbing her shins.

Her skin.

Her warmth.

"Rhys?" Her voice was raspy, but she was trying to sound like she was unaffected.

"All good." I mumbled then cleared my throat. She moved back on the bed so her ankle could stay lifted and I backed away and stood up.

Glancing around her room, I took in everything that defined who Ash was. There were clothes tossed over an old dresser, soccer gear in the corner, and a small table next to her bed. Books were stacked high, all about mathematics and finance, proving she was serious about her goals in life. A few newspaper articles about the team were tacked on the wall, but other than that, they were bare. It looked like a dorm room, temporary, but functional for a student. The only thing missing was pictures—of her family and friends.

"Okay," I nodded, knowing it was time to leave. "If you're good then..." I trailed off when my eyes caught the corner of a magazine. It was sticking out from a stack of books that laid close to the bed where I had been kneeling. Reaching down, I picked it up, and stared at myself on the cover.

"Got that at the last game I went to," Ash shrugged, like it was no big deal.

"I know exactly what game this was. You went to this one?" I turned the magazine toward her, showing her the image of me on the front in my jersey, and a soccer ball being squeezed between my hands as if I was trying to pop it. It was a game day program, with the date stamped on it so there was no questioning which game it came from.

"Yeah. You had a hat trick."

Yeah the game was good until halfway through, when I looked up to where Mel had been sitting, and she was no longer there.

While Ash explained in the background of my consciousness that Colin had given her and her friend the tickets, I was trying to keep the thoughts of my ex from riling me up. Yet the memories of that night flashed in front of me like an old movie.

Chapter Ten

Rhys

Two months ago

Levi and Colin were sitting in the stands at my request, waiting for the game to be over so they could watch me propose to Mel. After almost a year together, she told me she was ready to share our story with the world, and I warned her I was going to make that happen in a big way.

No one in my life had met her yet, and Levi and Colin had no idea Mel was sitting behind them all night. It was part of my plan, to make sure their seats were close, so every time I looked into the stands I could see the people that meant so much to me, without losing too much focus on the game.

When the whistle blew for an injury early in the game, I took the moment to walk to Cruz near the goal.

"Look up behind the bench. Third row, behind Colin and Levi."

"Is that her?" He squeezed water into his mouth while he inconspicuously eyed Mel. It was far away, but close enough for him to see that she was really there, that she actually existed.

"Yeah," I sighed, acting almost like a teenager. I was so in love and happy, that it was hard not to float on cloud nine.

"Does she have any clue what you are doing tonight?" Cruz laughed.

"I warned her I was going to make a scene, but she doesn't know I have a ring."

"I'm hanging around for the show," he nudged me as I walked back to midfield.

"You better," I shouted.

The whistle blew again and action resumed. It was Mel's first game, and I wanted to show off for her, make her proud to be my girl. By the time the whistle blew for the half, I had scored three times–a hat trick–and we were leading the game against Seattle, my former team.

Little did I know that when I smiled up at Mel, and winked before heading into the locker room, it would be the last time I ever saw her. When I returned to the field for the second half, I couldn't find her during our short warm up. But worry didn't set in because I assumed she had gone to the bathroom or the concession.

When play resumed, I kept looking up to see if she was back in her seat, but she never was. I got antsy and unfocused. Something felt wrong, and eventually, I had to ask Coach to pull me from the game.

For thirty minutes, I tried calling and texting her from the locker room, leaving her messages that I was worried. I even texted Levi and told him she had been behind him all night, and asked if he had seen her move anywhere.

The answer was no.

When the game ended, I made my way back to the field and scoured the stands for any sign that she had just moved seats, or had seen someone she knew. Maybe she ended up chatting and lost focus on her phone and the game.

Colin and Levi were eyeing me with concern, Cruz was waiting alongside me, and a few teammates were waiting around to see me propose. But eventually, the stands cleared out, and the guys hit the showers.

A girl had come up to Colin, and was talking to him, while Levi made his way to the field. Whoever Colin was talking to turned my way and my eyes locked onto hers. We both stared as I got lost in her eyes for a minute, feeling so much familiarity and comfort, that everything felt okay for a moment.

Not until she turned away and walked up the stairs of the stadium did I remember what I was supposed to be doing. Mel, I was looking for her, and I was worried.

When Colin said all his goodbyes and joined me on the field, my first instinct was to ask him who the girl was. In fact, the words were right on the tip of my tongue when my phone finally buzzed with a message.

> Thank the gray haired guy in front of me tonight for discussing your plans, it spared you the embarrassment of me having to tell you no to your face. Why couldn't you just be happy with the way things were?

"Was it her? Is she okay?" Levi asked.

"What happened?" Colin added.

I tossed my phone at Colin, the gray haired, big mouth bastard, and walked away, leaving Mel's message at his feet, and my heart shattered into a million pieces.

Chapter Eleven

"That was you," Rhys mumbled, coming out of a daydream.

"What was me?" I asked as Rhys backed away toward the door. It was like he was looking for an escape, but curiosity was keeping him close.

"You were talking to Colin after this game. I saw you."

My heartbeat had barely evened out from the way he had been touching me when it picked back up again. *He remembered seeing me.*

When I had spotted Coach in the stands, I made a point to go say hello and thank him for the tickets. But then I locked eyes with Rhys, and for a moment, I couldn't look away. I never understood what happened, or why that moment felt so intense, but I practically ran from the stadium to my car, needing to catch my breath.

"Your eyes," Rhys said, bringing me back to the moment. "I will never forget those gorgeous eyes."

Blushing seemed to be all I could manage and I tilted my head down to try and hide what his words were doing to me. Somehow, those words hit deeper than when his hands were on me. It was as if we hadn't just met, and had known each other for months.

"That shade of red on your cheeks, it is the only color that rivals the green in your eyes," he added before opening the door behind him. "I'm gonna get your bag from my trunk."

His escape gave me a minute to take in what he'd said, making me feel entirely too many emotions at once.

"Everyone has a crush on him," I told myself. "You're not any different. Just don't act like Rachel."

I finished my self-pep talk before the door opened again, thankful I'd spared myself being the crazy one.

The few minutes it took him to get my bag also seemed to do him good, since he came back sporting what looked like a half-smile instead of the haunted look he'd had before.

"I got a text from Colin," he explained. "He wants me to update him all weekend about everything we do."

"See?" I started to stand, but the weight on my ankle made me hiss in pain. Rhys cut across the small room and sat me back down. "Now we are big liars."

"We won't lie," he smirked, moving some of my dark hair from my face. "Sorta. I'll pick you up at ten in the morning. Be ready."

"I cannot practice on this ankle. Not with you, at your speed."

"Colin wants me to help you focus. Doesn't mean it has to be on soccer."

He wasn't looking at me anymore, he was walking around and fixing my apartment so that I had something to hold onto when I walked myself around later. He even created a place to elevate my leg in my bed. Then he grabbed his phone and clicked on it a few times before holding it up and showing me that he'd ordered a Cuban sandwich from the place up the road, and was having it delivered.

"You're all set," he nodded with a straight smile. "Be careful on that foot tonight. Call me if you need anything."

Then he was gone, and I was still sitting there trying to figure out what the hell had happened, when the knock on the door came. I hobbled over, using the chair Rhys had put halfway between my bed and door to stabilize my walk.

The delivery guy held up the food with a smile when I opened the door. "Late dinner is served."

"Thank you," I grabbed the food and placed it on the counter in the kitchenette before turning back to the door. "Let me get a tip."

"You left the tip on the order, ma'am. Very generous, thank you."

He was gone as quickly as he came, and I shook my head in disbelief. Rhys ordered me dinner, left the tip, carried me, rubbed my shins, iced my ankle, called my eyes gorgeous, and told me he liked the color of my cheeks when I blushed.

"What the hell is happening right now?"

"It's just a sprain and it already feels better this morning." I was applying a little mascara while I talked to Erin so I didn't look as tired as I felt.

"Hunter is going to lose his shit," she said for the fifteenth time.

"Just remember not to tell anyone I sprained my ankle. I don't know what Rhys has up his sleeve but he definitely didn't tell Coach."

"So if you aren't going to practice, what are you doing all weekend?"

"I have no idea. Some part of me feels like I need to tell Rhys no, that I am going to go to practice like a good girl."

"But the other part of you wants to be a baaaad girl," Erin laughed.

"It's almost like a blessing in disguise. I'm tired of soccer, so I sprained my ankle and got a few days off. I would be crazy to turn that down."

"I can't argue with that. But can we also admit that turning down a weekend with Rhys Peyton would be crazy as well."

"He's just a means to get by," I laughed, playing off how right she was. "Gotta go, though."

My timing was impeccable, as a knock on my door followed those words.

"Say hi to the sexy superstar," Erin sang before hanging up.

"Coming," I yelled, taking my time navigating the short distance from my bathroom to the door. My ankle really did feel better but I could feel a twinge where the pain was prominent the night before. It was definitely too sore to walk on all day, but getting to the car wouldn't be a problem. I just hoped Rhys didn't plan on sprints down the field, or a scrimmage. Maybe he would take me to a movie and let me sit in the dark with my feet up.

"That would be a date, you idiot," I scolded myself quickly before opening the door. "H...eeyyyyy." Without even saying hello, Rhys scooped me into his arms and kicked the door closed behind him. "What are you doing?"

"No need to walk on that foot now that I'm here."

"It feels better," I laughed. "You can't carry me all day."

"I can if you stop squirming."

I steeled myself, and pulled back to look at his face. He had a few days of growth on his jaw, his dark eyes were sparkling with excitement, and he smelled like peppermint and sandalwood. It was a definite contrast to seeing him on the field. Less sweat, his hair somewhat in place, and he wore jeans instead of his normal workout clothes.

"Anything you need to grab?" He asked, turning me around in the room to look.

"Just my bag," I pointed to the hook on the door of the bathroom where I kept a crossbody bag. It served as a purse, gym bag, school bag, and whatever else I needed it for. Rhys walked to the door and lifted me up so I could get the strap over the hook, then he settled me back down and made his way to the door.

Once I was placed into his car, I watched as he rounded the front of the hood, tapping it twice as he passed by. My eyes caught the watch he wore, paired with a few leather bracelets, along with a long-sleeved Henley that was too hot for Miami. It made me think that whatever he had planned would be indoors.

With the music up, and the windows down, we drove away from the university toward the stadium where the Miami Inferno played. I was wearing flip flops and cut off jean shorts, so to keep myself from freaking out, I picked at the strands of fabric at the bottom of my shorts. Rhys shifted the gear in the car smoothly, and his hair was blowing in the wind. His sunglasses covered his eyes, but I could see a soft smile on his lips. The combination was sexy, and I started to pant like a dog. Only I was able to keep my tongue in my mouth—thank God.

I didn't know what Rhys had planned, but I knew one thing for sure. The heat taking over my body was not from the weather.

Rhys just made Miami *extra* hot.

Chapter Twelve

Rhys

"Here, put this on." I handed Ash one of my Inferno jerseys and grabbed another one for myself. "Over your shirt is fine."

I pulled my Henley off, and stood there shirtless for a minute while I took in Ash's confused stare. She was holding the jersey on one finger and was silent, her eyes trying to look anywhere but at me.

There was nothing special about what I had planned, but I knew she would say no if I told her before I got her where I wanted her. Ash seemed like the good girl type, and even though our day was going to consist of far less offenses than drugs and human trafficking, she wouldn't go through with it willingly.

"Put it on." I urged, snickering at my own words. Never in my life had I said those words to a woman as gorgeous and tempting as Ash.

"Can I ask you a question?" Ash found her voice, but her eyes were still trying to stay off of my naked torso. "What happened last night?"

"What do you mean?" I knew what she meant, but I needed to

buy time while I thought of an honest answer, without telling her the truth.

No one knew about Mel except those closest to me, and there was no way I was going to start spilling my guts to Ash. Especially when she was somehow making me feel human again.

Why did she have to be so curious?

I was two seconds away from telling Ash to relax all weekend, that our lie to Colin would just have to stand on its own. Anything to avoid her asking more questions. Didn't she see how uncomfortable I got?

"I mean," Ash sighed. "You got lost last night. Backed away. Spooked. I don't know. You ordered me food and rearranged my apartment, then walked out like 'nothing to see here.' But then showed up this morning acting like nothing happened. So, what happened?"

Damn her.

"Just remembered that game. No big deal. It was a rough night."

"You scored a hat trick Rhys. Three goals in one game and still had time to hit the showers early. How was it rough?"

"Personally," I snapped, reminding her there was more to me than what she saw on the field that night.

Ash could finally see my anger surfacing, but she didn't bite back. She settled on retreat, backing away a little, and nodding her understanding.

"Sorry." I practically growled the words. I was angry at myself again for not keeping my fun-loving persona at the forefront.

"No," Ash started adjusting the jersey in her hand, getting it ready to slide over her head. "I'm sorry. We aren't 'share your life story' friends, and trust me, I get that. I don't want to talk about me either."

She slid the jersey on while I took in what she had just said. There was more to all of us, but why did I think Ash was immune to any turmoil or drama in her life? Probably because she still had goals, and when you maintained your motivation and set sights on your goals, you hadn't yet learned how reckless that can be.

Ash was only twenty-two years old so she wasn't there yet. I had twelve years on her and in those years, I lived a lot of life, and learned a lot of lessons. We were in two different seasons of our lives.

But she had exposed that there was more, and I was a fiend for information when it came to that green eyed girl. Even if that did make me a hypocrite.

I could acknowledge how unfair that was.

"How about this?" I decided, about to go against everything I had just said for the sake of knowing her a little better. "I will answer one question. Just one. But you also have to answer one. Because we *are* friends, Ash. I want to *stay* friends. So baby steps."

I slid my jersey on while I waited for her response, but when I locked my eyes on hers again, I could tell she wasn't buying some of my bullshit. She saw right through me. The unfair nature of me wanting to keep my past private, while wanting her to expose herself to me.

She mulled my offer over, though, because as unfair and absurd as I sounded, she was intrigued. Ash was just as much of a fool for information as I apparently was.

"Deal." She licked her lips and nodded, looking around the empty locker room again. "But not now. If I only get one question, I want to think it over."

"Sounds good to me." Because, me too. I wanted to think it over.

"But, I mean...I'm going to ask you a lot of questions, Rhys. I may need to preface my big question with the fact that it's my big one, so you know."

My eyes squinted with my smile. She was overthinking. Which again, was something I could relate to with her.

"Like, what the hell are we doing here? That is a valid question, but it's not my big one."

I laughed and nodded, "Touché." Mel, the game, Colin, and anything else that was making me pissy, was forgotten as Ash made her very valid point. "And good question."

I grabbed a few more things from my locker and started to scoop her into my arms again to carry her to the field. But she raised her hands up to stop me and shook her head.

"I can walk. It won't get better if I get atrophy from Rhys Peyton's special medical treatment of non-use."

"Hey, I'm practically a doctor," I laughed.

"Well, Dr. Peyton," she motioned toward all the stuff I had in my hands. "What the hell is this about?"

Fuck, she hit another nerve without meaning to. *"Do you realize when we get married, I will be Dr. Peyton?"* Mel's words from the night before she left came flooding back.

"What happened?" Ash asked. "No wait! That wasn't the big one. Shit, I said something to make you space out again. Okay don't answer that. Unless you want to, then okay. But it's not my big one."

Damn she was cute. She made it so easy to let go of those moments.

"Nah," I waved her off, not wanting her to take the moment too seriously. "Just remembered that Cruz was supposed to be here by now."

"Cruz Martin?" Ash squealed.

"Wait, should I be offended that you are losing your shit over just hearing his name, but you stomped away from me with an attitude when we first met?"

"You kicked a ball into my stomach. I was mad."

"So if I hadn't done that, you'd have screamed my name too?" I got closer to her, my voice dipping low, and my double entendre creating that pink across her cheeks that I loved so much.

"You were there to make me play more soccer when all I really wanted to do was go home and study. You were at an unfair advantage from day one."

Her words were breathy, barely able to get them out from the effect our proximity was having on her. I should have stepped back and given her space, but I only drew in closer, taking my fingers to the strands of hair that always seemed to find their way from behind her ear. Gently, I pushed the hair back into place, and suppressed a groan when her breath hitched from my touch.

It would be so easy to kiss her. Everything about her was drawing me in, and with my eyes locked on hers, I was having a hard time remembering why kissing her was a bad idea.

"Just once," I bargained with myself, even though she could hear me fine. Her eyes moved to my lips and then back up to my eyes–the universal sign that she wanted me to kiss her.

"Just once," she repeated my words, no doubt telling herself that one kiss wouldn't hurt. If anything, it would help us move past the tension that had been brewing since she stormed in anger toward me on that field during our first practice.

I moved a hand to her waist with resolve and pulled her toward me so that there wasn't as much space between our bodies. I was standing at my full height, and our significant size difference made me feel like a king.

"One time," I reminded us both. Her slight nod was all I needed to bend down and push my lips to hers, gently, barely touching, before I stopped. If I only got one kiss from her, I wanted to go slow, to savor it in all its stages. Just like our *one* question, I wanted it to be a big one.

Before I could push further, to actually taste her lips and feel how soft they were, a door slammed and she jumped backward. Our eyes were wide, locked again in another stare down. This time in disbelief.

We almost kissed.

We almost caved.

And while I should have been relieved that the noise snapped some sense into one of us, all I felt was hunger and thirst. A tiny brush of her lips was not enough, and I became a man possessed with the urge to pull her back to me and demand we finish that *one* kiss.

If it wasn't for the fact that the slam of that door down the hallway meant Cruz was there, I would have. I just hoped she didn't take my retreat as surrender. Because come hell or high water, my new goal in life was to kiss Ash Keller.

Just once.

Chapter Thirteen

Ash

How did we go from talking to almost kissing? It happened so fast that I wasn't even sure where the transition was. I was going to let him kiss me, just once, like he said, and then try to act like it never happened. I wanted to know what it felt like to kiss him.

The intense moment made Cruz Martin walking in less thrilling than I thought it would be. The world's best goalie was right there for me to meet in person, and I wanted him to leave. Luckily the door he came through was down a hallway that led to the main part of the locker room, and it gave both Rhys and me a minute to get our shit together. But when Cruz introduced himself, I was still less than focused on anything besides almost kissing Rhys.

"Cruz is here to take pictures." Rhys' words were proving that he was less affected than I was, because he was actually able to form thoughts and sentences. I couldn't even manage to ask what the hell he meant by *pictures*.

Scooping me up into his arms, Rhys made his way down another hallway that had a light at the end. It was the field, and excitement started to course through me again. I was headed onto the Miami Inferno's field wearing Rhys Peyton's jersey, with Cruz Martin following us for some unknown reason.

"What the hell are we doing?" I finally asked.

"Is that the big one?" Rhys teased, only I couldn't tell if he thought I was asking about the field, or asking about the kiss.

"No. And why are you carrying me?" I kicked. "I told you I could walk."

Rhys' voice was low enough that Cruz couldn't hear him. "I have two good ankles but am still having a hard time keeping my knees locked right now. Be still."

Goosebumps formed on my skin as he unexpectedly admitted that he was affected just as much as I was. Without thinking, I squeezed his neck, and felt his groan making his chest vibrate. I had never doubted that I was physically attracted to Rhys. Hell, I knew that much before he even showed up at my practice. No girl was immune to Rhys' good looks and athletic body.

What I didn't expect was to be so drawn to him as a person. He had charmed me with his funny and caring side. I was in awe of how skilled he was with a ball. Mixed with whatever it was that occasionally haunted him, I was more than intrigued.

As we reached the end of the tunnel, Rhys took a few steps up from the bench area and onto the turf before he set me gently on my feet. Cruz joined us but his head was down, typing on his phone. He was either trying not to notice the tension between Rhys and me, or had something that was drawing his attention far away from whatever Rhys was having him do.

"Here." Rhys handed Cruz his phone and then took my hand, slowly leading me to the center of the field. "Be sure to get the stadium in the background but try not to get below our waists."

"Got it," Cruz laughed.

"Now can you tell me what we are doing?" I asked Rhys.

"Sending Colin some pics from our workout," he explained as if the answer was obvious.

"I'm not dressed for a workout."

"Neither am I. Here, let's spray some sweat on you."

He took a water bottle that he had been holding and started to spray my face. Then he turned to spray his own, and ran his hands through his hair to mess it up a little more than it already was. My mind started off trying to remember if I used waterproof mascara, but it diverted straight back to almost kissing Rhys when I saw the water falling from his cheeks and over his lips. His messy hair was begging me to run my fingers through it, and the smirk he gave me told me he knew exactly what I was thinking.

Cruz kicked a ball and Rhys stopped it between us before Cruz started yelling, "Okay now use the ball and school your faces. Act like this is a hard, and long ass practice."

"You cannot seriously be thinking of fooling Colin with pictures like this, can you?"

"Trust me," Rhys said with a tilt to his head. "This is me being nice to Colin."

"Being dishonest is being nice?"

"He needs to focus on his sister, not your ankle, and not your workouts. But I know he will ask, and I'm going to give him some proof."

"This is the craziest thing ever," I sighed, but still thinking he had a point. I absolutely did not want Coach worrying about the team.

"Without moving your feet, pretend you're trying to beat me one on one."

I did the best I could, taking a few suggestions from both Rhys and Cruz. The whole process shouldn't have taken that long, but Cruz kept saying something was missing, and snapped more and more pics with Rhys' phone.

After thirty minutes, Cruz shouted and started backing up farther away from us. "She looks sweaty but not flush. We need pink in her cheeks. I'm going to try from farther away and we can crop your legs out."

"Did you hear that?" Rhys growled. "You need to be flush. Pink. Maybe red. Needs to look like you just told me I was sexy again, or got mad at me for kicking you with the ball."

I definitely felt the effects from his words, but it wasn't enough to create the illusion that I had been working out all day. It made me want to smile.

"Don't make me touch you," Rhys warned. "Cruz thinks he's here to help me fuck around with Colin. He has no idea that when I graze your cheek with my fingers you turn that shade he's wanting to see in you."

"I can't just make myself look like that," I explained, but I was already breathing harder.

"You can imagine me almost kissing you again. How we both knew we needed just one. Picture me leaning down to meet your lips, and how if it wasn't for Cruz we may still be in there now. Tasting each other. Our arms holding onto each other for dear life. Trying to stop ourselves from taking it farther. The attraction we both feel, knowing it can't be any more than just one kiss to curb our—"

"Perfect." Once again, Cruz was responsible for reminding me how stupid I was as he ran toward us with Rhys' phone.

Rhys' words were cut off, but his thoughts carried on, and I could tell from the way he was still looking at me that everything he was saying was true. Not only were they true, but he was just as affected as I was.

"Here," Cruz handed Rhys his phone. "I gotta go, but this was fun. Fucking with Colin is my favorite past time."

Rhys smirked and nodded, thanking him, and somehow I was

able to give him a proper goodbye with a "nice meeting you", and "see ya around" tacked on. When we were alone again, Rhys started picking up the water bottle, the ball, and a few other things he had brought to the field.

I barely moved a muscle, but not from my ankle being in pain. It was from my knees feeling weak, and my brain not being able to erase what Rhys had said to me. Would a kiss be enough? Would we have kept going?

When we got back in the locker room, Rhys changed back into this other shirt and used his fingers to tame his hair.

"Colin won't know about your ankle." He assured me.

"Good. But I hate lying."

"You told me you didn't want him to worry. I'm just going the extra mile."

"Feels like we are playing him for a fool."

"It's just for fun, Ash. Colin isn't going to be butt hurt if he finds out."

I nodded, and trusted that he knew Coach well enough that he was right. But my stomach twisted into a knot. It wasn't very often I crossed the morally gray line of lies and deceit. It reminded me too much of my mother. She was a manipulator, and I vowed never to be like her.

Not even for a "good cause."

"Keep my jersey," Rhys smiled as I started to take it off. "Number seventeen looks good on you."

I nodded but took it off anyway. My head was somewhere else, hoping and praying I wasn't gradually turning into my mother. It was a fear that sometimes manifested in me when I least expected; and it was on the brink of taking over. I knew it was irrational, and unwarranted, but it wasn't like I had control of my triggers.

Suddenly, the room started to spin and I grabbed onto my

stomach. It had been a long time since my last panic attack, but I was mixing my unsure feelings for Rhys with lying to my coach. Add in a dash of overthinking about my mom, and I didn't stand a chance.

Chapter Fourteen

Rhys

The pictures were supposed to be funny, and we had fun taking them. But I didn't want that to be the end of our day. I wanted to show Ash the stadium, and let her see behind the curtain of the MLS.

"Let me give you the tour. We can even grab lunch at the cafe upstairs. It's open for the staff, and everybody that works here throughout the day. They have an awesome pastrami sandwich."

"Actually, Rhys, I just want to go home and lay down. I'm not feeling too well."

Her face was pale, and she was shaking a little. "You need me to—"

"Just take me home," she snapped, cutting me off.

"Whoa, okay. I'll take you home." She was more than ill, she was angry, but I had no idea what had changed, or what had upset her. "But can you tell me what just happened?"

"Nothing happened," she sighed, before mumbling, "And maybe we need to keep it that way," as she turned away from me.

Was she talking about the fact that we almost kissed? Because I was still thinking that was a good idea.

Maybe I was wrong.

Space. We needed space. Taking her home, letting her rest her ankle, and giving her space was a good idea. Space provided perspective, and I needed to remember all the reasons I told myself about why kissing Ash was a bad idea.

Because at that moment in time, I couldn't think of any of them.

"Let's go then." I flipped my keys in my hand, then motioned for her to lead the way. She wasted no time grabbing her bag and shuffling ahead of me to her escape. There was still a slight limp in her stride, but she had been right about it being a small sprain. Heat and ice tonight would have her back in shape as early as tomorrow.

On the ride back, the windows were down and reggaeton was blasting through the speakers. It was my only hope of distraction—for myself. The music seemed to be lightening her mood as well. Her fingers were tapping to the music and there was a slight sway in her shoulders. Her mouth moved to the lyrics, words spoken in Spanish that I had no idea how to translate, but a beat so sexy that it was one of my favorite songs. Watching her love something I loved, and reacting to it the way I did, was making me feel less and less like I should drop her off and let her be.

It's a bad idea, I repeated in my head.

When I pulled up to her apartment, and the music stopped, she closed off again and barely looked at me. Without a word she climbed out of the car, managing a short look back at me before unlocking her door. I rendered her a small salute as a goodbye, then hit the gas and sped off, wasting no time creating more distance between us.

My head was all over the place. I hated driving away when she didn't feel well. It went against every instinct in my body.

By the time I got halfway home, my phone started ringing over

Bluetooth, making my music stop. I grabbed my phone and looked at the caller ID before answering, hoping it was her and prepared to do a U-turn in the middle of traffic to get back to her if she needed me.

Cruz.

"Already miss me?" I answered with a laugh and a hint of disappointment.

"Something like that." I could hear laughter in his tone as well. "You alone?"

"Yeah, why?"

"Because holy shit, Ash is fucking gorgeous."

What the fuck did he think he was doing? Did he seriously want to play rough? Because after the shift in Ash and barely saying goodbye to her, I was primed for a fight.

"Yeah, so?" The laughter was gone, and in its place was a robot—monotone, small words, and clipped responses.

"Just wondering if she is your rebound."

Rebound?

"You need one," he continued. "That last chick has been gone for two months now. Time to take that anger and bullshit out on someone else. Just not the same way you took it out on Garcia."

"Ash isn't a rebound. She's just a girl that Colin has me coaching."

"No fucking way was that coaching, Rhys. If I hadn't been there you two would have been *metiendo mano en la malla*."

I sighed as Cruz continued to laugh at himself. The very last thing I wanted was a rebound, but now that he had said it, I couldn't stop wondering. What if my attraction to Ash *was* a rebound? What if it wasn't real? How did that not cross my mind?

What if she picked up on that?

"I had to bail on you two and go rub one out from all the damn tension I felt."

"Ash is too young to be a rebound," I argued, gripping the steering wheel and gritting my teeth. I was desperately trying not to let the picture of him stroking his dick to Ash's image get to me.

"She's not too young," he countered. "And she is the complete opposite of the last one."

Ash was definitely the opposite of Melanie. Cruz didn't know enough about either of them to properly make that assessment, but he wasn't wrong. Where Melanie had fair skin and blonde hair, Ash had a darker complexion and dark brown hair–almost black. Mel was a doctor, but she kept herself high on a pedestal of prim and proper. She wouldn't have been caught dead on a soccer field. Not to mention my reggaeton music was banned when she was around.

"Look," I sighed as I pulled into the parking garage to my building. "Ash is fucking beautiful, definitely not Mel, and we have a lot more in common than I thought we would. But I'm not stupid enough to sleep with her. I may not mind messing with Colin about fake soccer practice, but that was just supposed to be fun. Fucking one of his players is crossing the line. Especially if I was just using her."

Cruz continued to laugh as I started over explaining myself in an attempt to make *me* believe the bullshit I was spewing. "What he doesn't know won't hurt him. Besides, it's not his kid, and you're both adults."

"Very funny." I jerked my car into park and started strumming my fingers on my leg.

"Eventually you're going to want to get that dick wet again and..."

I pressed END on my phone and hung up, not wanting to hear Cruz talk about my dick. A text popped up before I could even climb from my car with what looked like twenty laughing emojis from Cruz. Why did he like getting under my skin and pushing my buttons?

I made a mental note to return that favor one day. Eventually, he'll grow up and some poor girl will make his head spin.

Instead of heading up to my apartment, I took the stairs to the ground floor of the parking garage and out the door to Bayfront Park.

When I first moved to Miami, it wasn't my intention to live downtown, but I already had the place and it made sense to stay there. It ended up being the best decision because the access to the park was one of the things I loved most about where I lived.

The park was full of life and it always grounded me. Mel hadn't been a big fan of anything outdoors so I spent our entire relationship avoiding the fresh air, unless I was on the field. Now I soaked it in every chance I got.

Sitting down in the grass, I rested my forearms on my knees, holding my phone in one hand as I looked around. Friends were laughing, families were spending time together, and kids were running around.

It was my dream life, so simple and joyous.

"Fuck Mel," I whispered to myself. "Why did you have to spook so easily?"

Even knowing how different we were, I'd trade the fresh air to have her back in my life. No matter how angry I was, she was the first woman I ever loved.

I had respected her wishes and never contacted her after that night, but talking to Cruz about Ash being a rebound made me wonder if I needed more closure with Mel. It also made me wonder if I had made a mistake not trying to get in touch with her. She may have needed me to reach out, explain, and fix whatever was broken that night.

Ash's anger was a sign that I had been headed in the wrong direction. That it wasn't time to close the book on Mel, yet.

Lifting my hand slightly, I thumbed through my phone and found Mel's number in my contact list. My finger hovered over the *call* button as I made a deal with myself. If she answered, then I would go from there, if she didn't, then I would be able to at least say I tried.

Chapter Fifteen

The weekend of silence was refreshing. I was able to get ahead on my school work, rest, and stretch my ankle out. I didn't hear from Rhys at all. He could tell I was icy when he took me home Saturday, and I could tell he was responding by being cold to me as well. It may have been easier to tell him the truth; that I was overwhelmed and started to panic. But it was embarrassing, and would have opened the door to discussing feelings I shouldn't be having toward him, and feelings I hated having toward my mother.

It was easier, and though he may not forgive me, or understand, I've always taken care of myself the best way I knew how. I did what I had to do.

Of course, I told Erin everything when she brought me dinner Sunday night. We sat on my bed and ate, filling each other in on our weekend.

"He almost kissed me," Damn, I sounded more like a twelve year old than a grown woman.

"What?" Erin screamed. "Why *almost*? Why not all the way?"

"Cruz Martin came in and slammed a door making me fly away from Rhys like he had cooties."

"You got to meet Cruz Martin?"

"Geez you're starting to sound like Rachel."

"Hey now," she laughed and pointed her fork toward me. "I'm a fan, but you will never see me throwing myself at one of them like Rachel."

She was telling the truth there. Cruz was the newest addition to the Miami Inferno and already had a huge fan base because he was originally from Miami. Erin was part of that, but she would rather die than get labeled a squealing fan girl.

"Okay back up, don't try to distract me. Tell me the rest of the story."

"Not much to tell. We kinda quietly agreed to kiss once. Just so we could let go of the tension, ya know? But, it didn't happen. And I'm thankful for that. It kept me from making a huge mistake. Then we took some pictures for him to send to Coach. I felt guilty lying to Coach, and I randomly started thinking about my mom. From there I just spiraled into a panic and shut down. But it was a good thing, because had self-preservation not kicked in, I would have kissed him when the opportunity came back around, and I wouldn't know what to do with that."

"You'd enjoy it!" She screeched.

"I doubt I'm strong enough to enjoy just one kiss and walk away. And since I'm not what he's looking for in his life, it's best if I don't risk getting attached."

"Hey, there is nothing wrong with having a fling. Sex has been known to relax you and help you focus."

"Wow," I deadpanned. "This escalated quickly. How did *one* kiss turn to sex and a fling?"

"My mind goes where it goes, Ash. There are no straight roads up here." She tapped her temple, making me giggle.

"Well, now that we've had time to cool down. I'm sure we'll be back to normal. I really do like being his friend."

"Boooooo." She gave me a thumbs down, and then threw a

cashew at me for good measure. I knew I needed to change the subject before she took me wedding dress shopping.

"How has Hunter been acting?"

"Ugh." Erin put her food container down and pushed it away, making a show of losing her appetite. "Whatever is going on with him, he needs to chill the fuck out."

"That bad?"

"It's not that he's doing anything wrong, he's just acting differently and, I don't know... scary?"

"We need to say something to Coach when he gets back."

"Say what? That Hunter's angry and barely talks? That isn't exactly a good reason to raise hell."

"I'll be back at practice tomorrow. Not that I can help, he creeps me out too. But at least we'll be together."

"Yesssss," she pointed at me and then stood from my bed. "I'm glad you got to rest this weekend, but practice will be better with you there. Ankle good to go?"

"Yep!" I stretched my leg out and twisted it around for good measure, showing her I was ready to get back to business. It felt weird even wanting to go to practice since I had been actively trying to avoid playing soccer for a while. But I had to give Rhys credit, playing soccer with him was fun, and it brought back the fire I had lost somewhere in my studies.

After Erin left, I took a quick shower and climbed into bed. It was still early, but what else was I going to do? Papers were finished, textbooks were read, and I didn't have a TV. Watching YouTube, or reading a romance book was at the top of my list, and since I wasn't feeling lovey-dovey, I opted for videos of the best soccer goals of all time.

Naturally, Rhys was on there more than once, and though I could have scrolled past it, I found myself rewatching them over and over again. Only when a text popped up did I realize I had been watching the same video for nearly 20 minutes.

Practice tomorrow at 7

K

He wasn't exactly sending me warm and fuzzy vibes, so my short response seemed valid.

Bring a change of clothes.

K

Wait! Why?

Because we are going to learn to focus tomorrow.

My heart started racing thinking about what he could have meant. Focus on what? I didn't need a change of clothes to focus on soccer.

K

Dammit, I should have said 'Hell no,' but I was way too curious and as long as I remembered Rhys was just a friend, spending time with him wasn't hard. It only got hard when we made it awkward, and there wasn't a chance we would make that same 'almost' mistake. Right?

Feel better?

Yes. Sorry about that, by the way.

You don't have to apologize.

Did you have a good weekend?

Yep. You?

Sure.

Sure? Sure wasn't an answer.

Ankle feels okay?

Yeah, full range. I'm all better.

Good. Now Colin won't kill me.

Did you send him the pics?

Surprisingly, he didn't ask for any. So I didn't
even send them.

A sigh of relief escaped and I relaxed farther into the pillow behind my head. It made me feel a little better that Rhys didn't have to send pictures to keep up the ruse. But another thought crept in. I had to face Hunter, and I'd lie through my teeth to him with no issues. Especially if he gave me any issues about missing practice.

Send me a pic in case Hunter asks.

image sent

Night Ash.

Night.

I opened the file he sent and saved it to the pictures on my phone. The redness of my face and his angle made it look like we really were scrimmaging on the field. But that was not what was happening.

In the picture, you couldn't see Rhys' face, but I knew his mouth was moving and saying all sorts of things to create that look on my face. Things I wished, at the time, were real.

Monday started off normal–exactly was what I needed. Classes and then practice.

With Hunter leading the team though, practice dragged on longer than normal, or at least it felt like it. I was drained, both mentally and physically.

Hunter never questioned me about missing practice over the weekend, but I felt like I paid the price with how hard he pushed us. Coach never rode us that hard the night before a game. Hunter had us unsure if we were going to be able to walk, much less play.

While everyone else left the field, I stayed behind and waited on Rhys. He was always there when we finished practices, but it was nearing seven-fifteen and he was nowhere to be seen. Had he not texted me to confirm, I would have assumed he was standing me up, deciding my little breakdown had been too much for him and he was out. But since he had, I laid down in the grass and waited a little longer.

Finally, I heard his car and lifted my head from the ground just enough to see him slamming his door and walking toward me. He wasn't in clothes for practice, he was dressed in jeans and a graphic t-shirt with flip flops. His hair was done–as done as Rhys' wild mane ever got–and he had on the watch and bracelets that he'd worn on Saturday.

I rolled to my side and got up, trying to hide the shakiness in my knees so he didn't know practice had gotten the best of me. He was marching across the field, almost angry, definitely on a mission.

He looked around as if someone was calling his name, but there was no one around but me, standing alone in the goalie box. I probably should have met him at midfield, maybe even tried kicking a ball, but the look on his face made me freeze.

Something was wrong.

Very wrong.

Chapter Sixteen

Rhys

When I showed up at the practice field, I had to pull over on the side of the road before I could go into the parking lot. I wanted to wait for everyone to clear out so they didn't see me dressed casually. The problem was, the girls looked drained, and took forever getting their stuff together.

Then there was Hunter.

He had followed the girls until he reached the edge of the field, then stood behind a tree while he watched Ash. She was alone, laying down and catching her breath. It took everything I had not to confront Hunter and ask him why he was creeping around. The only thing that stopped me was the likelihood that I would end up punching him, or hitting him with my car. I didn't want the night to go in that direction.

After ten minutes, he left, trudging back to the locker rooms and offices without saying anything to Ash. I waited till he was completely gone to drive up into the lot and then made a beeline to Ash as if she were in danger unless I was right next to her.

"Get your stuff," I commanded. "We're leaving."

"Wh–"

"I told you to have clothes, Ash. Don't act surprised that we aren't sticking around here tonight."

"You seem angry, what the hell is going on?"

"I asked you that same question on Saturday, and got nothing."

My face was red, my anger at Hunter getting the best of me. And she didn't move. Scooping her up by the waist, I threw her over my shoulder like a caveman. I wasn't going to be able to calm down until I was away from the temptation to find Hunter and ask what his problem was.

"Rhys what are you doing?" She squealed and kicked.

I remained quiet and grabbed her bag, leaving everything else scattered on the field. It would be fine where it was, or I'd send the university everything to replace it if it wasn't.

I didn't even care.

Getting to my passenger side, I pulled the door open and carefully put Ash down. "Get in."

She quickly slid into the seat, not arguing with me, though she was clearly annoyed. Her arms were crossed and she was eyeing me like I had gone mad.

I rounded the car to my side, jumped in, and flew from the lot as quickly as possible. Ash just kept her arms crossed and shook her head every so often. Not until I was away from the university did I start to calm down. Turning the music off, and then running a hand down my face to clear my head, I decided I had finally calmed down enough to tell her what got me so upset in the first place.

"I was late because Hunter was leering at you from behind a tree. Hiding, or some shit. I had an early dinner with a teammate and didn't have time to change. And didn't want him to see me dressed casually and realize that we were not practicing, so I waited him out. But the more he stood there, the angrier I got.

Ash, I literally pictured myself ramming him with my car. Dammit, every time I see him, I hate him a little more."

Without looking at her, I placed both hands on the steering wheel and squeezed, hoping she took my stance as casual. It wasn't normal for me to feel that way. I had no idea what was happening.

"He's harmless."

"You keep saying that, but how long has he coached you?"

"Just this year."

"Exactly. Not long enough for you to know who he is."

"I've known him longer than you, but you're the one that carried me off that field. You're the one that threw me in the car and drove off like you were kidnapping me. What if he saw you and thought the same thing?"

"A few nights ago you were freaking out because you thought he texted you. Now you're defending him?"

"I don't want him texting me or calling me. And to be clear, he hasn't actually done that. He gives me the creeps, but until he crosses a line, it's all just a gut feeling that a few of us have. I don't want you to do something crazy."

"I'm different," I explained, my tone finally easing back into the casual, playfulness that I tried to give everyone. "You wanted to come with me."

"What makes you so sure?"

"When I texted you last night, you said 'k.' If you didn't want to go, you would have said, 'nope.'"

She laughed and I finally looked over at her, seeing for the first time how weary she was. Practice must have been brutal, and I also wondered how much of that was still lingering from the weekend.

"You scared me Saturday," I confessed. "I didn't know what happened."

"I think I started to panic." She looked out the window and sighed, the confession weighing on her.

"I don't want to be the reason you panic."

No response. Just silence for a few more minutes as we drove through downtown.

"You intrigued me," she finally said. "And I'm curious where we're going."

"My place," I smiled, enjoying the way her head whipped toward me and her eyes widened with shock. "Scared of me now?"

"No. But why are you taking me to your place?"

"I have a good setup for getting my body ready for a game," I reminded her. "You don't need to always grind the way we have been."

From the corner of my eye, I could tell she was staring at me while pulling at her lips with two fingers in a fidgeting manner. The plan was solid though, and had nothing to do with Hunter creeping around. It was my plan from the get-go, the only change being the venue.

Originally I was going to take her to the stadium to use the ice bath. But a few of the guys mentioned they were going back after dinner, so I had to make a new plan on the way to get her. I wanted to take her somewhere more secure, safer. Somewhere neither one of us had to look over our shoulders and worry about who was around.

After the shit Cruz gave me on Saturday, and then again at practice on Sunday, he would never let me live it down if he saw I had Ash in the ice tub.

I pulled into my parking garage and Ash jumped from the car, holding her bag and looking around while she waited. I grabbed my own bag from the trunk and took her hand, guiding her toward the private elevator that went directly up to my penthouse.

"Fancy," she mumbled.

The mirrored walls of the elevator surrounded the space, and I looked at the reflection of us standing side by side, our hands together, and our bodies close to one another.

I expected her to drop my hand, maybe even step away to create space between us, but instead her eyes locked on mine in the mirror. We stayed that way for the rest of the ride to the top floor, until the doors opened making the mirror disappear.

The elevator opened directly into the foyer of the apartment, which was open to the kitchen and a dining area. Straight ahead was my living room. The far wall was nothing but glass windows and doors that led to a balcony. It wrapped around my entire side of the building, and you could look across the bay and the skyline of South Beach.

Ash let go of my hand and started walking around, taking in the decor and the view. Her fingers lightly floated over the back of my couch, then a lamp, and landed on a picture frame I had on the end table.

"Is this your brother?" She asked, bringing the picture closer to analyze it a little more.

"Yeah, Levi. He and I actually own this place together, but he lives in Atlanta so it's all mine for now. We got it before I signed with Miami, as a little getaway place, but for the last six years it's been home sweet home.

"He coaches in Atlanta, right?"

"Yeah football, the Jets."

She nodded, placed the picture back down, and began looking around her in every direction. I poured two glasses of water and two glasses of wine, then balanced the four glasses in my huge hands until I was in front of the couch.

Without having to ask, Ash rounded the couch to join me and took the waters from my grasp, setting them down. We both lowered to the couch, sitting at an angle so we faced one another. She was still in her practice gear, including her cleats and shin guards. Her hair was falling from her ponytail and her arms still had pieces of grass stuck to them from lying down after being so sweaty.

"Here," I handed her water. "Drink this first."

With no arguments, she took the glass to her lips and drank the water without even a breath. I handed her the next glass and watched her throat move as she drank that one as well.

"Lay back," I suggested when she was done. "Let's get these off."

I pulled her legs up into my lap and started undoing her laces one at a time. I could tell she was close to arguing and pulling them from my grasp, but she stayed quiet and eventually gave in.

Just like the night she sprained her ankle, I rubbed at her shins, trying to make the embossed design from her shin guards disappear. Only her soft moan reminded me that I was off track and toeing the line of insanity with her once again.

Pushing her legs down, I stood up and cleared my throat, needing some space to remember what the hell my original plans were.

Think, Rhys. Think.

Oh yea, she needed to relax.

"Follow me."

She padded her bare feet across the tile and stood next to me where I had stopped near a staircase. Without her shoes on, I towered over her even more. The way she looked up at me, with so much trust in her eyes, was making me want to stay just like that, standing there and soaking her in.

Why did I think I could erase our connection over the weekend? Despite her anger, and despite my motives, I wanted to kiss her again.

"After you," I motioned for her to head up the stairs ahead of me.

"I'm not going up those stairs till you tell me what the hell we are doing."

"Swimming," I said immediately. "Just swimming."

"You didn't tell me to pack a suit."

"Well swimming wasn't my original plan," I confessed. "I'm improvising right now."

"It feels like..." she trailed off, not sure she should finish her sentence. Nor did I want her to. I knew what it felt like. It felt like I was off the rails again, back in that moment when I leaned down and told her I needed to kiss her just one time. But I wasn't, that wasn't what this was at all. I was past wanting to kiss her just one time, I wanted to kiss her a million times.

I wouldn't

But I wanted to.

Chapter Seventeen

It felt like he was trying to seduce me. Like he had decided he wanted that kiss and was putting the work in so that I would give it to him, instead of running away.

I didn't bother finishing my thought, though. If I said it, it would make it real again, and I still wasn't sure I could handle kissing him. Not even once.

Shrugging, I visibly gave up the thought and started walking up the stairs that I assumed led to the pool. They were winding and at the top was a sliding glass door that was already open to the rooftop.

Rhys' penthouse was unbelievable. Something I imagined was too rich for even the likes of doctors and lawyers. This kind of lifestyle was reserved for the super-rich, the ones that played sports, or made movies. At least from what I could guess. I had no experience being around anything that lavish.

"Wow," I breathed, as I stepped close to the edge. "This view is amazing."

"It's like being on top of the world." His voice seemed in awe of his surroundings, like he couldn't believe that was his life. I didn't even want to speculate how much money a place like this would cost, but I was willing to bet that our view that night was sponsored by *adidas*. I was a freshman in college when it was reported that Rhys had signed with *adidas*. A very lucrative sponsorship contract, and I knew to this day he still wore all their gear, and was in plenty of their commercials.

"You must be pretty used to it, though."

"I never get used to shit like this," he shrugged. "I will never forget where I'm from, and how hard life was growing up. I try to soak in my blessings every chance I get. Or at least I used to, and I'm trying to start again."

Rhys was irresistible. Seeing him in real life, as opposed to on TV, or even at a game, he was just like anyone else. He didn't have an air of entitlement following him around. It felt no different talking to him than it did any other guy.

With the exception of the insane sexual tension he created.

No guy I had ever talked to before made me feel so weak with just a glance or a casual touch. Rhys was superior in that department, but it wasn't because he was rich and famous, it was because he was just Rhys, no matter what.

"I don't have a suit," I reminded him, breaking us away from the view and back to business.

"You have on *Dri-FIT* shorts and a sports bra. It's practically a swimsuit."

I licked my lips and turned around to face the pool. Lights had come on around the rooftop as the sun was fading. I peeled my practice jersey over my head and tossed it onto a chair before dragging a foot into the water to test the temperature.

"You coming too?"

Rhys swallowed and slid his hands into his jean pockets, shaking his head slightly to tell me he had no intention of getting in. "Just relax. Let the water cool you down."

Taking the steps gingerly, I tried gradually adjusting to how cold the water was, not wanting to lose my breath by diving in.

"How is it so cold? It's on a roof in the middle of Miami, shouldn't it feel like a bath?"

"I have a cooler on it, for this very reason. I do laps after practice sometimes. Well, I did before I started coming to the university."

"Then I don't understand why you're not joining me now, didn't you have practice today too?"

"Yeah, but it won't be very relaxing if I join you."

"Why is that?"

"Don't play dumb, Ash." He rested his hands on the back of a chair in front of him and leaned over, eyeing me. "You know why."

"Honestly," I huffed, "I don't know anything anymore. Being around you is like having a serious case of whiplash."

He stood straight, his mask slipping to show me he knew exactly how I felt. Like we couldn't decide if we were coming or going, hot or cold, north or south. I left him to figure it out while I dove backward and submerged myself the rest of the way into the water. Under the water, my thoughts were quiet, and my concentration was on my task. Using the wall, I pushed back the other way and didn't come up again until I was right where I was standing moments before.

Rhys was still in place, but the look on his face changed. He nodded to himself a few times before flicking his wrist and catching his watch as it fell off. He took the bracelets off as well, then reached behind him and pulled his shirt over his head to reveal his chest.

My heart started racing, knowing that calling him a case of whiplash had spurred anything holding him back. He was about to prove a point, that joining me in the pool was about to be the opposite of relaxing.

So far, he was right, because I could barely handle it when he flicked his belt open and unbuttoned his jeans. Kicking his flip flops to the side, he let his zipper down and his jeans fell, showing me he was a boxer-briefs guy.

Thank you, adidas. Thank you.

Like a panther, he started walking toward the deep end, his eyes on me and his gait steady and calm. I followed his gaze, turning as he got farther away. When he stopped at the deep end, he smirked, and shrugged one last time before muttering. "No more whiplash."

Then he dove in head first and I watched as his body got closer and closer to where I was standing. The water was coming to my stomach so when he was directly in front of me I could see all the way to the bottom. He pushed on the floor of the pool and came up, so close to me that the water dripping from his hair splashed me in the face, making me turn to protect my eyes.

Without even getting a chance to look back, his hand was on my cheek and he was pulling me back to face him. His head tilted and he brought his lips close to mine. "Just once," he whispered, before closing the small gap between us.

Our lips touching was like an imprint, molded as if they were always meant to be together. We breathed in the feel of our connection while both of Rhys' hands held my cheeks gently. He pushed harder, slipping his tongue between my lips, and demanded entrance to my mouth.

My hands found his chest and I traced the lines of his muscles before grabbing onto his shoulders and holding myself as close to him as I could. His resounding groan sent chills down my spine, and I knew why romance novels always described kisses as melting, because that was exactly what I was doing.

Cold in the pool, but miraculously melting in Rhys' arms.

Rhys moved his hands from my face and ran them down my body, finding the backside of my thighs and pulling me closer. I wrapped my legs around his waist, my arms around his neck. I could feel how hard he was and I moved my pelvis against him, begging him for more.

"Just once."

Rhys' words played again in my head and I knew he was right. He had been warning me, knowing that whatever feelings had started boiling between us weren't going to be satiated until we had just one kiss.

When I finally came up for air, I realized we were no longer in the pool. Rhys had carried me from the cold water and was laying me on one of the loungers. His body hovered over mine as we continued to kiss like it was our only way into heaven. I no longer cared that it was a bad idea because it had become glaringly obvious that we were always going to end up like this.

Just once.

Chapter Eighteen

Rhys

The way I felt when I saw Hunter watching Ash should have been my first clue that I was in too deep with her. But in my defense, I had never been so captivated by a woman that I had never even kissed. Even with Mel, it took weeks to realize she was capable of changing my life and turning it upside down.

I barely had to look at Ash before I knew how remarkable she was. Her fire, her boldness, and her beauty all smacked me in the face that first night I met her. But that didn't mean I had to kiss her.

I didn't have to protect her.

I didn't have to bring her into my home.

Now that I knew how she tasted, I was fucking done for. Kissing wasn't enough. Not for either of us. The only thing holding me back was Cruz in the back of my mind telling me she was a rebound. Ash didn't deserve to be anyone's rebound.

That should have been all I needed to make me pull away but when she started moving her body against mine, those thoughts dissipated, and I allowed myself to give her more.

Laying her on the lounge, I pressed my cock into her core,

wanting to know what she sounded like when she felt me. Rebound or not, no one ever accused me of being a good decision maker. Hell, when it came to decisions, I was downright reckless. So why stop when I had Ash under me, willing to let me take her anywhere I wanted to go?

"I'm going to kiss you again," I told her, grabbing her by the back of the head to keep her close. I thrust my tongue into her mouth, our teeth almost hitting as I seemed to be losing control. I could barely pull my lips from hers to talk, so overwhelmed with the need to stay connected to her.

"You have to," she groaned against my mouth.

"No choice," I agreed.

"Please."

I moved my mouth to her neck, placing open mouthed kisses on her skin. Her nails found my back and she ran them up to my shoulders, leaving marks on my skin. So deep it made me hiss and jerk, but knowing I would feel them and remember that moment tomorrow, made me want more.

"Damn, baby, you trying to kill me?"

She giggled, fucking giggled. I had heard her laugh, but her giggle was special. Like hearing her moan when we were close, or the way she grunted when she kicked the ball. Noises that may as well have been big red easy buttons straight to my dick.

"I just need more."

This was not what Colin had in mind when he asked me to take care of Ash. Fucking her was not his idea of helping her focus. But I would bet my entire *adidas* contract that she was going to be focused for a while. Her attention was going to be on me, on how many times I could make her come, and all the ways she could beg for more.

"Take your bra off. Let me see those tits." I demanded. She reached for the elastic of her sports bra and pulled the wet material slowly over her head. Her dark nipples were fucking perfect and I took a hand to my dick to calm him down, making her lick her lips while she watched.

Grabbing her small shorts, I yanked them down and tossed them somewhere behind me, not caring if they flew over the wall and down the forty flights. She was bare and her legs fell open, giving me a view of how wet her pussy was. She wasn't shy about showing me exactly what I was doing to her.

"So young," I teased, getting off on the fact that she was still in college. "How experienced are you, Ash?"

"Enough to know what I want," she snapped. "Enough that you don't have to worry about being noble and virtuous. Don't be nice to me, Rhys."

Oh fuck. Her words were like poetry. I wanted to tattoo them on my body. *"Don't be nice to me, Rhys."* As much as I loved the fact that she wasn't innocent, I wanted to kill anyone that had come before me. All I could do was make sure she forgot they ever existed. And I was determined to make sure that anyone who came after me was compared to how good I was going to make her feel.

Reaching to her nipple, I pinched, making her hiss from the pain before I rolled it between my fingers and grabbed onto her entire breast. It was like testing them, and her, seeing what she liked, and what made her squirm. I wanted to study everything about her body.

Straddling the lounge chair, I opened her legs wider and got as close to her as I could. Her nipples needed to be in my mouth. I wanted to flick my tongue and play with them until they were hard enough to cut me.

"Your tits are perfect," I mumbled, almost unaware that I had even said it out loud.

"Put your mouth on them, Rhys. I could come with just a flick of your warm tongue."

So responsive, and telling me what she wanted was a fucking

turn on. Leaning down, I did as she requested and swirled my tongue around. Her pussy was close to me because of how we were sitting, but not close enough for her to find the friction she started rooting for. Laying one hand over her clit, I let her ride my fingers. She was so confident, seeking her pleasure and using my fingers like they were her personal toy.

My tongue kept working her nipples until her legs started to shake and a few mumbled whispers spewed from her mouth. I pressed a little harder on her clit, giving her more than she was taking, wanting to make sure she had no choice but to come. Her eyes rolled back in her head and she screamed as the waves of pleasure ripped through her body.

I had never seen anything so beautiful. More powerful.

More...

"More," she pleaded. "More Rhys." Like she could read my mind, she begged, using the only word I could register.

I shook my head in disbelief and when I spoke, my voice was raspy and rough. "You're fucking perfect, Ash. And trust me, we aren't even close to being done."

Taking my fingers that were on her clit, I ran them through her cum and then brought them to her nipples, circling the dark area and making a mess for me to clean up. I put my mouth back on her and sucked like I needed her tits to survive.

She instantly started to shake again, and I knew the buildup in her body had come right back to the point of unrestrained desire.

"So needy," I growled. I pulled her by the thighs until her pussy was against my stomach and added, "Use my body baby. I wanna see more."

Just like she did my hand, she ground her pussy on my stomach and started shaking, moaning, and holding on tight to my neck for leverage. I kept my tongue on her nipples, giving each of them the attention they deserved, and trying to keep myself from coming in my shorts.

"My cock wants you so bad," I hissed. "He's jealous of my stomach, getting to feel how wet you are. Fuck, Ash, I may come right now. Just like this. You want to see me emasculated by how bad I need you?"

"Rhys," she cried, my words hitting her right where I wanted them. "Oh God."

Her climax was better than the first one, so raw and unrefined. It made my chest hurt, in a good way, to see her like that. She was panting for air, her eyes were unfocused, and the whole moment felt surreal.

Pulling her up from the chair, I held her in my arms while I made my way back inside, down the stairs, and to my bedroom. She was lethargic, but strong, and held on tight until I laid her down on my silk sheets. By then, she was refocused and ready. Her need seemed to be endless.

Ash watched me while I dropped my boxer-briefs and stroked myself. Somewhere in the back of my mind, I knew I needed to get a condom, but I was having a hard time breaking the stare down we were having as she waited for me to pounce.

I knelt on the edge of the bed, buying time so I didn't have to reach for that protection. I wanted as much of my bare skin on her as I could get before the magic was dimmed by responsibility. "Come suck my dick."

Getting on her hands and knees, she crawled to get close to me and looked up with her bright green eyes. They were glowing with lust, so bright we could have found our way around in the dark. Her hair had come loose from the bun she'd had it in earlier, and I pulled the tie out to let it fall free and frame her face.

Her tongue snuck out to taste the precum from my tip, and my knees locked tight at that first feeling of her warm mouth. I put my hand behind her head and shamelessly guided her down my shaft, wanting to keep control so the night wasn't over anytime soon. It was new to me, to be practically vibrating from small touches, and I wasn't sure I could trust myself.

My hips moved when she got to my base and she opened her throat to take all of me as far as she could. Her small gag made me thrust forward, wanting to hear her struggle. I wanted to be too much for her, and push her to her limits.

The decision to dive in and kiss Ash was calculated, spurred on by her doubt and confusion. I knew I had been back and forth, fighting myself on what was right, and what was needed, but she felt it too. It was making us both crazy and I knew that kissing her was the only option. But I had no idea that I would be taken over by instinct, and unable to pull away from her.

It wasn't just me, either.

Ash was receptive and moving on impulse. She was sucking my cock like she was applying for a full time job and I offered shit, like benefits, and a 401k.

She'd have been hired.

Probably promoted.

But I had to stop her. It was too much. And if I only got one chance, I didn't want her mouth being my final destination.

Chapter Nineteen

Ash

Once Rhys' lips were on mine, the entire world shifted on its axis. School didn't matter, soccer was third rate, and any goals I had for myself were no longer relevant. All that mattered was that even though it was supposed to be an inch, we were taking a mile.

Rhys may not have planned things that way, but being secluded, on top of the world, and alone, was all the temptation we needed. It wasn't very often that I found myself with no books to read, no papers to write, no ball to kick, no coach to yell, and no goal to focus on. Rhys may not have realized it yet, but he had given me more than what either of us knew I needed that night. More than relaxation and conditioning.

Freedom.

Watching him fall apart with me was exhilarating and I was eager to please him. I wanted him to remember my mouth, think about it every time he walked into his bedroom. I wanted him to stop mid stride, look at his bed, and picture me on my hands and knees, sucking him and pleasing.

Before I could take him too far, he pushed me backward onto

the bed, forcefully, as he growled at me to stop. His eyes connected with mine, a look of confusion was all over his face, and for just a moment, I wondered if I had done something wrong.

"Let me get a condom. Open your legs." His voice was hoarse but deep, demanding. He moved quickly as he pulled his side drawer open and returned with a condom in his teeth. When he was back between my legs, he pushed my knees, opening me wider then kept his eyes on my center as he ripped the package open and sheathed himself.

I wasn't normally insecure, but as Rhys climbed over me, I started thinking about the last time I had sex. It was my sophomore year of college. The guy I was seeing took me to a frat party then we ended up back at my apartment. It was our first time together and he left immediately afterward.

Later, I heard through mutual friends that he said I was just a little too strong and muscular for a girl. I didn't take offense because I wasn't a girl, I was a woman. An athlete. It wasn't my fault he was insecure about how hard I could take it.

But that didn't mean it didn't cross my mind again in that moment with Rhys. It shouldn't have mattered, but I started to close off, scared he too would think my thighs were too strong, too thick.

"Keep your eyes on me," he whispered, his mouth close to mine. "Where'd you go?"

Wrapping my arms around him, I suppressed that old memory and made sure he knew I was still there, still ready. His weight was on his forearms and he was gently tapping the outside of my entrance with the tip of his cock.

"Come on Rhys," I urged. "Fuck me."

His mouth smothered my words and his tongue started mingling with mine. He eased himself forward and I squeezed him tight as he hit me somewhere deep inside. Neither of us could suppress our moans but they were muffled as we continued to keep our lips together.

Once he was all the way in, he pulled back and looked at me like he was memorizing my face. His eyes were moving to each of my features and landing back on my gaze. "You feel so good. Like you were made to be mine."

All I could do was press my forehead to his, accepting that his words were just... words. Because I could never be his. It was just one time, one weak moment.

"More," I groaned, as he moved slowly in and out of my body.

His motions got less intimate and more erratic, as if he remembered that we were just fucking. He lifted himself up onto his knees and he pulled my legs onto his shoulders, hitting me deeper, making me scream. I was chanting, "Yes," over and over again, hoping he never stopped. Sweat started pouring from his forehead, his forearms were flexing as he held onto my calves, and his teeth were biting his bottom lip.

"I can feel you shaking, baby. You're gonna come for me again, aren't you?"

"Yes," I moaned.

He turned his head to the side, leaving his eyes on me, and sunk his teeth into the skin of my leg and sucked a mark onto my body. I had no choice but to let go, coming as he pumped inside of me and licked the pain away on my leg at the same time.

"Good girl." He took my legs off his shoulders and leaned down to kiss me again, then down my chin and to my neck. When he got to my nipples, he sucked hard and bit down a little making my clit tingle like it hadn't just come three times already.

"One more."

"I can't," I cried.

"You're moving that pussy up and down my cock, Ash. You want more, you can take more."

Moving and grinding, I was doing anything I could to get more friction while he gave his attention to my nipples. Never in my life had I come so many times, but now it seemed like I was a machine and Rhys knew all the right buttons.

"One more," I finally nodded.

He pulled his cock from my body and flipped me over, bringing my ass into the air and pushing my head into the bed. The wet condom touched the back of my thighs as Rhys kneaded the skin on my ass, taking his time before deciding to reenter my body.

When he finally lined himself up, he didn't waste time easing in. Quickly, he pushed into me and hit somewhere even deeper, somewhere I had never been touched before.

"You're squeezing me so tight," he hissed. "Your pussy was made for me."

His hand snaked around to my clit and with one press, I started quivering again.

"Rhys."

"Keep saying my name, Ash. Scream it."

With his cock stroking my core, his fingers playing with my clit, and his voice in my ear, I didn't stand a chance and came. Just like he told me to, I screamed his name as tears formed in my eyes. My tired body was starting to sink down, being held up only by his arm wrapped around my waist.

An animalistic grunt fell from his lips each time he pushed back inside of me. Then he stilled, and his deep moan of pleasure was better than any sound I could ever imagine. I could tell he was spilling himself inside of me and my only regret was not being able to see his face as he came.

When he pulled out of me, I fell to the bed and curled into myself, unsure if I was okay, or not. My body seemed pliant and satisfied, but my brain was scared. I wanted to cry from being so wrecked, but I also wanted to run away and hide.

"I better go," I suggested, thinking Rhys was probably wanting me to leave. There was no need to make things more confusing for either of us.

"The fuck you are." He laid next to me, having disposed of his condom somehow. He pulled me closer to him, trapping me in his grasp, and covered me with his silk sheet. "Close your eyes."

I didn't want to leave, I just thought I should, but I took my cues from him and closed my eyes. Comfort, along with the lack of responsibility and my body being weak, made me fall asleep quickly.

When I stirred awake, I was alone and the clock on his nightstand read two o'clock in the morning.

"Fuck," I pushed from the bed, looking for my clothes and remembering I left them outside. My bag was out in the living room as well, so I wrapped the sheet around me and went in search of something to put on and my phone to call for a rideshare.

When I walked into the living room, I stopped short and froze when I realized Rhys was standing by the window looking out toward the South Beach skyline. It was dark, but the moon lit up the room enough for me to see he was shirtless with gray capri sweatpants hanging low on his waist.

He brought a drink to his lips and took a sip then turned to see me standing there watching him. I pulled the sheet tighter and started looking around the floor for my bag, not sure what else to do.

"Did I wake you up?" he asked, staying put by the window.

"No, I was just..." I walked closer to where my bag was and reached down to get it, showing him what I needed.

"What time are your classes tomorrow?"

"Nine and eleven."

"Then go back to bed. I'll get you up at seven and take you home."

I snorted and looked up at him, seeing if he was serious. His face was unlike the happy-go-lucky Rhys he showed me most of the time. He was stone, and thoughtful. Something was on his mind and instead of worrying that it was regret over us having sex, I shook my head.

"Just once," I whispered to myself as I turned and made my way to the bedroom to change. "Just freaking once."

Chapter Twenty

I fell asleep with Ash, but woke up a few hours later feeling like I had slept for days. I hadn't slept that hard in months. Either the intense sex exhausted me, or it was the girl I had with me making me feel so content. Fearing I would wake her up, I eased from the bed, thinking a drink may lull me back to sleep.

But as I stood there looking out the window, my mind drifted to Melanie, and the way my finger had hovered over the call button as I sat in the park came flashing back.

A call I didn't make.

I wasn't ready, or I didn't want to. I still wasn't sure which. Despite how much I loved her, she hurt me. Led me on. Then took back everything we talked about, and planned, in a fucking text.

Why did I still think about her? Ash was in my bed, fully fucked, and I had never felt more like a man than I did when I made her come. I should have been contemplating more ways to do just that, but Mel crept back into my thoughts and I couldn't go back to bed until I let those thoughts go.

When I tipped my drink up for a sip, I saw Ash's reflection in the window. Then I turned and saw her wrapped in my sheet, and

I had to mentally glue my feet to the floor to keep from scaring her. I wanted to run toward her and fuck her again, use her body to make me forget all the thoughts of Mel, once and for all.

Ash looked unsure, lost. Her eyes were scanning the room, and when she raised her bag in the air, I knew she planned on leaving.

"Just once," I heard her whisper when she turned toward the bedroom. "Just freaking once."

No way.

Three long strides and I caught her, grabbing her by the elbow and pulling her back to my chest. I threw her bag back to the floor and ran my nose up her neck and behind her ear.

"Don't leave."

"You told me to go back to bed."

"You were going to leave."

"I don't want to overstay my welcome."

"You're always welcome here, Ash."

"Why are you awake?"

I pulled back to turn her and look her in the eyes, wondering if she could tell my mind had been distracted. All I cared about was making sure she knew I had no regrets. Even if she was a rebound, even if I was hung up on my ex, Ash was special, and I wanted to soak in the peace she unknowingly gave me.

"I slept so well. When I stirred awake, it was like I had been sleeping for years. Thought I would try a drink to get me back to sleep."

"You looked upset, maybe lost in thought."

So insightful.

"I had something on my mind. Someone. But one look at you and my mind went blank again."

"Coach?" She asked, her voice giving away her concern.

"No, not Colin," I laughed softly.

"You laugh, but I may be doing laps for years if he finds out about this."

"Then I will kick his ass." I was serious, and I tried to convey to her that Colin wouldn't do shit. "We are both adults, and I'm not your coach. Nothing is wrong with us meeting each other and doing whatever we want to do." Although I could see why she would want to hide the facts.

"He wanted you to look after me."

"And I have," I smirked, then growled. "And I will again."

"Just once, remember?"

"I'm a fucking liar." I leaned in and kissed her before adding, "Once was never going to be enough."

"Rhys," she moaned against my lips.

"Back to bed." I scooped her up and cradled her in my arms, carrying her to my room. I didn't want to give her a chance to tell me no.

I threw her back onto my bed and unwrapped the sheet from her body like a present. Climbing between her thighs, I kissed from her knees to her pussy, watching her shake as she anticipated me tasting her.

When my tongue licked up her slit, her legs gave out and fell all the way open inviting me in for more. I closed my lips around her clit and sucked, then pushed my tongue as far as I could get inside of her.

Her fingers found my hair and pulled, and it made me smile against her pussy. Leaving was no longer on her mind. She was ready to lay there and let me eat her pussy, tempting me to keep my mouth on her until she could no longer walk.

Sliding two fingers inside of her, I started flicking my tongue against her clit. She pulled at my hair harder, her head was thrashing back and forth, and her thighs closed around my head.

Ash was an athlete, so fucking strong, and I savored the feeling of her crushing me between her legs, keeping me close. I laid my hard cock on the silky sheets and started grinding the soft fabric, teasing the head of my shaft like her mouth did before we fell asleep.

"You're making me crazy," I moaned while nipping at her some more. "You see what you're doing to me? See how desperate I am? How weak I am for you?"

She looked at the movement of my hips and her mouth fell open. Her eyes stayed on my body and I dove back into her core for another taste. When I curled my fingers inside of her, she started to shake again, letting go and coming as she watched me torture myself.

She rode out the wave of pleasure while I humped the fucking bed, but once I knew she was satisfied, I pulled up and grabbed another condom from the nightstand.

I made quick work of covering my dick and then lined up to push inside of her. "This pussy is the only place I'm coming." I thrust hard, driving my point home.

"You're going to make it hard to walk," she moaned. "Much less play a soccer game."

"Good. That means every time you kick that ball, you'll be thinking of me."

Keeping our eyes locked, I started driving harder inside of her. The change in her eyes as she got closer to coming was hypnotic, and without meaning to, fucking her became something else. Something intimate.

Something like before, that neither of us were ready for. Something I had to chase away.

Leaning onto my arms, I started pistoning my hips quickly, in pursuit of my own satisfaction and hoping I took her along with me. I had to erase the way we were just staring at one another. It was irresponsible. That kind of moment was where feelings were formed.

"Rhys," she moaned again. "I'm coming..."

I let her squeeze my cock and ride out her orgasm, then I let myself spill into the condom that was between us. I closed my eyes and hid from her, not wanting to feel anything other than pleasure until I was fully sated.

When I fell to the side of her to catch my breath, I held onto her hand, and even though I knew it was still a risky decision, I couldn't help myself. "Don't leave."

"Not sure I can walk," she laughed softly. "So I couldn't if I wanted to."

"Good. If it crosses your mind again, tell me first so I can fuck you unconscious again."

I pulled the condom off and tossed it to the floor with the one I had on earlier. Then I lifted the covers over us and pulled Ash into my arms. I knew I was playing with fire—a damn inferno—but I just had to go with my gut.

Don't treat her like a rebound.

Don't fall for her.

Keep her close.

Selfish prick, I thought to myself.

Soon, Colin would get back, her season would be over—as would mine—and I would be headed to Atlanta to spend time with my brother, like I did every year. Everything would sort itself out, and in the meantime, I was going to take advantage of the distraction.

Chapter Twenty One

Ash

I woke up to Rhys slapping my bare ass playfully. But when I didn't make a move to get out of bed, he scooped me up and carried me into his shower. Thankfully, he had started it before he did, and it was warm and soothing. I slid down his body and stood, letting the water fall down on me from all directions.

"What time's your game?" He was casual, soaping his hands with body wash as if we always showered together and had small talk.

"Six." His hands started rubbing me, cleaning me. Even the warm water couldn't keep me from shivering.

"I'll be there."

"What?" I stopped him from rubbing my body and made him look up at me. "What do you mean?"

"I mean...I'll be there. I have practice this afternoon so I will head to the university when I'm done."

"Why are you coming to the game?"

"Are you ashamed of me?" He teased me. "Afraid I will embarrass you in front of your friends?"

"No, but just because we fucked doesn't mean you have to go

to my game. I don't want you coming because you feel obligated. I'm just fine with us being a little fling."

"I don't feel obligated. I feel like I want to make sure Hunter is well-behaved, see how you play after the ankle sprain, and just, ya know, return the favor. After all, you came to my game a few months ago."

I rolled my eyes and laughed. "I didn't come to see *you*."

"I'm going to pretend you didn't say that." His smile was bright and infectious, a fake pout falling on his lips. I couldn't help but be drawn in by his charm.

"Fine. Then I'll see you tonight."

"Bring extra clothes," he winked.

"We can't keep making this mistake."

"One more time," he whispered, holding up one finger and sticking his bottom lip out.

"Damn, this pussy must be magical."

His laugh echoed off the shower walls and I mentally patted myself on the back for making him look so happy. "You have no idea."

With a lightness, I kept the smile on my face while Rhys and I finished cleaning ourselves and each other. I half expected him to initiate more sex seeing that his dick stayed hard the whole time. But he never did. He just toweled me off and got dressed.

I must have seemed disappointed, because when we got in Rhys' car to head to the university, he reached across the console and grabbed my hand. "You okay?"

"Yeah, I just..." I waved at the air, knowing I was being silly. We were naked in a shower together, and I was completely wet for him. His cock was hard.

"You have a game tonight, remember? You have to save that strength."

I looked over at him and furrowed my brow. How did he know what I was thinking?

"I saw you eyeing my dick this morning. I know you wanted it."

I could feel my cheeks burning, so I turned my head and looked out the window without answering him. He chuckled and squeezed my hand, keeping us connected as we drove through downtown.

"Your apartment? Or straight to class?"

"My place, I need my books."

He took the turn and in no time, we were pulling up to the curb near my building. I stalled before getting out, not really sure what to say. *"Thanks for the sex,"* seemed like a bad idea. So did just getting out and walking away. Why was I being so weird?

"See you tonight," Rhys tugged my hand, forcing me to look at him. He kissed my knuckles and I practically floated across the console of the car to kiss his lips in return. It may not have been what he expected, but I wasn't thinking anything through, just going with whatever felt right.

"See ya."

He waited by the curb while I unlocked my door and with one more wave, he drove off and I was finally able to take a deep breath.

Holy shit.

What the hell happened? What did I do? Will I get in trouble?

According to Rhys, we were grown adults, but something told me if Hunter knew I spent the night with Rhys, he would bench me out of spite. He'd make up some conflict of interest or other bullshit. Anything to flex his new power. But my scholarship payments dictated that I play a certain number of games. I should have warned Rhys about that, told him to make sure no one knew, so that Hunter didn't find out.

I pulled my phone from my bag to send him a quick message, but before I could type it up, my phone started to ring.

Erin.

"Hey!"

"Hey," she sounded solemn, almost sad.

"Whoa, you okay?"

"I'm in so much pain," she whined. "After practice last night I practically died in my bed. I just woke up and thought I should call and check in on you since you had practice with Rhys afterward."

"I hate you're hurting," I deflected. Erin was my best friend but I wasn't sure she was ready to hear about Rhys rubbing my own cum on my nipples and sucking it off. "Are you going to be able to play tonight?"

"I have to. Lauren had to go to the fucking ER after practice for fluids. She was worse off than I was and she's my only backup."

"Fucking Hunter," I muttered.

"So I'm assuming Rhys didn't make it worse?"

No, no he didn't. My muscles were loose and rested, maybe a little sore on my inner thighs where I was squeezing as I came on Rhys' tongue, but other than that, I was rested and ready to play.

All of that I kept to myself, but I started pacing the small room and smiling like a lunatic.

"You there?"

"Yeah, sorry, I spaced out. Rhys is coming to the game tonight."

"Are you serious? The one game I'm going to probably die in?"

"Dramatic much?"

"Just need a day off, or a night out. Oh, how about Friday? We don't have practice Saturday. Let's go dancing."

"Count me in." I loved to dance, but I hated going out. For Erin though, I tried to make the effort when she asked, which wasn't very often. "Just not that dingy place we went to last time."

"Rachel was telling me about a place downtown. A rooftop

bar, dance floor, a pool, and a gorgeous view. I'll get the name of it."

Rhys' rooftop pool popped into my mind and I smiled, thinking about him diving in and then coming up to kiss me. The view was gorgeous. His chest was dripping with water, his lips were puffy, his eyes were boring into me like he was on a mission to devour me.

"Hello?"

"Sorry, I keep spacing out. Trying to get ready for class. I'm in. Just tell me where and we will make a night of it."

"That's my girl," Erin shouted. "Okay you get to class, I'm going back to sleep until my afternoon class."

She hung up and I glanced at the time, seeing I only had a few minutes to get across campus. I grabbed my books, quietly thanked Rhys for the morning shower, and started running so I wasn't late. I got into the lecture hall just in time to slide into a seat and get my books ready.

Forgetting all about the text I was going to send Rhys.

Chapter Twenty Two

Rhys

No matter how much I denied it, Cruz saw straight through me and knew I fucked Ash. He did a double take when he saw me walk into the locker room for practice and immediately called me out.

"I'm all for it," he rambled on next to me as we dressed out. "But don't let that anger you had toward Mel go. You've played better the last few months than you have your entire career. That is literally saying something. Although it helps when you don't punch anyone and can stay on the field."

"It's not *literally* saying something," I scoffed. "I just haven't focused on anything else. And I *Googled* what Hugo said to me, it wasn't nice. He had it coming."

His laughter followed him through the locker room as he headed to the field. Meanwhile, I was stewing on what I had just said. I hadn't been focused on anything but soccer, so I was playing at a high level. Colin's main concern with Ash was that she wasn't focused enough. I had to wonder if we were both going to play like shit now that the only thing we could focus on was getting back in bed together.

"I don't even care," I laughed to myself after a few minutes of trying to be mindful of the issue. "Worth it."

"Alright guys," Coach Sandy started clapping his hands and ushering us to the field. "Away game in Atlanta this Friday. Let's have another good practice."

Fuck, I had been so wrapped up with Ash in my head, I forgot that I got to see my brother at the game in Atlanta. We were going to have dinner afterward. It was perfect timing, because by Friday, I was going to need to start washing Ash out of my system. A trip out of town would do me good, remind me how reckless it was to get attached to someone else so soon after a heartbreak.

I ran to the field with a new resolve and practiced like I was going to take special joy in beating Atlanta. Miami versus Atlanta was the only time Levi didn't root for Atlanta. He had friends on that team, tried getting me to sign with them, and pulled for them to win.

Just not when I was in town.

When practice ended, it was close to Ash's game time so I took a quick shower and started to head out. Cruz stopped me though, looking at me with a smirk on his face.

"Wanna grab a drink tonight?"

"Headed to the university for the game."

"Going to her game?" Cruz whistled. "Sounds serious."

"How the fuck is it serious? I just met the girl a week or so ago."

"But you've fucked her, and when you spend so much time together, it's easy to think it's been months. Hell, you've probably seen more of Ash this week than you did Mel all of May. Remember? You kept telling me how she had to do this or that, or we had an away game, or—"

"Are you done?" I bit at him, not wanting him to keep reminding me of my ex. It was like he had a hard on for bringing her up and making me squirm.

"Yeah. Let me grab my things, I'm going with you."

"No you're not."

"Yes, I am. Because as much as it's no one's business who you sleep with, it's going to discredit Ash if everyone finds out. If we both go, you look less like a lover boy and more like a spectator."

I wasn't sure his logic was sound, but once he said that being with me would discredit Ash, I practically blanked out. That was not what I wanted for her, so I nodded toward the car and told Cruz to hurry up.

We bought tickets at the gate like anyone else and sat as close to the field as we could. When we got settled, I immediately scanned the field for Ash, wanting to see her in the final minutes of her warmup.

She was with a red head, laughing and bouncing a ball from knee to knee. The red head was shaking her legs out, twisting her neck, and stretching her back out. She seemed less relaxed than Ash, and I snickered under my own breath at how I loosened Ash up the night before.

When the redhead bent over to touch her toes, Ash scanned the stands. She was looking for me, and my chest puffed out a little waiting for her eyes to land on mine. When they did, her lips quirked but her eyes didn't linger. They went right back to the redhead and I slid my sunglasses down from the top of my head to cover how long I stared.

Cruz leaned back in the seat next to me, relaxed. I could tell he was scoping out both teams and enjoying being in the stands of a game instead of on the field. There was no way I could lean back. I wasn't as relaxed. I had my elbows on my knees, my fingers steepled in front of my lips, and my eyes zeroed in on Ash.

Then I saw Hunter, walking up to her with his drill sergeant stride. He was wearing slacks, a polo shirt, and a hat. Trying too hard to look like the head coach, but I hated him for some reason and that may have skewed my observation.

Ash didn't seem worried. Hunter was telling her something and she was just nodding along. When a whistle blew, Hunter and Ash both started jogging side by side from the field and down toward the end of the bleachers.

The soccer stadium wasn't much bigger than a high school football stadium. It shared a parking lot with the practice field and the locker rooms were in between. When it was time to leave the field, they didn't go under the stands like we did, they went around and out toward the separate building that housed their lockers.

I kept my eye on her as long as I could, and right before they disappeared, Ash shot me one last glance and smiled. She knew I was probably wondering what Hunter was saying, sitting up there being tense. Not until that smile did I lean back in my seat and relax.

Taking a deep breath, I wiped a hand down my face and confessed to Cruz. "I hate that guy."

"I can tell," Cruz responded without even having to ask who I was referring to.

"He freaks Ash out."

"Probably because of you. Colin has you stomping around his turf and he has no idea why. He probably just thinks Colin doesn't have faith in him when in reality, Colin was just trying to give you something to do."

"Maybe. But he needs to be careful and not give me a reason to beat his ass." At this point, I was willing someone to give me a reason to throw my fists.

"Let me know and I'll help." Cruz was that kind of friend. He teased and busted my ass, but he was loyal and loved his friends. Without question, I knew if I wanted to beat someone's ass, he would jump in head first and ask questions later.

The game started with Ash at left wing, my same position. We had talked about the fact that we played the same position, but seeing her in action was different. She owned that side of the field, and her left foot kick was unmatched by everyone else. I was so fucking proud, watching her focus and dominate.

It was different than watching her with me, because against me, I was able to keep control over her more often than not. But against her teammates and opponents, I could see why Colin wanted her in top form. She was a head above the rest.

By the seventy-minute mark, Hunter pulled her from the game and the trainers came over to tend to her. They stretched her out and made sure she was good before leaving her to watch the rest of the game.

There was so much pride swirling around my heart for Ash. I played no part in her being as good as she was, that was all Ash Keller. All she needed was to refocus, and every athlete went through that from time to time.

"Damn." Cruz had been chatty as the game went on, cheering and getting into it with all the fans. But at the end, he sat there and watched as the teams shook hands and started their way off the field. "That was intense. Ash is good."

"She's amazing," I muttered.

Right before she was behind the bleachers, she glanced up at me and smiled. "I'll take a ride share home. You go get your girl."

"She's not my girl. Just a little fling."

"A few days ago, she was a rebound. Before that, she was a friend. Sooo, sure man. Sure."

Cruz patted my back as we stood and made our way down the bleachers. I didn't even give him a response to his summary, just let him have his fun.

Standing outside in the parking lot, a few people recognized us and we posed for autographs and signed a few things. It helped us kill time while Ash showered and did whatever else her post game routine consisted of.

When she finally emerged, her eyes started scanning the

crowds and she smiled when they found me.

"Sorry," I said, interrupting the last few fans. "I need to see my friend."

Cruz pushed me in jest and I tilted my head up at him, thanking him for coming and not depending on me to get him home. I didn't want to waste any time getting Ash back to my place so I could praise her for a job well done.

When she saw me approaching, she looked around to make sure none of her teammates were there, then started running. She leapt into my arms and I swung her around, refraining myself from kissing her senseless.

"Good game, baby." The sentiment fell off my lips without meaning to. It was one thing when we were naked in the bed, but another when we were celebrating her win—as friends. "Sorry," I mumbled, putting her back on her feet.

If she heard me, she didn't let on. Just grabbed my arm and pulled me further into the parking lot toward my car. "Let's get out of here before Hunter is done talking to the press."

When we were safely behind the tinted windows of my car, we turned and looked at each other. Both of us with goofy smiles and awkward silence.

"Was that Cruz with you?"

"Yeah he wanted to come. Hell, I think he wants to come back. He loved it."

"What about you?"

"I stopped paying attention after the seventieth minute."

She bit her lip and smiled sheepishly, making me reach across the console and run my thumb on her cheek. I had to know if she was as warm as she was red when she blushed like that.

"Come home with me again."

She lifted her bag that sat in her lap. "I packed extra clothes like you told me to."

"Yeah my bad, you won't need them."

Chapter Twenty Three

Ash

"**S**o what did Hunter say to you right before the game?"

I knew he would be curious when Hunter singled me out. I did a good job not looking bothered, though. I had to make sure Rhys didn't let Hunter know we slept together. If I had shown any sign of discomfort, I was afraid Rhys would come barreling down to the field. If the way he acted the night before was any indication, Hunter was a trigger for Rhys.

"He told me he saw that you were there. Then he asked why."

Rhys' knuckles whitened as he gripped the steering wheel, his jaw had a slight tick in it. He had waited until we were almost to his place to ask, and I bet he did that on purpose. Distance seemed to tame Rhys' crazy.

"Relax. I told him you were there to see how your *student* was doing since we worked all weekend on my lefty push kick."

The car grew quiet after that. Rhys was probably mulling over Hunter, but I was enjoying the music that was playing softly as we drove—Unchained Melody by The Righteous Brothers. It was my grandma's favorite and I knew every word by heart. It was soothing, taking me on a trip down memory lane.

A tear fell from my eye and Rhys put his finger under it to

catch it. I hadn't even realized he was paying that much attention. "Tell me."

I laughed and wiped my eyes. "Did you forget we aren't the sharing type of friends?"

"Then what are we?"

My silence lasted until we turned into the parking garage and into his designated spot. He turned to me, still waiting for my answer so I shrugged. "Friends who play soccer, and apparently, have sex."

His smile made his eyes gleam, but there was an ominous undertone. "Let's get inside."

He shoved from the car and led me to the elevator. It was a long ride in the private lift and with him leaning against the rail with his arms crossed it seemed to last forever. Through the mirror, I could see his eyes were on me so intently, like he was planning an attack.

When the doors opened, I made myself at home, flopping on the couch. Rhys followed me, bringing glasses of water and two glasses of wine like he did the night before. Only I skipped the water and went straight to the wine.

"Not gonna lie," Rhys started, leaning back on his side of the couch. "After this morning, I thought I would have to lure you into my car with candy. Wrap you up with rope and throw you in the trunk."

"Turns out, I'm a willing victim."

His smile brightened again, and the same questions I'd seen scrolling through his eyes earlier, still lingered. "What caused the tears?"

So we are sharing?

"My grandparents," I said point blank. If I let him guess, he would assume the worst, and even though it sometimes hurt to talk about them, I didn't want him thinking it was him. "The song on the radio made me think of my grandma. It was her favorite and Grandpa would make her stop whatever she was doing when it came on and dance with him."

"They're gone?"

"Yeah a few years now. They were all I had. And they loved each other so much. Grandma passed away in the hospital from pneumonia, and Grandpa died of heartbreak at home a month later."

"Shit I'm so sorry. How old were you?"

"Senior in high school. Just about to graduate. Soccer afforded me a scholarship with just enough left over to get my apartment. I got a little savings from selling their house. And I do have their old car I can drive if I need to. So they raised me, and left me with enough in this world to give me a head start."

Tears had started falling again and I tried wiping them away before Rhys made a big deal about it. The only other time I opened up about my grandparents was to Erin. Not because they were a secret, but because I hadn't had anyone in my life worth telling.

"What about your parents? What's that story?"

I rolled my eyes and waved my hands in the air, wiping that question away from the space between us. "I told you about my grandparents to keep you from assuming my tears were something else. But if you want to know about my parents, that will cost you the one big question that we agreed on."

"I don't think I can limit myself to one big question anymore. I want to know a lot more about Ash Keller."

"Then you better start answering a few questions yourself. Starting with why you get a kick out of torturing Coach?"

"He and I go way back. I stupidly held him responsible for my life falling apart a few months back. Making him crazy sometimes helps me smile."

"How adult of you," I mumbled, making him laugh.

"Colin and I are good, Ash. He can be a pain in my ass, but he means well."

"You still didn't answer my question."

He twisted his glass in his fingers, debating what his next words were going to be. I tried to look like I meant business, like I wouldn't accept anything less than a straight answer. "I think I did."

"Elaborate. How did Coach make your life fall apart?"

"He didn't. He just...that night, at that soccer game you were at, he said some things without knowing my girlfriend was sitting behind him. She overheard and left the game. I haven't spoken to her since."

My jaw dropped, my eyes widened, and my heart started racing. "What did he say? Were you cheating on her?"

"The fuck?" He was instantly angry and stood up quickly. Pointing at me, he added, "That was your one question."

"You said we get a lot more," I argued.

"I lied," he snapped, raising his voice like I had never heard from him before.

He set his glass on the table and then took mine from my hand and set it down. Without any preamble, he picked me up and threw me over his shoulder. In a flash, we were in his bedroom and I was being thrown on his bed. Not like the night before, but aggressively, and with anger oozing from him.

"Lose the clothes, Ash. We both know why you're here, so let's get to it." He pulled his own shirt over his head and tossed it to the side.

I got on my knees, defiantly crossing my arms and snarling at him. "Why's that, Rhys? Tell me why I'm here."

"To fuck Rhys Peyton."

His mood had shifted, his words were mean and unnecessary. I shoved at his chest and got off the bed, not willing to let him speak to me that way. I wasn't there because I wanted to fuck

Rhys Peyton, I was there because I wanted to fuck Rhys— *'my friend who I played soccer with and fucked.'*

I got to the living room and grabbed my phone and bag, trying to pull up a rideshare app to take me home. Rhys was on my heels, though, and snatched the phone from my hand. "You get to assume I was cheating on my girlfriend and then act like I shouldn't be upset?"

"You're not going to act like *this* and still get between my legs. I'm not here for your status Rhys, I'm here because I like spending time with you. I came because I figured why the hell not."

I was yelling, irate. But I realized as I started backing away from him that I was mad at him for the same reason he was mad at me. We both voiced an assumption of the other one and we were both wrong. Not only were we wrong, but that assumption was a mark on each of our characters.

"I'm not a cheater," he countered. He was in his jeans, barefoot and shirtless. His hair was a mess, his eyes were an inferno. "She left because I was going to ask her to marry me. She wasn't ready, and Colin mentioned it during the game. She sent me a text telling me she heard him talking and I was crazy to think she would marry me."

As he spoke, his voice got louder and louder. I knew he was angry with me, but I could tell that he was angrier with her. His defense of himself turned into a vent, and I nodded, telling him I could take it. If he wanted to keep venting, yelling, and getting it off his chest, I was there.

"I wanted to be a dad, and a husband, and I wanted it with her." His voice was eerily quiet this time, but his face still projected the ire he had inside his veins. "I never would have cheated on her."

Hell, I never even knew he was dating someone seriously enough to marry them. Not that I should have known, but he was all over the media. Surely it would have been mentioned. It made me think, for just a minute, that his story was fiction. Something he made up to keep me from knowing anything else about him.

But I didn't dare project that opinion, or voice it in anger. That would just be another assumption. He was angry enough to have lived it, I just wondered how no one knew.

"She was my doctor," he explained, like he could read my mind again. "We kept it between ourselves, out of the public, until I was no longer her patient."

I stayed quiet and motionless. Hating myself for trying to find flaws in Rhys. My subconscious knew it would be easier to walk away from him if he was a cheating liar underneath all the smiles and charm.

"And I'm not here because you're Rhys Peyton," I finally reminded him. "And you know it."

My words snapped him into motion, and in three steps, he was close enough to grab my neck and pull my lips to his. We had come to an understanding. No more talking, no more yelling. I wrapped my arms around his neck and let him lift me into the air. Instead of taking me to his bedroom, though, he took me up the round stairs and out to the rooftop.

Our lips were smothering each other, our moans were loud. I wasn't in the right headspace to think about why he took me to the roof, but it didn't matter. We went from wine and laughing, to yelling, then kissing. I was suffering from another Rhys Peyton whiplash and keeping my lips on his seemed like the best way to make it stop.

Rhys, on the other hand, had a different way.

Chapter Twenty Four

Rhys

I crossed the line, but so did she.

She assumed something about me because of who I was. In doing so, she hit a nerve and I snapped. I told her way more than I intended and the only way I knew to change the subject was to kiss her.

Instead of going back to my bedroom, I took her to the roof. We needed to start the night over and wash away the anger.

Without warning her, I jumped into the pool letting the water come between us and our lips parted.

"Rhys!" She screamed. The pool had been cooled again so she had to catch her breath from the unexpected plunge. Fight or flight kicked in and she tried pushing away from me but I held her tight, not letting her go.

"Let's start over tonight," I insisted.

"I was letting it go without the swim."

"This was for me. I just took you with me."

She was holding my neck, her legs once again squeezing my waist. I could feel her irritation starting to wane. Her eyes looked calmer as they flickered to my lips, wanting to kiss me again.

Instead, she took me by surprise with her words. "I'm sorry."

"Fuck, me too, Ash. I didn't mean what I said."

I nipped at her nose and then her top lip, making my way to her cheek and down to her neck. Our words needed to be kept at a minimum. I had already said too much, let her see more than anyone else since Mel left.

I hadn't told anyone how I was feeling, or how I was dealing with Mel's disappearance. Yet, I wanted to keep talking and tell Ash everything. Just the few words I got off my chest felt like I was letting it go. But it also made me wonder if I wanted to let it go. I may not have called Mel the other day, but every time my phone rang, I hoped it was her.

Or I used to.

I pushed Ash's shirt up and over her head, knowing that the best way to get past wanting to tell her more was to lose myself inside of her. Cruz's words once again floated in the back of my head, making me regret that Ash really could be a rebound. I was using her, but I couldn't stop.

"Get your shorts off," I demanded. Her legs came off my hips and she started pushing them down while I cupped her breasts and thumbed her nipples. We were just deep enough that the water came to her neck, making it hard for me to suck on her without drowning.

As I moved her toward the shallow water, she reached for my jeans and tried taking them off. I had to grab her wrist and stop her, not ready for that barrier to be gone. Those jeans were the only thing keeping my dick from pushing inside of her, and I didn't have a condom in the pool.

"Not yet," I growled. I turned her around and pressed her back into the side of the pool. Her tits were finally above the water and I knelt down to put them in my mouth while I looked up into her bright green eyes. The reflection of the pool was making them look like they were sparkling.

My teeth clamped down onto her pebbled nipple and I tugged.

She seethed at the spark of pain, keeping her lips open but her teeth clamped shut. Then I twisted my tongue around her to soothe it.

I had learned really quick how sensitive her tits were. A whole night could be spent just watching her reactions as I played and toyed with them.

Running my hands down her arms, I lifted them to the edge of the pool. Staring for a minute, I tried to make sure she knew I wanted her arms open and still while I kept playing with her. But when she started to reach for my shoulders, I had to push them back in place.

"Don't move," I warned her. "Move and I stop. Your arms are the only thing that's going to keep you from drowning."

"I can reach the—"

I cut her words off by pushing my fingers into the folds of her pussy. "Your legs are about to be useless."

Finding her hole, I inserted two fingers and placed my thumb on her clit. My eyes couldn't leave hers and she returned my stare as she spread her legs wider for me. When my mouth found her nipples again, I moved my fingers to the same rhythm as my tongue, working her up. Her breathing was getting heavier, and despite the water surrounding us, I could feel her warm cum wrapping around my fingers as they moved inside of her.

"You make this so easy on me, baby. I've barely touched you and you're already about to come."

"It's you," she grunted as she tried riding my hand. "You do this to me. I've never...."

"Never what?" She stopped talking as her orgasm started to become imminent, so I pulled my hand away and stopped, desperately wanting to know what she was going to say. "Tell me."

"I've never been this quick and ready. Not with anyone else."

"Has anyone else ever given you an orgasm?"

"Not like you have. Not given. But I've taken them. Used whoever I was with to get myself there."

"Is that why you keep trying to ride my hand?" My pride was swelling again, my smirk was unmovable. I felt so fucking satisfied that I was giving her something no one else had. "Afraid I won't deliver without your help?"

"You've done it before. I trust you to do it again. But Rhys?" My name on her lips made me look into her eyes, and she was leaning forward as if to make sure I was paying attention. "If you don't make me come right now, the movement of this water will, because I am so close it hurts."

My fingers dove back between her pussy and she clamped around them, coming as soon as they entered her body. "You can take whatever you want from me. Watching you come is better than a hat trick."

Her legs gave out as her orgasm heightened from my words and her head fell back against the edge of the pool. I pulled on her nipples one last time and hoped the entire city of Miami could hear her screaming my name. My cock was pushing on my wet jeans so hard it was painful but I wanted to prove to her one more time that she never had to be in charge of her own orgasm from me. Not if she didn't want to be.

Her head raised up when I pulled my fingers from her, but her legs were still too weak. Grabbing her by the waist, I picked her up and set her on the edge of the pool. She leaned back on her arms and I spread her legs, getting my mouth close to her pussy.

"You don't have to take this one, either."

"Rhys," she whined. "I can't..."

"Of course you can." I nipped at her folds, teasing her as I watched her head move back and forth. She was telling me she couldn't, but her eyes were begging me to prove her wrong. "You came four times for me last night. I have new goals for tonight."

"Goals are reckless," she cried. "You said so yourself."

"Trust me. I'm well aware how reckless this is." I closed my lips over her and pressed my tongue to her clit. The way her body shook and her mouth fell open urged me to go harder, not wanting to waste any time before she came.

My hands kneaded her thighs and my nails scraped her skin just enough to make her feel me there. *Remember me there.* From the way she was looking at me, though, I knew she wouldn't forget us in my pool anytime soon.

Moaning to create a vibration on her clit was the last straw, and she came again, harder and louder. Her eyes were struggling to stay open, but she somehow kept them on me. She knew how much I loved her eyes and how they affected me.

When her body started to settle back down, I lifted myself from the pool and onto my knees between her legs. Water was dripping down my chest and from my hair, leaving drops across Ash's naked body.

As she watched, I popped my jeans open and lowered them down just enough to free my dick. I stroked myself for her and sunk my teeth into my bottom lip. My hips moved into my hand, eager to be inside her pussy instead.

"We have to go back downstairs," I groaned. "I need to be inside you so bad."

She sat up from the pool deck making my cock level with her tits. Squeezing them together, she urged me to move my hand and wrapped her breasts around me. Then I started moving again, pumping myself between her soft skin. Her tongue peeked out and tasted the tip of me as I moved up and down.

"I don't want to move until I see you come, Rhys."

"So naughty," I whispered. "So perfect."

I had never fucked a woman's tits before. Hell, Mel's weren't even big enough to encase my cock the way Ash's were. Not to say Mel's weren't great, but Ash's were quickly becoming my favorite.

Ash's eyes were once again gazing into mine, watching my

every reaction as I moved. When her lips pursed over the tip of my cock, I barely kept it together but pulled back quickly to make that feeling last as long as I could.

"Touch yourself." I replaced her hands with my own, holding her tits around my cock but at an angle I could thumb her nipples. Ash's hands moved to her own pussy and even though I couldn't see, I knew the moment she found her rhythm. "That's it. Rub it baby."

"I'm so..." her breathing was ragged and her chest moved up and down as she got closer to another orgasm. It made it impossible to keep myself under control so I gave in, letting the tingles ride down my spine and into my shaft.

"Open your mouth," I demanded in an urgent tone. "Now."

Her head fell forward and her mouth found the tip of me just as my orgasm hit and I spilled onto her tongue. My moaning was loud and I knew it turned her on, so I wasn't surprised when she came right after me, not even having time to swallow.

"Fuck!" She shouted, making my cum fall from her lips and down her chin. I was tempted to run my finger through it and shove it back into her mouth, make her swallow every bit of me. Instead, I enjoyed the sight of her marked, completely zoned out and thoroughly satisfied.

When she finally looked at me again and started to wipe her mouth off, I stopped her and pulled her into my arms. I backed up a few inches until my legs were back down into the water then I pulled her with me.

My lips found hers and I could taste the saltiness of my own cum on her tongue. My jeans were still around my thighs, her arms were around my neck, and as we went deeper into the water, everything else washed away.

Including any lingering thoughts of Mel.

Chapter Twenty Five

Ash

"You're a bad girl," Rhys growled in praise as we swam around the deep end of the pool.

"I'm a good girl, Rhys. I just don't mind getting a little dirty." I backed away toward the shallow end, creating space between us before I showed him how much dirtier I was willing to get with him. I would have done almost anything to see him getting pleasure from my body.

Rhys started swimming toward me like an alligator, slowly and with only his head peeking above the water. His expression was serious, like he was on the hunt and I was a poor little raccoon at the water's edge just trying to quench my thirst. His arms snaked out to grab me before I could back up again and I was against his body and in his arms.

He turned me so my back was to his chest and pushed his cock against me, making me moan as I realized he was already hard again. "I'm about to race you to my bedroom."

With a gentle push, he urged me toward the stairs to the pool and I took his challenge. Up and out of the water without even drying off, I went down the spiral staircase and across his living room. By the time I reached the door to his bedroom, he had closed in on me and lifted me into his arms. Laughter bubbled up in me and when we fell into his bed, we were both beaming at one another.

"I even gave you a head start," he teased.

I turned to my side so I could face him and rested my head on my hand. Taking my other hand, I traced it up his torso. "I played hard tonight. I'm exhausted."

"Doesn't matter." He grabbed my hand and bit gently down on my finger before adding, "I'll always catch you."

My heart skipped a beat, my smile fell, and I squeezed my eyes shut to block out the sexy and sincere way he was looking at me. That look was one that would make me fall for him and falling for Rhys wasn't part of my plan.

"Come on," Rhys tapped my leg and I opened my eyes again as he crawled to the bedside table to get a condom. He ripped it open and leaned against the headboard as he pushed it down over his shaft. "Come sit on my dick."

Crawling up his body, I straddled his legs and held myself above him. He lined up to my core and pushed my hips down, guiding me slowly down until he was fully seated inside of me. Instead of moving, I just sat there and looked at him, wanting to know what he was thinking. He must have thought I was scared or nervous about being on top, though, because he nodded at me slightly before moving my hips back and forth.

"What are you thinking?" I dared to ask.

"How I've never, ever had sex without a condom but your pussy feels so good I can't help but wonder what it feels like bare against my skin."

My eyebrows almost hit my hairline in shock. His words were not what I was expecting and he was so matter of fact that it left little room to question its authenticity.

"Of all the things?"

"I'm not complicated," he groaned as I continued to move while we spoke.

"Somehow I don't believe that. You're way more complicated than you let anyone know."

"What about you? What's going on in that gorgeous head of yours?"

"Wondering how I'm already so close to coming again."

"I bet you'll never get tired of having me inside your body."

More words that hit too deep, too real. There was a chance that he was right and I would never have enough of what we started. In a way, I wished we could go back to the night before and erase everything that started this fast growing addiction. Then I wouldn't know how good it felt and it would be easier to walk away.

"Just once," I mumbled under my breath.

"Such liars."

As I nodded my agreement, his lips came up to mine and I moved faster over his body. His hands found my breasts and he pinched my nipples the way he knew I liked. I could feel myself starting to contract around him, squeezing so hard it almost hurt. Spasms started inside my core and I raced toward the release as if it would disappear if I started overthinking everything again.

Rhys' moans against my lips were fuel and he urged me to keep grinding on top of him. "Keep riding me, baby. Don't stop. Don't you dare fucking stop."

When I finally came, tears almost sprang into my eyes at how good it felt. Rhys was right behind me, controlling my body through his own orgasm as I fought to stay upright.

Instead of moving me off of him, though, he sat up and wrapped his arms around my waist, holding me still. His head nestled next to my neck and I ran my hands up his back and into his messy hair. We both were still breathing hard, still trying to make sense of whatever was going on. Even if it was only a fling, it was intense, and I knew he felt it in some way. It was hard to ignore.

"Food," he finally said, backing up to look at me with his easy going smile. "I need food."

I started to climb off of him but he held me down, making me furrow my brow and give him a side smile. "If you want to eat, I have to get up."

"Then screw it, food is for wimps."

My head fell back with laughter as I continued getting up. When he was no longer inside of me, I felt empty and alone. Cold. It made me want to go with his plan and stay connected. But my tummy rumbled at just the right moment and it made me back away toward the door to the bathroom.

While I splashed water on my face, Rhys disposed of the condom. Both of us in the bathroom together felt domestic and intimate, even more so when our eyes connected through the mirror.

Rhys reached up to a built in cabinet and opened a set of drawers, pulling out a pair of shorts and a shirt. He slid the shorts on and once he was covered, I snapped out of my stare and started toward the doors to find my bag to get dressed as well.

He didn't let me leave, though. He turned me around, and slid the white Miami Inferno shirt he'd grabbed over my head. I worked my arms through the holes and it fell right above my knees. "You don't need more clothes than this."

"I need some panties."

"No the fuck you don't."

He led me to the kitchen with our hands interlocked, and pulled a stool from the bar that overlooked the cooking surface. I sat down quietly and watched as he started moving around, getting ready to fix whatever we were going to eat.

"Why did I figure you for a take-out kind of guy?"

"Another assumption?" He winked before sparing me. "I guess because most of us single guys take that option."

"Not you though, huh?"

"I'm too old to eat like a kid. Plus, I did a lot of cooking growing up, helping out my mom." He shrugged and grabbed a few more things from the pantry before turning back around. "I like cooking. Reminds me of home."

"Which is Oakland, right?"

"A little bit outside of the city, but yeah. Mom still lives there, runs a non-profit that my brother and I started once we could afford it."

"And your dad?"

"I don't think it's any secret that I grew up without my dad. He bailed on us when I was young." He was annoyed by the question. It was one I shouldn't have asked. But he assumed I had read up and knew his history, when in reality, I never had. I knew more about his soccer stats than his personal life.

"I've never looked you up. I mean, about your personal life. Not that deep, anyway."

He shrugged like it didn't matter, but I could tell bringing up his dad was a sore subject. I understood that all too well, because I dodged his questions about my parents like a boxer in a ring, bobbing and weaving. I hated talking about them. It was humiliating.

That may have been what he felt as well and I found myself opening my mouth to share more than I planned to just so he knew I could relate.

"I don't know who my dad is," I confessed. He froze and looked up from the cutting board where he was chopping vegetables.

"I don't want that to be my one question," he smirked, trying to lighten the mood.

"I think we are past that." I rolled my eyes, giving up on our little game. "We said just one kiss, too. See where that got us?"

He went back to chopping as he laughed at my reasoning. He didn't ask for more information, but it felt good relating to him, talking to him. "My mother didn't want me so she gave me to my grandparents. Since she didn't know who my dad was, I just assumed she fucked so many people she really didn't know."

"You know where she is now?"

"She doesn't contact me unless she needs something. Especially since my grandparents died. But I can't stand the sight of her. I'm determined to be better than her in every way. I never want to rely on her or need her. It's been a while since I've even seen her and I'm a much better person when she isn't around."

Rhys pulled a pan out and turned the stove on, brushing the vegetables from the cutting board into hot oil. He grabbed an onion and started working on it, not immediately responding. He seemed to be mulling it over, barely focused on his task.

When the silence became too much, I sighed and ran a hand through my hair. "I hope you aren't thinking how pathetic I am."

He huffed and shook his head, not looking up until he finished his last slice of the onion. "I was actually thinking about how alike we are."

Chapter Twenty Six

Rhys

When Mel left, I knew every woman that came after her would be subjected to my private appraisal. Ash was my first attempt at life after Mel, and even though we weren't more than what we were, I still made the private comparison.

Surprisingly, the more I was around Ash, the more flaws I realized Mel had. She never let me cook for her. She liked eating out or having someone cook for us. She would have never sat in front of me looking freshly fucked in nothing but my t-shirt. I couldn't even remember her looking thoroughly fucked. She always got right up and fixed her hair and makeup, insisting that she always be put together. I didn't want her put together, I wanted her like Ash—looking satisfied thanks to a few lewd rounds with my dick.

As Ash told me about her parents, I realized we had a lot in common which was another difference I had with Mel. I never got to meet them, but Mel told me her parents were doctors, like she was. Well off, warm, and loving. She used to tell me she wanted a family just like she had growing up, and her goals aligning with mine was why I fell for her.

But there was something to be said for connecting with someone that knew how it felt to be missing a parent, to grow up with very little, and who used their love of soccer to claw their way to a better future. We both let our absent parents define our goals. I wanted to prove mine wrong; she wanted to avoid the mistakes all together.

Even though Ash and I were at different places in our lives, and had different paths for our futures, she was reminding me that letting go of what I thought I had with Mel was possible.

"I take a lot of shit in the locker room for wanting to settle down and raise a family." Our conversation had carried over to the living room as we ate the pasta I had thrown together. Ash had eaten almost every bite and it felt good knowing she loved what I had cooked for her.

"I imagine you do," she smiled. "You guys can get anyone you want. Why settle?"

"See? That gets old after a while. Cruz, for example, he's a few years older than you. Has a different girl in his bed every night. In ten years, he's gonna be exhausted."

She laughed and shook her head, placing her plate onto the coffee table. "Everyone has their own goals, their own dreams, and their own paths. But Cruz may wake up tomorrow with one of those girls he was taking pictures with tonight and be in love."

"Yeah, it's crazy to think you can always get what you want in this life. I was never like Cruz. I was always hoping my relationships were forever."

"Until now," she teased, referring to whatever we were.

I didn't respond because I didn't know what to think. Sleeping with Ash was never about a relationship or a future. Just a means to an end of whatever was drawing us to one another, and, as much as I hated to admit it, getting over my ex.

"It's okay," Ash nudged my knee. "I'm glad we got a couple of nights to let loose and focus on something besides the shit in our lives that creates distractions and havoc."

I could barely smile, barely acknowledge what she had just said. It was unspoken, but obvious, that we weren't going to see one another after that night. I had an away game, then she had to travel for a game, then Colin was set to return home. He wouldn't need me to keep mentoring Ash forever so I wouldn't have a reason to go to her games. And then when the season ended, she would finish school and move on.

My silence made her scoot closer to me, and she put her hand on my knee. "I'm sorry again, about earlier. I assumed things I shouldn't have based on what I *thought* I knew about you. And sorry you are dealing with heartbreak."

"You're not a rebound," I blurted like an idiot.

Ash, so graceful and gorgeous, widened her eyes and gave me a soft smile. "That is probably not true. But it's okay, too."

She lowered herself to her knees on the floor and crawled between my legs. Her green eyes looked up hesitantly as her hands ran up my legs and to the elastic of my shorts. My cock hardened quickly, knowing she was coming for him. When she pulled the band down, I ran my fingers down the side of her cheek and she leaned into my touch before scooting closer and taking her tongue along the bottom of my shaft.

I hissed at the feeling of her soft touch, trying to resist the urge to push her head down and shove myself into her mouth. Pulling my hand from her cheek, I rested my arms along the back of the couch and let her go at her own pace.

"Those eyes, Ash. They do something to me. That night at my game, when I saw you talking to Colin, it was those eyes that had my attention."

"You were devastated, distracted."

"But for just a minute, I saw those eyes and everything was okay."

"I don't mind making it okay for you, Rhys. I promise."

Anger at myself crept into my chest and I grimaced. Why couldn't I truthfully tell her she was wrong? Why was I letting her wrap her mouth around me when she knew I still had feelings for my ex?

Ash could see my mood shifting and she sheathed her teeth as she took me as deep as she could. The anger started to dissipate and the need for her mouth got more intense. Her nails dug into my thighs, her eyes were on mine, and she sucked hard up and down my dick. She got quicker and more aggressive every few strokes, like she was getting herself off by making me feel so fucking good.

Moans started coming from my mouth, growls from my chest, and I inadvertently began moving my hips in rhythm with her motion. "Fuck Ash."

"Mmm," she moaned, then swirled her tongue around my tip. Slurping noises were getting louder as her saliva coated me and mixed with my precum. I was so close to unloading in her mouth that I didn't bother pushing her away to fuck her. It was too late, I was too far gone.

"I'm gonna come down your throat," I warned her.

She nodded and moaned again, closing her eyes to savor the moment she felt me painting her tongue. I was groaning with my release as I watched her swallow, and when I couldn't take anymore, she pulled her mouth from me and climbed up onto my lap. Her pussy was still bare under the shirt she wore and I could immediately feel how wet she was as she started grinding her clit on what was left of my hard cock.

"No," I stopped her and started lifting her off of me. "You don't have to take your pleasure, remember? I'll give it to you, baby."

"Trust me," she purred, settling herself back on top of me.

"You *are* giving it to me. Just sucking your cock made me want to come. Let me use you."

I let her get a few more passes on top of me, grinding her clit to her own beat. When I was just about to take over and shove my fingers inside of her, she started shaking and moaning. I felt her warmth coat my dick and she squeezed my shoulders to ground herself as she rode out her release. Then she slumped forward and placed her head on my shoulder as she caught her breath.

"Fuck that was so hot," I confessed.

"You make me so desperate for you."

Her words reminded me she wasn't shy or high maintenance when it came to sex. She wasn't afraid to tell me how she was feeling, what she wanted, and how she wanted it. She had just ground her pussy on my dick like a toy, and I was in awe.

Dirty. She was a dirty girl—my dirty girl—and I was obsessed.

We sat there for a few minutes, collecting ourselves and regaining our composure. Then Ash stood up and walked toward her bag. My brows furrowed as I realized she was grabbing her clothes and I started to stand up to stop her.

"You're staying the night," I commanded without asking, making sure she knew I was serious.

"No," she smiled. "I'm not."

She didn't seem mad, she seemed... resigned. Like we had gone as far as we could and it was time to say goodbye. I reluctantly nodded, knowing deep down she was right—she wasn't mine. There was no reason to sleep alongside one another and create an awkward goodbye in the morning.

When she walked to the bedroom to change, I ordered a town car to take her home. I really wanted to take her myself but I knew she would refuse, and a rideshare at that late hour made me nervous.

She walked back in the room with tiny jean shorts and a tank top on. I crossed my arms over my bare chest and looked around the floor like I had dropped something. All I was trying to do was keep myself from feeling something as Ash finished gathering her things. But I gave up when she approached me and placed a hand on my chest.

"Have a good trip," she smiled. "Kick Atlanta's ass."

"Of course," I smirked. "Text me if you need anything. Oh, and I ordered you a car. The driver should be downstairs waiting."

She lifted onto her tiptoes and kissed my lips softly. "Thanks."

Thanks for what? I wondered as she walked toward the elevator.

For the car?

For my offer to contact me if she needed anything?

For not walking her down to the car and making it awkward?

For all the orgasms?

For helping her focus?

For opening up to her?

Dammit, what was wrong with me?

Chapter Twenty Seven

Ash

"I'll just meet you there," I insisted, while Erin tried to convince me she was going to drive downtown for our night out.

"I probably won't even drink," she explained, making me roll my eyes because that was definitely not happening.

"Let's both take rideshares and meet there. I plan on drinking, and so do you. Stop trying to pretend."

"I'm mostly just worried you won't actually show up."

I looked down at the Atlanta versus Miami soccer game that was streaming on my computer. Erin had a right to be worried that I wouldn't show up, since watching the game had me in my feels. I should have turned it off, but somehow, watching Rhys play and picturing those muscled thighs moving between my legs was my new favorite sport.

"I'm coming," I promised. "And I'll even beat you there." Erin wanted to meet up early so we could watch the sunset from the rooftop bar. It was her night out, and I wasn't going to let her down just because I missed Rhys.

He wasn't even mine to miss.

We made final plans and I flopped down on my bed to watch

a few more minutes of the game. It was four to zero Miami, with Rhys scoring two of the four goals so far. The TV camera kept scanning to Rhys' brother, Levi, as he sat in the crowd cheering.

"It's strange seeing Coach Peyton in Miami colors, isn't it?" one of the announcers said.

"Being the big brother to Rhys Peyton isn't always easy," the other announcer joked.

The camera went back to the action and Rhys drove up the field toward the goal before passing it to Tripp Maddux. Tripp drove up a little more and then took a shot on the goal. It missed, but the ball ricocheted off the goalie's hands and then out of bounds, creating a corner kick for Miami.

"Rhys Peyton will take the kick," the announcer said, as the camera zoomed in on Rhys' face. He looked focused and in control, determined. Sexy. It was a good thing I was alone in my apartment because while Rhys lined the ball up and licked his lips, I couldn't help but moan and think about all the places on my body those lips had been. He may have been in Atlanta, but he was still making it hotter in Miami as sweat formed on my chest and palms.

The whistle blew and Rhys kicked the ball from the corner. The camera panned out and showed the ball going straight to Tripp, who stood a foot taller than everyone else. He headed the ball and it went into the goal, and I knew Rhys used his super precision to aim and make that goal possible. He and Tripp probably practiced that every day.

My heart was racing as I watched them celebrate and line back up. Rhys tugged at his shorts again and his thigh flexed before the shorts fell back down. I was so screwed. My feelings for Rhys weren't supposed to get that far.

Slamming my laptop shut, I decided to let him go for the night. Erin and I were going to have fun, and maybe it was what I needed to keep myself from thinking about the man I couldn't have. Shouldn't have.

It didn't take me long to get ready and before I knew it, I was pulling up to the bar in my rideshare while Erin waved at me on the sidewalk like a maniac. I ran into her hug, like it had been years since we saw each other and soaked in her excitement.

"Let's get to the roof," she squealed. "The sun sets in an hour."

Hand in hand, we waited at the bar for a drink and grabbed a shot of rum for good measure. Then we found a table close to the view and smiled at each other like loons.

"Okay," Erin sighed. "Before we get to the fun part, I need to ask you a serious question really quick."

I started nodding, answering her question before she asked, unable to keep it from her a second longer. "Yes, Rhys and I slept together."

Her eyes widened and her mouth flopped open and closed as she processed what I had just said. Then she squinted and turned her head a little, shaking it as if I had answered the wrong question.

"I was going to ask if you had heard from your mother," Erin huffed a laugh. "But this works too."

My face reddened and I knew Rhys would have loved seeing me so flush, which made me redden even more. "Oh," I laughed, although it wasn't exactly a laugh, more like an embarrassed cry.

"You fucked him?"

"Shhhh," I looked around but the bar hadn't filled up yet since it was still early. "Yes. And no, I haven't heard from my mother. I'm sure she is in the middle of finding someone else to torture for a while."

"Poor soul," Erin laughed, knowing I was right. "But back to Rhys."

I groaned but smiled, kind of anxious to tell her the whole

story. So I did, and even added in how I had let my feelings get the best of me.

"We talked while he made dinner and then talked more afterward. Erin, it felt so good. But it was the wrong move, because I just wanted to keep talking to him and learning more about him."

"Why is that wrong? He clearly wanted the same thing."

"He wants his ex. He wants what she could give him. Not me."

"So then what? You two are just done?"

"We were never more than a fling. A couple of nights to use each other, but that couldn't last. It's better if we just get back to being friends."

"I guess," Erin shrugged. "If it was me, I would just ride that dick as long as I could."

"Yeah right!" I laughed, knowing she wouldn't be caught dead riding anyone's dick.

"I meant if I was you," she squealed. "But I know how to use a dick if I had to. Don't think I wouldn't."

I raised my hand in surrender and shook my head. "Change of subject."

"No way," Erin pushed the shot of rum toward me. "Shots, then you tell me more about Rhys' dick."

Raising our shot glasses to each other, we smiled and then tipped the drink down quickly. We made rum shots our little thing during our freshman year when it was all we could get our hands on. It made us feel like we were having drinks in a tropical paradise when in reality, we were holed up in our freshman dorm rooms.

Those were the days when Erin and I first connected. She made me feel like I wasn't alone anymore. But those days were ending, as Erin readied herself to go pro.

"Now," Erin said, a giggle from the rum making her nose scrunch. "Tell me how big it is."

It took me a minute to realize what she meant, but when it hit me that she was talking about Rhys' dick again, I laughed and shook my head. "I'll need a few more drinks before I start telling you how I'm ninety-nine percent sure he dilated my cervix."

"Oh daaaamn. This calls for more shots." Erin jumped up and ran toward the bar, not needing anymore of an excuse to get more drinks. I just giggled, feeling the first drink warm my body and make me feel lighter than I had in a while.

Going out was the right move. Not only was I getting much needed time with Erin, but I knew if I had enough to drink, I would forget about Rhys. In fact, forgetting Rhys was my goal for the night, and the shots that Erin brought back to the table were going to help.

Chapter Twenty Eight

Rhys

The game against Atlanta wasn't even close. My brother may have ruled that city as the head coach of their football team, but I ruled Major League Soccer in Miami and we stomped Atlanta's *Futbal* Club six to nothing.

Levi was waiting for me when I came out of the locker room and we made a quick Facetime call to our mom so she could see us together. It was kind of a relief she wasn't there, because I needed to just chill with my brother. I hadn't yet decided how much I was going to tell him, but I knew I needed to mention my lingering thoughts of Mel. Maybe he could help me make sense of why they're still there when I have no desire to do anything about it.

Levi had been the opposite of me our entire lives. He saw what our dad had done and never wanted to be with one woman forever. He was scared he would repeat our father's mistakes while I was eager to end the cycle.

What he didn't realize though, was that in my eyes, he ended the cycle a long time ago. Not because he found someone to love, but because he was my hero growing up.

After our dad left, Levi took over clapping on the sidelines of my soccer games. He would walk back and forth and yell at me to stay onside or use my left foot. When mom couldn't take me, Levi would skip his own practices so that he could drive me to mine.

Even if he never met his girl, he was already the opposite of our father. Meeting her was just icing on the cake.

"How's Charleigh?" I asked him after we sat down and ordered a beer.

"She is working in Detroit this weekend, or she would be here."

"Well I'm sorry I missed her, but kinda glad we get a chance to be alone."

"I know being around us isn't easy since Melanie left."

"Nah," I waved him off. He was right, it wasn't easy seeing him accomplish *my* goals. But he deserved it more than anyone I knew. I wanted him to be happy and being in love suited him. "I'm getting over her."

"Are you though?" He teased, nudging me as the waitress dropped off our beers.

I shrugged, trying to decide where to start. As much as I wanted to get his opinion about Mel, I wasn't ready to share Ash with him. I respected his opinion more than anything, and I was afraid if he told me what a mistake I had made, it would dim the high I was still on from spending time with her.

Ash was starting to take up more space in my thoughts, and as I sat there mulling over what to tell my brother, I realized my issues weren't because of Mel. She wasn't the first thing I thought about anymore; it was Ash.

Every left foot kick I made during the game, I thought of her. In fact, I was intentionally kicking lefty all night just so I had an excuse to think of her. It was a wonder Atlanta FC didn't figure that out.

"What's going on with you?" He asked seriously after I got caught up in my thoughts for too long.

"I don't know. I mean, I almost called Mel, just to get some closure."

"Almost?"

"I didn't hit the button."

"Good," he huffed and took a big swig of his drink. "She doesn't deserve your call."

"It wasn't for her, it was for me."

"Well you don't deserve to have to listen to her lies. She said she wanted to get married, have kids, and led you on. Made you think she was the one. Which wasn't her worst offense. It was that text she sent you? Fuck that bitch."

I smiled as he ranted, taking a drink of my own beer. My brother was always a fighter. He was always ready to put his gloves on, and go a 'round' with whomever he needed to, especially for the people he loved. A few months ago, he loved Melanie for how happy she made me. The second she sent me that text, she was dead to him.

"I'm not worried about her," I told him, hoping it calmed him down. "I'd love to know why she disappeared so quickly, but I'm over wanting to spend a lifetime with her."

He eyed me a little, like he didn't believe me. He could tell there was more, but I kept my lips sealed when it came to Ash. He respected me enough to change the subject. "What have you been up to then?"

"Well, Colin is trying to distract me. He's had me helping one of his girls. I was pissed at him for asking at first, but it's been good to work out and coach someone. I get why you like it."

"Yeah, it was on the news that you were at their game."

"What?" I almost yelled, shocked. "What news?"

"Just online, I saw your name and clicked. A picture of you and Cruz watching the game was with a short write up about you two taking in some college action."

"Geez," I laughed. There weren't any secrets in my world. As long as they didn't catch me shoving my dick in Ash, I guess I was okay. And since the only place we were intimate was my place, that was doubtful. "Everyone wants a story."

"No one knows that better than I do." He was referring to Charleigh, and how hard it was keeping their relationship out of the public eye.

"It was just a game. Checking in and seeing how they did in Colin's absence."

Levi was just about to question the truth in my words when my phone started ringing. My eyes practically popped out of my head when I saw Ash's name on the caller ID. I hadn't heard from her since she left my place the other night.

"Let me grab this," I mumbled to Levi before answering. "Hello?"

"Guess who's here?" Ash's voice was a high whisper with a slight slur. There was loud music in the background and I could hear another girl giggling close to the phone.

"Where are you?"

"At a pool, on a roof. Sound familiar?" Based on the continued slur in her voice, I knew Ash had been drinking. "And there is rum."

I looked up to Levi, who was trying not to smile at me, as he was pretending to play on his phone. He couldn't hear Ash, but I knew I had tensed up and he took notice. Holding up one finger, I told him I needed one more minute, then lowered my voice.

"Ash, where are you?"

"Club something. Not far from your place. I guess all these tall buildings have pools on top."

"Who's with you?"

"Erin." She spoke as if I knew who Erin was so I assumed she was a teammate. I still didn't have a clue, but at least she was with someone she trusted.

"Is that what you called to tell me?" I actually smiled, calming down a little. She was having fun, the pool probably reminded her of me, and I couldn't help but be glad I was on her mind.

"Noooo," she laughed again. "I called to tell you that Coach is here."

"Colin?"

"Hunter." She was back to a stage whisper and the other girl—Erin—was giggling again.

"Why is he there?"

"I don't know. He hasn't seen us, but he's with a girl. Can you believe there is a girl that wants to spend time with him? I guess I could see him being kinda hot if he wasn't such a dick. But not Rhys Peyton hot."

"Ash, baby," I slipped, getting worked up again since she mentioned Hunter. "What's going on?"

"Okay let me start over," she giggled. "Erin and I are by the rooftop pool, we had some drinks, Hunter walked in with a girl, and then I called you."

"It's only eight, barely even dark, what time did you get started?"

"We had three shots of rum. It's always party time in Miami, baby."

"*Four*," Erin yelled into the phone. "We had four because it's paaaarty time."

"Started strong, I see," grimacing.

"I was going to text you but did you know that spelling and rum don't go well together? Rhys, I swear...rum makes you dumb. So I told Erin, 'Ah ha. I can call him!'"

I rubbed my hand down my face and looked at Levi. He was trying to suppress a knowing smirk. Slipping up and calling Ash a term of endearment was not lost on him. Either was the fact that I had scooted my chair back and was ready to run back to Miami.

"Try to slow down. You're making me nervous."

"I'll be fine," she sighed. "No one worries about me when I go out because it's just me, myself, and I in my life. Don't start worrying now."

Too late.

"You plan on staying there all night?"

"Yeah, and I'm gonna dive in the pool. But Rhys.... Hunter is with a girrrrl."

"Does that bother you?" I instantly got jealous at the idea that *she* was jealous. Not to mention it wasn't lost on me that she had just said he was kind of hot.

"It bothers me that he is in my space."

"Maybe if we flirt with him, he will leave," Erin suggested. "I tend to scare men away."

"No!" I jumped up and started pacing, making other people in the restaurant take notice and look at me strangely. "Don't go near him."

"Are you jealous Mr. Coach? Rhys. Peyton. Man?" She was slurring even more, giggling at herself.

"You know I don't like him, Ash. I don't want him anywhere near you. It's bad enough he's your coach."

"Well don't you worry, Mister. I don't think his dick is as big as yours. And that is what I told Erin."

"For fuck sake," I whispered, looking around the room like everyone could hear her. "I'm in Atlanta, but I'm going to text you the code to my apartment. If you need a place to go, you both can go there for the night."

"I know you're in Atlanta. You kept lifting the leg of your shorts and those thighs, Rhysssss, those thighs. You have the best thighs."

"You watched the game?" I smiled again, not being able to help myself.

"Most of it," she giggled. "Enough to know you overused your left foot, and probably didn't drink rum before the game."

She noticed. Fuck, my chest was warming up. I had to squeeze my fist just to keep from rubbing the area where my heart was rapidly beating of my heart.

"Ash, just go to my place if you need to, okay?"

"Why would we need a place to go? Ohhh shit, Hunter just saw us... he's coming this way."

The phone call ended abruptly and I turned back to Levi. Before I could even say anything, he tossed me the keys to his car and took another pull of his beer.

"Leave my car at the airport and I'll grab it later. I already texted James and he's ready for takeoff."

Chapter Twenty-Nine

Seeing Hunter show up made us groan and take another shot of rum. How were we supposed to have fun with Mr. Creepy around?

I would have assumed he was there to spy on us and be weird if it hadn't been for the fact that he was with a girl. He seemed pretty into the poor woman, and hadn't even looked around for us since we saw him walk in. It was safe to assume he had no idea we were there.

Rum made me do some stupid things though. For starters, I called Rhys to tell him Hunter was there, and then proceeded to tell him his thighs were fucking hot.

I had confided in her about Rhys not being a fan of Hunter—mostly because I wasn't a fan of his. Then I said, "Watch this," and stupidly called Rhys to tell him Hunter was at the club.

Erin laughed her ass off until Hunter started walking toward us. We had been spotted and I hung up on Rhys so he didn't get mad at whatever Hunter had to say. Again, I knew that was stupid, but the rum was talking and I was losing control.

"Hey ladies," Hunter nodded at us, his eyes looking beady and angry.

"We can be here, we are not kids," I blurted, hearing my own self slur.

"I'm not here to say you can't," Hunter snapped. "But I wouldn't be much of a coach if I didn't come say hi and ask you two to be careful."

"We were hiding from you," Erin laughed even though she was trying to sound serious.

"You ladies are already drunk and doing a shit job of hiding."

"I called Rhys!" I practically yelled it, like it mattered to him, and I instantly regretted that as Hunter's brow furrowed and his snarl surfaced.

"Rhys Peyton?"

"You know another Rhys?" Erin waved her hand in the air and shook her hips. It was supposed to look sassy but she was too drunk to make it work.

"Why do I need to know you called Rhys?" Hunter tilted his head at me, his face turning red.

"You don't like him."

"You don't know anything about me, Keller. Why would you assume I don't like Rhys?"

"Because you have been Mr. Mood Swing since he arrived." Every time Erin answered a question or spoke, she stood up from her stool. Eventually, she was going to tumble over and I had to be the responsible one and calm her down.

"Hey," I patted her hand. "I got this."

"Keller," Hunter leaned in and got close to my face, closer than I wanted him to, making me lean back a little for space. "Stop assuming you know me or anything about what has changed my mood. It sure as hell isn't Rhys."

"Oh," I smiled. "Then we are all good."

"No, we aren't. You're drunk and I'm responsible for you two."

"No, you aren't," I mimicked his tone. "We are responsible for we."

"Hunter?" I heard a soft feminine voice, and Hunter backed away so I could see her behind him. "What's going on?"

"Nothing," Hunter snapped. "These are two of my players and they're fucking drunk."

"Geez," the girl said with a laugh. "They're having fun. Leave them alone Coach Crazy."

"Oh that's a good one!" Erin laughed.

Hunter backed away without introducing us to his friend, but his eyes stayed on us with a warning until he grabbed her hand and turned around.

Once we were sure they were far enough away, Erin and I started laughing again. "Coach Crazy!"

"That is now his new name," Erin confirmed. "Oh, let's drink to that!"

She disappeared from the stool and shimmied toward the bar. I knew it was my job to watch our table so I stayed put and pulled my phone back out from under my dress. I had three missed calls from Rhys and two text messages asking me where I was. I knew I should have answered him, maybe even apologize, but I also knew the rum was doing the talking for me. It was safer if I called him in the morning.

Nearly twenty minutes later, Erin returned holding four shot glasses in her fingers. She set them down and took her seat, then wiped the sweat from her brow. "The line is long so I ordered double to keep us occupied."

"Good thinking!" I slurred again. I lifted one of the shot glasses and nodded at her to get one as well. "To us. May we not remember tomorrow that I drunk-dialed Rhys."

Erin's head flew back laughing while I took the shot. When she stopped laughing, she took her own shot then raised the other glass in the air. I took my second glass and waited as Erin made her own toast.

"To us. May we go home with strangers!" Her words had me

giggling, because going home with a stranger was Erin's method of operation. She refused to date, but loved sex, so our evenings out always involved her finding someone to fuck.

I envied that side of her. She was carefree and strong enough to know what she wanted. Sometimes she would joke around that she was a slut, but I would give anything to feel that sexually empowered.

Until Rhys, sex wasn't even that fun for me. It was just a connection between two people that was supposed to lead to long standing relationships. But I had only managed one relationship that lasted six months and he did the bare minimum in the bedroom.

Maybe going home with a stranger was exactly what I needed. No names, no expectations. Just sex. The kind of sex that would make me *not* want to call Rhys.

"I'm gonna drink to that," I finally slurred, then downed another shot. "I need to fuck Rhys away."

"I thought you two just fucked. Why do you need to fuck him away?"

"Because he was a goooood fuck," I laughed quietly. "So goooood."

Erin nodded knowingly, like she had no doubt Rhys was good in bed, or the pool, or the couch. Thankfully, she changed the subject and we spent the next hour letting the rum settle as we recounted our days at Miami University. The nights we had together were few, and as we carried on, I started to get emotional about how different our goals in life were.

"Hey," Erin took my hand and held it, then shoved a napkin in my other hand. "We will always stay close."

"Yeah," I sniffed and dabbed at my makeup. "We will."

"Shit. Fuck this. Let's dance."

I stood, excited about the change and ready to sway my hips to the Latin beats the DJ was playing. Erin held my hand as she led me to the dance floor that was right next to the deep end of the pool. She turned me and held my hips, grinding behind me as we started moving to a new song that had started.

Facing the bar, I locked eyes with Hunter, who was watching us intently. That same feeling he always gave me creeped back in and I was tempted to go tell him to fuck off. How dare he watch Erin and me like that. Much less when he was clearly on a date.

Instead of leaving the dance floor, I sent Hunter a middle finger and then turned so that I could no longer see him. Erin was too lost in the music to even notice. Plus she was using my body to shield herself and hold herself steady.

For a few songs, her hands were on my hips behind me and I was able to let loose, feeling safe in our space. But then the beat of a familiar reggaeton song started, the one that played in the car when I first rode with Rhys. The one that helped distract me from a panic attack after the first kiss we almost shared.

Erin pulled her hands from me and I reached back to put them back. I wasn't ready to separate, not ready to leave the dance floor. But instead of Erin's small and dainty fingers, rough and strong hands covered mine and held onto my hips.

I stopped dancing, realizing Erin wasn't behind me, and I turned to see who the hands belonged to. Holding me in place, those hands on my hips stopped me from turning. They started to move my hips, insisting I keep dancing, but it wasn't until I heard the voice in my ear that I complied.

"I just took a private jet from Atlanta so I could have this dance. Don't you dare stop now."

"Rhys," I whispered. It was too low for him to hear me, but telling myself who it was made my fears dissipate. I leaned back against his chest, resting my head back on his shoulder and looking at the sky above us. I missed him more than I should have. Dancing with him was making me feel too much.

Yet I didn't stop. I let the song play and even though it was upbeat, Rhys and I swayed slowly together. Every few beats, I would move my ass against his cock and I felt him getting harder each time. By the end of the song, his hands were roaming over my tight dress and I could hear his breathing getting more erratic.

"You better be careful," he growled. "I will fuck you right here on this dance floor."

"That's what I'm going for," I teased. The rum was still talking because I was not the kind of girl that wanted to fuck on a dance floor full of people.

"No it's not," Rhys called my bluff. "But if you want, I can turn you around and let you watch Cruz and your friend doing just that."

"What?" I stopped dancing and turned around, looking for Erin as I had completely forgotten about her once Rhys' hands were on me.

"Don't worry," Rhys moaned. "I brought Cruz with me to keep an eye on her. She's in good hands."

"She is a bigger slut than Cruz. But she isn't interested in what he has to offer."

Rhys laughed, catching on to what I was trying to say. He leaned down, close to my lips and smirked. "No one is a bigger slut than Cruz, but it sounds like they have a lot in common."

"She's drunk!"

His lips finally met mine, making me stop talking, and stop thinking. I forgot why I had even been talking in the first place. Erin was a big girl, and if Cruz tried anything, she could take care of herself.

When Rhys pulled back on our kiss, he turned me to just the right angle and I saw Cruz and Erin dancing, just like Rhys had said. They were practically fucking and it was hot to watch as they pulled another girl in between them and kept moving.

Okay so it was safe to assume Erin was fine.

Turning back to Rhys, I wrapped my arms around his neck

and kissed him, letting go of any worries I may have had. His hands went to my ass and he pulled me close to him, rubbing my stomach on his still-hard cock.

"You flew home to dance with me?" I asked in disbelief. A slow song had started and we began to sway again.

"I flew home because you had me fucking worried. My brother and I had already arranged a charter flight to bring me home so we could stay and hang out together. It was nothing to change the flight time to 'as soon as possible' and get here."

"I'm sorry I hung up, it's just that Hunter had—" thoughts of Hunter creeping at the bar made me stop my sentence and turn around to look for him. "Oh shit, Hunter!"

Chapter Thirty

Rhys

I texted Cruz to meet me at the jet. He was my back up in case I had to beat Hunter's ass, and he needed to attest that the fucker deserved it. But when we got there, he ended up being my wingman.

And Hunter ended up being an ally.

After we landed in Miami, I turned my phone back on and it immediately chimed with an incoming text.

> It's Hunter, Keller's coach. Got your number from Colin. Look, I don't know what is going on between you two, but if you're nearby, she's at Rosa Sky. She mentioned she called you, or I wouldn't have even considered sending you this message.

> Just landed at the private airport. Twenty minutes away.

When Cruz and I walked into the bar, my eyes landed on Hunter first. He was with a woman at the bar but was watching the dance floor more than he was talking to her. My eyes followed the direction of his and I found Ash and her friend right away.

Had he not texted me to tell me where they were, I would have gone to him first and pulled his eyes from his head. Now I was considering the fact that he may have just been keeping an eye on her for the sake of her safety.

This dude confused the fuck out of me.

He glanced toward the door casually and spotted me, and I saw his entire body relax. He gave me a slight nod toward Ash and turned around to face his date, leaving Ash in my hands.

Cruz saw Erin grinding on Ash and told me he would happily entertain her. We pulled Erin away and I replaced her position with my own. The way Ash leaned into my body when she realized it was me made me grow hard and hot. I loved that her body craved being next to mine.

"Oh shit, Hunter!" Ash had gotten past the haze of us dancing and it clicked that Hunter was somewhere in that bar.

"It's okay," I tried pulling her back around to face me. "He's with his date."

"You saw him?"

"When I walked in. Ash, calm down."

"Oh my God!" Tears sprang in her eyes and I had to pull her from the dance floor to the wall overlooking the city. "You were in Atlanta."

It was like everything was starting to sink in and she was sobering up as she remembered what had transpired.

"You came because of Hunter."

"I came because you scared the shit out of me. I came because the idea of you being drunk in a bar and possibly taken advantage of made me see red."

"Because Hunter was here. I should have told you when he left our table that we were okay. I should have called you back."

"Wouldn't have mattered. I was coming the second your name showed up on my caller ID."

Her shining green eyes looked up into mine, so many questions swirling in her head. They were probably the same questions Cruz asked on the entire flight.

What is going on here?

Is she more than a rebound?

Why do I care so much?

"Fuck I love your eyes," I whispered, ignoring the questions, and my answers, like I always did. I took my hand to her cheek and caressed her until my thumb fell to her bottom lip. Her eyes continued to look up into mine, and for a second, it was like we were alone at my place. It was hard to remember that there were hundreds of people only a few feet away.

Before I did anything crazy, like pushing my dick up under Ash's dress for the whole world to see me fucking her, my phone vibrated with a text.

> Now that the girls aren't alone, I need to get my date home.

I looked around but didn't see him.

"Who was that?"

"Hunter."

Her eyes started to get big again and she looked around with me as well. She was on alert and the soft moment we had between us was gone. "No he didn't..."

"It's okay," I assured her. "How do you think I found out which roof top you were on? He texted me."

She looked confused, and while I completely understood why Hunter creeped her out, and pissed me off, he kept an eye on her and told me where to find her. It was making me think that whatever was going on with him couldn't have been because of me. Or Ash for that matter. He knew enough to know I would come if she needed me, and he felt like she needed me. I may wake up the next day and hate his guts again, but I was thankful for him that night. I was going to cut him a break–a small one–and hoped that this all meant that whatever crawled up his ass didn't involve me being close to Ash.

"He's gone." I held up my phone and showed her his text, letting her draw her own conclusions so that we no longer had to make him the topic of our conversation.

She nodded and started to melt back into my stare as my phone buzzed again with another text. "Fucking hell."

> Erin is wasted. I'm getting a ride share and taking her home. You good?

> Your home or hers?

> If she wasn't Ash's friend, I'd take her to mine. But no, you idiot, I'm taking her to her place.

> THEN LEAVING.

> Thanks man.

Ash read my screen as I replied to Cruz. She seemed content that Erin was okay. That Hunter was gone. That I was there.

"Take me home," she whispered. "Your home."

Without a response, I took her hand and led her toward the elevator. We were only a few blocks from my place and I decided to walk, hoping the time and the quiet city streets sobered her up a little.

"You're not going to fuck me, are you?" She asked as we got closer to my building.

I laughed, finding her pout endearing. "No ma'am, I'm not."

"Ma'am?" She stopped walking. "Do I look like your mama?"

"My mama taught me to respect the women in my life. Pardon my manners, they peeked out for a minute."

"I don't like your manners," she slurred a little, proving she was still feeling her rum. "I like when you're unmannerly. Rude. Impolite."

With each word she spoke, she was trying harder to enunciate. By the time we got to the elevator and up to my apartment, she had come up with eleven more words to describe how much she liked when I was ill-mannered.

"Straight to bed." I led her to my bedroom and started unzipping her dress. She let me get her completely naked except for her thong then fell backward onto my silk sheets. "Stay there. I'll be right back."

"Bring a condom," she giggled.

As much as I wanted to be inside of her, it wasn't going to be on a night when she was that drunk. Coming back to Miami to fuck her wasn't my intention. It was to take care of her, make sure she was safe, and I had done just that. If she woke up in the morning and still wanted to fuck me, then I would show her how *rude* I could be.

I brought water and a few ibuprofen back from the kitchen and managed to get her to swallow some of it before she laid back down. Within minutes, she was sleeping so I laid the sheet over her and grabbed my phone.

First, I was going to make sure Cruz was good. Then I was going to send Hunter a message that Ash and Erin were okay. Lastly, I was going to text my brother.

Levi never even asked questions when I took Ash's call. He saw something in me that told him I was gone. Not just from dinner, but lost to the enchantment of a college girl whose goals in life didn't align with my own. He could have told me to sit down, to get my shit together. Instead, he texted the pilot and had him ready to get me to Miami.

I needed to set him straight. Tell him Ash was just a friend. That was all I was going to tell him if she came up at dinner and since nothing had changed, the truth was all he needed to know.

Even if I didn't believe me, I needed him to believe me.

Grabbing my phone from the counter, I started to scroll to Levi's name when another text came through. Not from Cruz. Or Hunter. Or Levi.

Not even from Colin.

We need to talk. I miss you.

Chapter Thirty One

Ash

I didn't have to open my eyes to know where I was. Hell, I remembered almost everything from the night before, but the silk sheets and the smell of Rhys was all around me. The only thing missing was Rhys as I felt next to me and came up empty.

Looking over, I saw it was five o'clock in the morning and I was alone. He had told me sex was off the table and I knew that because Rhys was too noble to risk taking advantage of me being drunk. But I figured he would at least sleep next to me.

Climbing from bed, I slid a discarded shirt of his over my head and walked out to the living room. Rhys was in his jeans from the night before, with no shirt on, and his arm was thrown over his eyes as he slept. A glass of bourbon was half drunk on the coffee table next to his phone and I smiled at the thought of how tired he must have been.

Afterall, he played an entire game, then flew back to Miami and took care of me. No rest in between all that, and not to mention I made him crazy when I brought up Hunter.

I grabbed the glass and took a small swig. Not enough to get drunk again, but enough to clear the dryness off my tongue. Then

I climbed on top of Rhys and laid down, letting my head rest on his chest.

His arms came down and held me tight, his chest rumbled with content pleasure. I kissed his bare skin and my fingers ran the line of the waistband of his jeans. I wanted to soak in the fact that we were getting one more chance to be together.

"Wake up," I whispered.

"I'm awake."

"I was talking to your dick," I joked, lowering my kisses down to his stomach.

"He's awake, baby. He's always awake for you."

The giggle I made was the one that only Rhys brought out in me. The one that made me feel cheery and careless. The one that hadn't surfaced since I was a child who hadn't yet figured out how hard her life would be.

My eyes went to his as he watched me undo the button and zipper of his jeans. I tried keeping my eyes on him because I knew how much he loved them. But it was hard when I wanted my mouth on him as well.

"Get up," Rhys commanded, in what I now knew was the tone he took when he didn't want to explain himself or have any questions asked.

When we were both off the couch, he led me slowly to the bedroom and sat me down on the edge of the bed. As he undid his jeans, and let them slide down his legs, I started to take the shirt I was wearing off but he froze and shook his head, making me stop.

"I'll do that."

My mouth kicked up on one side and leaned back on my arms to watch as he discarded his boxers as well. His fingers ran through his untamed hair as he lowered to his knees in front of me. Just the vision of him on his knees was making my clit pulse and my stomach twist with pleasure.

I started taking deep breaths, and I leaned up to touch him at the same time his hands started running up my legs. They made their way under the shirt and grabbed the edges of my thin thong, ripping them on the sides so he didn't have to bother taking them down.

He pushed me to lay back and wrapped my legs around his neck while holding my thighs with his hands. My insecurities about my thighs began to trickle back in, but I let them go just as quickly.

Rhys seemed to love them, kneading and nipping his way closer to my pussy. "I want to make you feel so good that I won't be able to hear you tell me to stop. Press these legs around my ears, make me feel it."

When I tightened, he groaned with pleasure as he kneaded them more. I had never told him about my hang up with my thighs, but it was the second time he had made me feel less like a freak and more like a goddess. My strength was my superpower and he wanted to use it like a drug.

His tongue gently swept up my folds and I shook with the anticipation of him going deeper and harder. My body knew him now, and knew what kind of pleasure he could give. I didn't have to overthink it or hope it would come, it was there the moment he showed me his intent.

"Rhys," I pleaded. "Go easy on me."

"Back at you," he growled.

Our eyes locked for a moment, the meaning behind our words seeming to change in context as we stared at one another. Then Rhys shook the moment away and his mouth covered me, attacking my pussy like it was a meal. His tongue pushed inside of me and then to my clit, messy, but somehow controlled.

I squeezed my legs without meaning to, locking his head between them again and keeping him completely at my mercy. When my pelvis started to move against him, he pushed me down and held me still, reminding me we both still had control.

Glancing down, his eyes were watching me and his tongue slowed and pressed over my clit. With a deep exhalation, I came, and he watched me shake as I lost control of my now limp legs. They fell open and he rose up, taking my shirt with him.

"I tempted to shove my cock inside that pretty mouth of yours," he smirked. "But I will send cum right down your throat, and you know that's not where I want it."

I nodded, understanding. He had said before that coming inside of me was claiming me, marking me, and I knew as he scooted my body up that he wasn't even going to bother with a condom.

His eyes were warning me while also begging me to say no, but I couldn't bring myself to be responsible. If he wanted inside of me, I wanted him there, bare. I wanted to feel how good it was to have him without the barrier between us.

He lowered himself on top of me and kissed me passionately. It had more meaning than words, and I nearly started to cry as I waited for him to push his cock inside of me. When he was lined up, he looked into my eyes one more time and took my silence as his okay to keep going.

Slowly, he moved his hips and I felt his warm skin enter me like no one ever had. It felt different, and raw. So good that I could see why people said, "*Fuck that,*" and had sex without protection.

"I've never felt this," he admitted. "Never took this risk before."

"Me either."

"I just couldn't let you go this time without feeling all of you."

"Don't let me go," I let slip, confessing what I wanted. We agreed on once, then twice, but did we have to ever stop counting? We knew we weren't going to make it forever because we were both going in different directions. But did that mean it had to end now?

Instead of answering, he kissed me and started to move, making love to me in a way that felt so perfect, yet so final.

Within minutes, I was close to coming and he closed his eyes tight trying to make it last longer. I could feel myself squeezing him and his control waning by the second.

"Don't try to hold back," I urged him. "And don't make me come alone. I want us to feel everything together."

His eyes opened and once again locked on mine. I gave in to my body's need and came, moaning and shaking beneath him.

"Fuck," he growled and sped up to his own release. "Fuck you're holding me so tight."

"Come inside of me, Rhys." I urged him again, knowing we were making a mistake but unable to stop myself from wanting it more than anything.

"Dammit, Ash. I need you to know how it feels to have my cum dripping down your leg."

Then he stilled, and I could feel him releasing as his muscles jerked from the pleasure. His face, his passion, and the way he completely gave in, was making my heart want to explode along with him.

"You'll be okay," he whispered as he moved inside of me. "I promise you will be okay."

I didn't think that was true. How would I ever be okay after having Rhys in my life? Every moment would pale in comparison to the one we were having.

He moved to the side of me and laid back, catching his breath. I moved to get up—to clean up—but he stopped me and pulled me into his chest. "Stay dirty for me."

I curled into his hold and rested my head on his chest. "Good things happen when I come looking for you."

"Yeah," he laughed, then kissed the top of my head and ran his hand down my arm. "It should be a new tradition."

"I know I was drunk, but was I so irresistible you had to sleep on the couch?"

He huffed another small laugh at my sarcasm. "Yes, and no. You're always irresistible, but I decided to have a drink and think about some things. Guess I just fell asleep."

"Sleep here. I don't have classes tomorrow and no practice until later. We can sleep late."

"Nowhere I'd rather be." He yawned and pulled me tighter. I could tell he was ready to close his eyes so I stayed quiet and listened to his heartbeat. When his breathing evened out, I relaxed even more and closed my own eyes.

Before I could doze off, though, my phone started ringing and I realized I had no idea where my phone even was. I kept it under my dress in a holder when I went out, but that holder and that dress was somewhere on the floor.

The ring was coming from the living room, so I figured Rhys set it aside when we got to his place. It was nearly six in the morning, who would call me?

"Erin," I mumbled to myself. She probably wondered what happened to me and was worried. The phone started ringing for a second time and I eased away from Rhys so I could go get it and answer the call. Knowing Erin, she wouldn't stop calling until she knew I was okay.

By the time I got into the living room, the calls had stopped and in its place were a few text messages. "Coming!" I groaned and began walking toward the source of the noise.

It was coming from the coffee table, Rhys' phone not mine, and I paused unsure what to do. Leaning down, and without touching the phone, I looked at the messages that had popped up. Because the phone was locked, I could only read the last one that was sent from *Mel*.

I love you too.

Chapter Thirty Two

Rhys

I had been unbearable since I woke up without Ash. It had been nearly two weeks and while I didn't act out the way I had when Mel left, it was glaringly obvious to everyone in my way that I was not happy.

It just wasn't the same feeling.

With Mel, it was anger, embarrassment, and confusion—disguised as heartbreak—and I took those feelings out on the field and with my fists.

With Ash, I just fucking wanted her.

Missed her.

There wasn't one emotion or feeling that I could pinpoint.

For the first few days, I was fine, because Ash leaving was exactly the way it was supposed to be. We were never meant to see each other that night, it was not supposed to happen. She made it easy on both of us by heading out while I slept.

Then I told myself that if she drunk-dialed me again, that she was on her own. I couldn't keep worrying about her and obsessing. Mel had been trying to call me and that was all I could handle as far as women went.

But that didn't last long.

By the end of the week, I was pissed–mostly at myself. I just couldn't decide if I was pissed because I should have called her, or because I *wanted* to call her. It seemed unreal that a young girl, still in college, was capable of digging so deeply under my skin. I had no business trying to turn her life upside down when I couldn't even get a handle on my own.

Through Sandy, I knew Colin had rejoined the team and he wasn't going to ask me to keep working with Ash. She had been playing well and I was supposed to be focusing on my own team for the rest of the season.

I should have been relieved.

But I wasn't.

To make matters worse, Mel was still trying to weasel her way back into my life and I had no idea why, or what prompted her to reach out. That first night she texted me, I laid on the couch and considered what I would tell her if we actually talked. But I realized I didn't even care anymore. Even as her texts continued to roll in, giving me a million reasons she wanted to see me, I just wasn't interested.

And it wasn't because I was choosing Ash–she wasn't even an option. I was choosing myself, finally realizing that Mel didn't deserve me. It was like I had been so desperate for a wife and kids that I disregarded things about Mel that I didn't love at all. I hated myself for the time I had already wasted on her, so I blocked her number and took a deep breath, closing that chapter of my life.

If only that solved all my problems.

Toward the end of the second week, I knew I was fucked. Ash never called or texted me so I was sure she was doing fine, but I continued to spiral from my need to reach out to her. I found myself hoping she lost focus again and Colin would call me to help. All I needed was one tiny excuse and I wouldn't be able to stop myself from seeing her.

"You're back to being an asshole," Cruz shoved me, almost knocking me off the stool in front of my locker.

"Yeah," Tripp agreed. "What's up with you?"

"Don't worry about it," I growled, giving Cruz a warning to shut up with just a look. The last thing I needed was more people knowing about Ash. It was already going to be a shit show if Hunter decided to tell Colin I had been sleeping with his left wing.

"Wanna grab a drink tonight?" Tripp asked both Cruz and me.

"Actually," Cruz licked his lips and started rubbing his hands together. "I'm going to the university and watching the ladies' soccer game tonight."

"What?" I yelled, standing from my stool.

"What?" he echoed me, a tiny laugh highlighting his accent a little more. "There's a girl there that I am dead set on fucking, and she asked me to come."

My eyes beaded at him while Tripp looked at me obliviously. "So just us?"

"Actually," I answered, without taking my eyes off Cruz. "I'm gonna go to the game, too."

"I thought you had dinner plans with your brother," Cruz smirked.

"I can do both."

Tripp snorted and turned around to leave, giving up on Cruz and me. "Okay, you two go have fun with that. I'm not messing around with co-eds."

"You're practically a co-ed yourself," Cruz yelled at him as he got further away.

"I make too much money to risk becoming someone's baby daddy." Tripp pushed open the door and left the locker room, but I waited until I heard it click shut before turning on Cruz again.

"Are you after Erin?"

"Maybe," Cruz winked. "She and I have been discussing hooking up. Just once, of course. That much we agreed on."

"Yeah, I've said that before," I groaned and grabbed my wallet from my locker. Cruz was giving me just the opening I needed, and I was too fucking weak to not take it. "I'm going with you. Levi's plane doesn't land till nine."

And he's only coming because I've been a pain in the ass again.

Cruz laughed and started walking toward the exit. "You drive."

Fine by me. I grabbed my keys and jogged to catch up.

"So what's up?" He asked as we made our way through traffic.

He was vague, but I knew he was asking the same thing Tripp asked earlier. I tapped my fingers on the steering wheel and thought about what I could say that would make sense to someone like Cruz–young, carefree, a father he actually talked to.

"Mel has been calling."

His eyes widened and he spoke a few words in Spanish under his breath.

"Exactly," I replied, even though I had no idea what he was saying. "I blocked her number. I feel like a fucking idiot for falling for her in the first place."

"Did your rebound help with that discovery?"

I hit my hand on the wheel and Cruz barely budged, almost like he was taunting me on purpose. "Ash wasn't a rebound. Mel was just a mistake."

"So your fling with Ash is over?"

"Yeah, it has to be."

Cruz nodded like he understood, then shook his head when another thought popped into his mind. I waited for him to say whatever it was, but he eventually turned the music up and let the conversation go.

And I let him, because there was nothing more to say.

When we got to the stadium, Cruz led me to the side and around to the guest pass entrance. We walked through with a nod from the girl working the gate and straight onto the field where the teams were warming up.

"Did you call ahead?" I wondered.

"I know people," Cruz nodded toward the center. "They knew I was coming."

Colin was watching the girls stretch and get ready. Hunter had been moved back to being the assistant coach and was lining balls up in front of the net for the team to strike.

I tried not to zero in on Ash, so my focus stayed on Hunter. I still didn't care much for him, but he showed me he may not have been the fucked up creep I tagged him as. That didn't mean I trusted him, but I had a little more respect. Whatever he was going through, I just hoped he learned not to take it out on the team.

"Rhys," I heard Colin's voice and tapped Cruz to let him know I was veering off to talk to him. Cruz was already eyeing the team trainer who was prepping her station on the sidelines. He waved me off, not caring where I went so I walked onto the field toward Colin.

So much for Erin.

"Hey," he smiled knowingly. My own smile fell, worried Hunter had filled him in on how close Ash and I got while he was gone. Then I wanted to kick my own ass for assuming otherwise. Of course he told Colin, that was his job.

"Hey," I sighed, waiting for him to let me have it and prepared to remind him Ash was an adult.

"Thanks for coming tonight. Big game for us."

"Yeah, Cruz's idea. How's your sister?"

"She's home now. Justine is still out there helping her, and as soon as the season ends I'll go back. She has a long road ahead, but in good spirits."

"Fuck man, I'm so glad to hear that."

"How did it go around here? With Ash?"

That bastard beaded his eyes at me and I was tempted to knock his teeth out. He wasn't her dad, why was he giving me shit? If she wanted to fuck me senseless then who was he to judge?

Damn, I really was a walking whiplash.

And maybe a little unhinged.

"Fine," I eyed him back, gauging his mood a little more. He may have been fishing, but he wasn't going to hear anything from me. Not because I cared, but because Ash probably did. I didn't want to make her life on this team with Colin and Hunter any harder than it already was. "I haven't heard from you since you got back. I assumed you'd call and check in."

"Hunter gave me an update. Ash filled in the gaps. Figured you were back to being your sullen self and I didn't want to mess that up for ya."

I cracked a smile, enjoying him teasing me. Before I blamed him for Mel's disappearance, he was like a father to me, in a way. He mentored me, got on to me, grinded my gears, then loved me through all my growing pains as a player. I had been so mad, I almost forgot how good it felt to be on his good side.

Why the hell was I on his good side?

"So what did Hunter tell you?" *Two could go fishing in this pond, Colin.*

"Just that he saw you two practicing each night, the work was good, the payoff was perfect. Ash had been back to her old self, kicking ass the way she always had before. Although the fire seems to have dimmed in the last couple of games."

"All I did was scrimmage with her. I'm not much of a coach."

"Sometimes, all anyone needs is something else to focus on. Something to break the cycle. Something to give them perspective." I swallowed, unsure if he was talking about me, or Ash. Before he asked me to help her, I was the one spiraling and losing focus. Did Ash break that cycle for me?

"Yeah," I mumbled, more to myself, but Colin was still there and heard me.

He patted my back and squeezed my shoulder before laughing a little. "Enjoy the game." He walked off toward the team, blowing the whistle, and I glanced up and around me, my eyes locking with Ash's. She tilted her head in question, and I shrugged because I wasn't sure which question her eyes were asking.

I was sure the main question was, *"Why am I there?"* But I didn't know that answer any more than I knew what the hell that conversation with Colin meant. Hadn't we established that I was clueless?

Heading toward the stands, I took a seat next to Cruz on the front row, right behind the team bench. Hunter started jogging toward the bench and looked up at me. He shook his head slightly, then reached down for some cones before turning back and heading to the field.

He didn't tell Colin.

I wasn't sure how I knew, but that small movement of his head was him telling me he didn't say a word. It brought both relief and disappointment to the forefront of my brain. My head was spinning, and I leaned forward to rest my elbow on my knees and bow my head toward my feet.

"You okay?" Cruz asked. "Colin make you feel bad for pounding his left wing?"

"I don't think he knows."

"Then what's the problem?"

"I think I wanted him to know. I think I want everyone to know."

Chapter Thirty Three

Ash

Rhys showed up to my game and kept his eyes on me the entire first quarter. It was intense, and I was having trouble focusing on the game the way I should have been.

At halftime, we headed around the bleachers and toward the locker room. Coach raised a hand toward Rhys and waved him down to join us as we walked.

They spoke behind the team quietly, and before we got inside the locker room, Coach was calling me back to join them.

"Talk to Rhys," he grunted quickly and then joined the team. I turned slowly to Rhys who looked like a deer in the headlights.

The sun had set and no one was around, either being in the stands, or in the locker room. Four whole minutes passed before Rhys took charge and grabbed my hand. He led me around to the side of the building, back to where no one would see us if they walked by.

He pushed me into the hard bricks and held me by my shoulders, licking his lips. "Why did you leave?"

"I doubt that's why Coach wants you talking to me."

"We both know you focus better when you're not overthinking."

"I'm not—"

"Yes you are. You left, we haven't talked in two weeks, and now I'm here distracting you. So let's clear the air so you can focus."

I slumped a little at how accurate he was. With Coach back in town, I hadn't planned on seeing Rhys again. It had been a tough couple of weeks without him, but it was all the more reason I was glad I left. It was only going to hurt more if I watched him rekindle whatever still lingered between him and his ex.

I got too close. The way he made love to me in those early morning hours at his place was intense, and affected way more than just my orgasm count.

"I left because I needed to leave. You shouldn't be here either."

"Cruz was coming to get in your friend's pants. Think I was going to let him come alone?"

"So you're cock blocking for him? That's the only reason you're here?"

"You know it's not," he growled, dropping his hands from my shoulders and running them through his hair. "You need to focus, Ash."

"Hard to do when I keep looking up in the stands, mad that you're here, and at the same time, hoping you don't leave. You have me messed up. We messed this up, Rhys."

There was no way I was going to admit that I saw his text. It was irrelevant, and it wasn't like it made me mad. Rhys had been up front about her, about his goals to be a dad and marry her. A few weeks ago, he may have thought that was a lost cause, but now what?

"Fuck Ash," he moaned quietly and got closer to me. "We can't take that back now."

"You were only supposed to help me with soccer. Find my focus and play my game."

"Turns out you play best when your mind is quiet, when your worries are forgotten, and your body is satisfied." His mouth was close to mine, and I could tell he was struggling with whether or not to kiss me.

"It couldn't last forever," I tried to argue.

"But maybe one more time?" His hands skimmed the bare part of my thigh where my shorts and socks weren't covering anything.

"Right here?"

"Right now."

"Rhys, this is more than reckless. This is dangerous." *To my heart.*

"Open up," he nudged my legs apart and I complied, not able to stop myself from wanting him again. I didn't even put up a solid argument, nor did I care that I was in the middle of a game with thousands of people just around the corner from us.

His hand dipped into the waistband of my shorts and into my panties, his fingers finding purchase on my clit. I shook my head but no words came from my lips.

"Let me calm you down, help you focus. One more time, baby."

"How many 'one more times?'" I cried, but pushed into his touch.

He could have already been back with his ex. My coach could walk out and find us. People that were walking in front of the building could possibly hear us.

Or I could fall in love.

"This is bad. We are bad." I said to myself, but loud enough for him to hear.

"I always want to do bad things with you," he whispered back, his lips hovering over mine.

"So dangerous," I added as his lips touched mine and we found the same pulse we had developed before. A connection so natural and right.

Rhys' took two fingers and opened the folds of my pussy before pushing them inside of me. We didn't have long, in fact, we only had a few minutes, but Rhys seemed to understand that—as did my body.

"Soak my fingers, baby. Let go for me. Let me feel it."

I moaned again, louder, and he suppressed the noise with another kiss. His movements got faster and his thumb found my clit, barely touching me before I started to shake. My knees threatened to give out and I was worried Rhys was wrong. He may have been distracting me from everything else, but my legs were going to be Jello for the rest of the night.

"I feel you," he spoke against my lips. "You're squeezing my fingers. You're already there."

Tears pricked the corner of my eyes. Always feeling so much at once and not knowing how to react any other way. Rhys just kissed them away, not the least bit worried they were there. I grabbed onto his shoulders as I came, and moved my body as if I was grinding on top of him. With anyone else, it would have been embarrassing at how needy I felt, and how hard I came.

Rhys loved it.

It made him insatiable.

Desperate.

When he pulled his hands from my pussy, I waited for him to turn me around and fuck me from behind, against the brick wall with my shorts around my thighs. Instead, he took two steps back and nodded toward the field.

"Go focus on the game. Use your left foot. Your legs should be nice and loose."

"But..." I wanted more. There was always more. "What about..."

"No time." He raised an eyebrow just as Coach came around the corner.

"You fix her?" He asked gruffly, looking at Rhys then down at his clipboard.

"She's ready," Rhys nodded, his eyes staying on me while his wet fingers subtly caressed his bottom lip.

My breathing started to get heavier as I realized how close we were to being caught. I was still shaking my head at Rhys, my eyes boring into his. I still wanted more.

I would always want more.

"I gotta go," Rhys smiled, putting the tip of one of his fingers inside his mouth. "Dinner plans."

Coach nodded and turned around, joining the team as they walked back to the field. I followed along, completely unaware of what Rhys had said because I had been too focused on the way he was tasting my cum right there in front of my coach.

When my head cleared, I kicked ass in the second half of the game because I was no longer thinking. The orgasm Rhys gave me made nothing else matter, and since I was no longer wondering why he was in the stands, or if he would leave, I focused on the game and the back side of the opponent's goal.

"What did Rhys say to you?" Coach asked as we left the field. I could hear humor in his tone, as if Rhys handed me the other team's playbook and made it easy.

"He said to use my left foot."

"You already knew that."

"I guess coming from him it hits differently." I cringed because I could hear in my own voice how that sounded. Like Rhys could tell me it snowed in Miami, and I would think it was gospel.

"Then I may need to make sure he's here every night. That win secured our spot in the Women's College Cup."

He jogged off before I could tell him no. Keeping Rhys around was a bad idea. He may have figured out all the buttons to push to help me clear my head for a bit, but when it was over, I was consumed with thoughts of him.

That was when it hit me, his excuse for leaving the game. *"Dinner plans."*

Did that mean with his ex? *Mel*, as the sender from the text read. What a dumb name. I hated that name. Despised it. Probably short for Melvin.

Ugh I was petty.

I moped on my stool in front of my locker while Erin tried to convince me to go out and celebrate. I wanted to curl under my covers and be alone, though. There was no talking me away from that plan.

"Aren't you supposed to be going out with Cruz?"

She eyed me and shook her head with an evil smirk. "He's coming. But you know damn well that nothing is happening."

"But does he?"

"Of course! I wouldn't lead him on. Although he is trying to talk me into going out and us finding a girl for a threesome together."

That got a laugh out of me. Leave it to Cruz to find out Erin was into chicks and then try and manufacture a threesome. "Well don't let me know if that actually happens."

"It won't be happening. I have no desire to share with Cruz, much less have his dick anywhere near me."

"Something was lost in translation then. Rhys told me Cruz came to the game to get in your pants and he tagged along. I had already told Rhys that Cruz wasn't your type."

"Rhys is playing dumb then because Cruz only said that as an excuse to come to the game and drag Rhys along."

"Why?"

"Oh sweet Ashlynn." Erin laughed. "Rhys has been in a bad

mood for two weeks and thanks to my new friend, the goalie of the Inferno, I have been kept apprised. Cruz was hoping getting Rhys here would fix him again."

"Well," I cringed and lowered my voice. "Bad news. He may be fixed, but he broke me in the process."

Chapter Thirty-Four

Rhys

Seeing Ash, kissing her, making her come.

I needed her more than ever, and that one moment between us was all it took to get my head out of my ass and go to her. I didn't know what the future could hold for us, but I knew I would regret not trying.

It was late by the time I finished dinner with Levi and took him back to the airport, so I went straight home. Cruz had been calling all night, probably wondering what happened, but I couldn't talk to him and kept silencing his calls as I paced my living room. I just wanted to talk to Ash and waiting for daylight seemed like a waste of time.

Leaving my phone, I grabbed my keys and hit the button on the elevator. I was impatient as I waited for the doors to open and I practically dove in head first when they finally parted. I hit the button for the parking garage a minimum of 24 times, hoping that it got the hint to hurry.

Since it was so late, the roads were practically empty, and I made it to the university in record time. Leaving my phone seemed like a good idea at the time. It was a distraction that I didn't want to worry about. But as I parked across the street from

Ash's apartment, I instantly regretted that decision. I should have called, or texted her. Instead, I was about to possibly scare the shit out of her.

Making my way to her door, I took a deep breath, and knocked lightly. I had planned to knock a little louder every two minutes until I woke her up, but the door flew open quickly, making me jump.

"What are you doing here?"

"I'm...I'm..." I was startled and couldn't talk. I was also enamored by how her eyes seemed to shine even in the dark. "Fuck you're gorgeous."

"Rhys." She shook her head, pulling a blanket tighter around her shoulders. "Are you drunk?"

Snorting, I gave her a half smile and licked my lips. "Haven't had a drop. I just needed to see you."

"Your magic worked, if that's what you wanted to know. Gave me a nice little orgasm and sent me back onto the field. We won."

"That wasn't..." I took a deep breath and leaned against the door jam. "Can I come in?"

"We usually end up naked when we're alone."

"Ash," I sighed. "If I wanted to fuck you, I wouldn't be worried if we were inside or not. I'd fuck you right here on the front step. And to be clear, I always want to fuck you. But right now, we need to talk."

"It's late."

"I'm not leaving."

She saw how adamant I was and backed up, making room for me to enter. She had her laptop open on her bed, a movie paused on the screen, and a dim lamp in the corner.

I took a seat on the edge of the bed since it was the only thing she had in the small space that could serve as a seat. Keeping the blanket wrapped around her, she sat down and crossed her legs facing me.

"What do we need to talk about?"

"First, I need to know what's wrong. I feel like you're pushing me away."

"I am!" She practically yelled. "I have to, remember? I'm a rebound. A casual fuck. A short fling. Definitely not the girl that can make all your hopes and dreams come true. Did you forget all that?"

"I guess I assumed we would always be friends," I bit back, knowing damn well I wanted to be more than her friend. "And you left, but there were things I needed to tell you. Things we needed to talk about."

"Look Rhys," she steepled her fingers and pressed them between her eyes, making small circles to relieve some tension. "I know what we needed to talk about. I saw the text from your ex on your phone. She said she loved you *too*, which told me you had said it to her and she was replying. Which is fine because..."

I stood up quickly, making her stop talking and her eyes grow with fear. "What?"

"I wasn't prying, I didn't read all the texts. After you fell asleep, I thought my phone was ringing so I went to look for it and saw it was yours. I saw the most recent text and it said she loved you too."

I started pacing, completely forgetting what I went over there to tell her. She let the blanket drop, showing me her tight shorts and a white tank top with no bra. Her dark nipples were peeking through the thin cotton as she got on her knees on the bed, holding her hands up to try to get me to stop.

"Rhys, I'm sorry. I knew what the deal was between us, but I started *feeling* too much after our last time together. The way we made love, bare, and so intimate. I'm weak, Rhys, and I realized I could fall for you if I didn't bail."

Her words finally made me stop, and I looked directly into her bright eyes. "I haven't spoken to her. I haven't texted her. All her random messages have gone unanswered. Hell, I blocked her. All I can think about is you. I never chased her like this, Ash. I never showed up at her place and begged her to let me in."

She looked sad while she was trying to decide if she believed me.

"I had my fingers in your pussy a few hours ago, Ash. I've told you before, I'm not a cheater. If Mel and I were back together, I wouldn't have followed Cruz to your game. I wouldn't have touched you."

"It's been two weeks," she tried to reason. "I just assumed you two were working it out."

"We already know not to make assumptions, Ash. My silence has been torture. Nothing more than me trying to let you go. It hasn't fucking worked, it's been worse than anything I felt for my ex. Seeing you tonight made me realize I cannot make the same mistakes I did before."

Her mouth was hanging open, but her eyes never changed their intensity. I reached into my pocket to grab my phone, to show her the texts had gone unanswered, but I came up empty. "Fuck, I left my phone at home."

"I don't understand," she spoke softly.

Climbing onto her bed, I got in front of her on my knees, and took her hands in mine. I pressed my forehead to hers and took a few deep breaths before I could speak again.

"I know we are at different places in our lives. I know Colin will kick my ass. I know I have baggage with my ex. But you're all I think about. Like we both have said, one time wasn't enough, and I want to keep counting. I want to try to be more."

"I cannot give you what you want," she cried.

"Didn't I tell you that having goals in life is reckless? You can work and strive for anything in the world, but the world ulti- mately gets to decide your fate. We only know what we want right now and the rest is dictated by those decisions."

"You're going to break my heart."

"Not on purpose. And I will make it my new goal to never let that happen."

"This is such a risk."

"It could be worth it."

She leaned forward to kiss me, just a peck and sighed. "I can't say no to you."

"Good," I kissed her lips softly again. "Because I really need you to say yes."

She nodded and wrapped her arms around me, holding tightly to my neck.

"As soon as I get my phone, I'll show you the messages. I haven't answered her, I promise. I only left it because Cruz was blowing it up and driving me crazy."

"I believe you," she sniffed. "It's like you said before, you're not a cheater. You wouldn't be knocking on my door if she was back in your life."

Damn, her faith in me was everything. She believed me without proof. That wasn't something I'd ever had before. It was just another moment between us that made me think that we could be more than just a fling.

"When did you know this was what you wanted?" That wasn't what I was expecting her to ask, but I knew the answer immediately.

"Would you believe me if I told you it was the second I saw you?"

She smiled, our noses still pressed together, and our arms holding on to one another.

"No. I was kinda mean."

"Well, I did kick a ball into your stomach. You had a reason. But that wasn't what I was talking about." She put her hands on my cheeks and held me gently while she waited for me to finish my thought. "The first time I saw you was when you were at my game. You were talking to Colin, remember?"

"Rhys," she whined and shook her head. "That doesn't count. You had just had your heart broken."

"But for those few seconds, I forgot about all that. And every game since, I've look into the stands, hoping to find that same moment again."

Her smile grew and her nose nuzzled mine. "So charming, Rhys Peyton."

"Those eyes," I reminded her. "Every time I've looked into them I've wanted you. And even for the past two weeks without them, I've wanted you."

I pushed her back on the bed and laid down next to her, pulling her blanket around us. Her head settled on my chest and I laced my fingers with hers on top of my stomach.

"I left tonight because I had dinner with my brother, otherwise I would have waited for you. We would have had this conversation earlier."

"Your brother?"

"Yeah I tend to get moody when I care about a woman I can't have. He got worried I was getting ready to riot or something."

She giggled. "I thought you were having dinner with, um, *her*. After the text, I just assumed..."

"Yeah, well had I known that was circling around in your head, I would have been specific."

"So how was dinner?"

"Quick," I huffed. "Apparently I wasn't good company. And he called me a pussy."

"You are a little soft," she teased.

"Because I love hard and care so deeply?"

"Those are your best traits, Rhys. You feel so much and I bet everyone you've ever cared about has imprinted a mark on your heart somehow. But I was saying you are soft because you got beat by a girl."

My chest shook from laughing and I wrapped my other arm around Ash as I lowered my voice to a growl. "Oh baby, you only beat me one out of every ten tries."

"I said a *little* soft. You're a pro and twice my size, Peyton. You shouldn't have let one slip by."

"I was just taking it easy on you."

"You know I don't like it easy," she purred, sending those words straight to my dick.

"Fuck," I whispered.

She giggled while I got my shit together and my heart felt like it was going to beat out of my chest. "I saw your game the other day."

I glanced down at her and tilted my head. "Which one?"

"Against New York. You weren't using your left foot, Peyton."

"I couldn't," I cringed, thinking about how shitty I played. "Every time I use my lefty, I think of you, and I was desperately trying not to think of you."

She was quiet for a while, but I could almost hear the wheels turning in her head. Then she finally asked, "What changed?"

I knew she was no longer talking about the game, she was talking about us. About me. Why I could no longer resist the need to be with her.

"I woke up wanting to kiss you," I whispered the confession. "And I want to wake up and kiss you tomorrow."

"You can kiss me whenever you want," she smiled.

Our conversation flowed into other things that we had never talked about. She asked me about my college days and I asked her about her favorite foods. I also found out that while she didn't speak Spanish, she was able to memorize her favorite songs. Like me, she had no idea what she was saying.

For nearly three hours, we talked and laughed. We connected

on another level, and made plans for things we wanted to do together. But then she started to yawn and several minutes of quiet went by before she spoke again.

"Who's telling Coach? Or maybe we don't have to tell him at all?"

"I thought he already knew. He may figure it out when I come to all your games."

"Rhys," she pushed my chest and buried her head back into my shoulder. "You know I can't focus when you're there."

"We found a cure for that," I teased. "I just have to make sure you're very, very satisfied."

Chapter Thirty Five

I fell asleep in Rhys' arms and we never moved. When I woke up, I realized he was still dressed and his shoes were still on. He had an arm thrown over his head, while his other arm stayed securely wrapped around me.

It must have been early because the sun was up, but dim, as it peeked through the edges of my curtains. I had no classes, and nowhere to be, so I cuddled back into Rhys and closed my eyes.

When I'd heard that knock on my door, I'd known it was either Rhys, or my mother. Since I hadn't heard from her in almost a year, I jerked the door open expecting to see Rhys. I just didn't expect him to look so haggard and tired. The world had been weighing him down in the few hours since I had seen him.

It all made sense when he told me why he came, though. It was the same reason I had spent the evening curled under my blanket and fighting back tears. We wanted each other so bad, but both seemed to be using our baggage, and our goals, as a shield.

Rhys showed up and broke those walls down. All my fears of him reconnecting with his ex were gone, and for the time being, he was mine. Not just once, or for a few nights. We were together, and that fact was spiking my adrenaline.

"Rhys?" I whispered, needing him to wake up. "Rhys?"

He moaned and turned his head, then peeked his eyes open. His voice was barely a whisper, strained from still being half asleep. "Hey baby."

"Are you sure about this?"

His eyes got wider and his brow creased. "More than sure."

"Good." I leaned up and kissed his lips, then placed my head back down on his chest. "I thought maybe it was a dream."

I felt his chest shake a little as he laughed. "No. But I'm glad being with me is something you'd dream about."

I closed my eyes again with a smile on my face. Rhys kicked his shoes off and they fell on the floor at the end of my bed, then he turned and moved me to my other side, spooning me from behind. His mouth got close to my ear and his arms squeezed me around my stomach.

"I have to leave for Kansas City later for a game tomorrow. When I get home, I want to take you out."

"Like a date?"

"Yeah, like something couples do, instead of just fucking their way through my apartment."

"But we can still do that too, right?"

He laughed again and I felt the warmth of his breath against my cheek. "You don't even have to ask. Get some more sleep. I set your phone alarm for nine."

Closing my eyes again with a smile, I settled into his arms and let myself succumb to a few more hours of rest. It felt like I had blinked when the alarm started going off, but I felt rested.

Rhys sat up and turned my phone off, then ran a finger down my back. "I gotta go catch my flight."

I turned over and smiled, watching as he grabbed his shoes and pulled them back on. It was one of the few times he wasn't wearing flip flops, and something about the way his arms flexed as he tied the laces made my stomach flutter.

You're already too far gone, Ashlynn.

I rolled my eyes at myself and sat up next to Rhys. When he was done, he turned to me and kissed me gently. "I'll call you tonight when we get to the hotel. I'm flying back after the early game tomorrow, but it'll still be kinda late. Our date can be the next night."

I nodded and kissed him again. It felt weird, but good, knowing that we were going on a date, that we were an actual couple.

"You still have my code saved in your texts?"

"Yeah," I smiled.

"Use it, and be at my place tomorrow when I get back."

"Want me to be naked?" I teased.

"You better not be." I pulled back and looked at him with confusion. "I want to be the one that takes your clothes off."

I giggled, and he stood, grabbing his keys from my floor where he had apparently tossed them when he came in. He leaned onto the bed, his fists pressing into the mattress on each side of my legs, and kissed me one more time.

Then he was gone, and I fell back into the bed with a goofy grin on my face. How did life change so fast? How was this happening to me?

I had always been the girl who had to grind to get what she wanted. I set my goals and worked my ass off with no help from anyone, other than the encouragement of my grandparents, and the money I got from the sale of their house.

Soccer always came naturally, and although I didn't even want to play in college, I was recruited and given an offer I couldn't refuse. It had been all I'd thought about as I made my way through my four years. The occasional boyfriend and hook up came along, but nothing was ever enough to get my focus off my end goal.

Now Rhys was changing everything. I wanted to be with him

more than I wanted to graduate. More than I wanted to be in the Cup. More than I wanted to hear from my mom again.

I picked up my phone and considered calling my mom. Maybe with everything changing, she could too. Or maybe I could accept who she was with grace, rather than disdain.

Okay, Ash, that is asking for too much at one time.

I tossed my phone back onto my bed and shook the thoughts of my mom away. She wasn't something I could control, nor should I even be worried about it as I start a new relationship. But school work was never ending, and getting all caught up while Rhys was gone, was my new plan. That way, when he got home, I wouldn't have any distractions except for my own games and practice.

I brought my laptop up and grabbed my books from the side table of my bed. When everything was set up, I dove into my next paper on estimating L-infinity norms. A topic that only a few weeks ago made me giddy and excited.

Rhys was already changing me, making me obsess on something that didn't involve numbers. I closed my eyes and reprimanded myself, vowing that no one was worth throwing away my dreams. If Rhys and I were going to be anything together, I had to remember to make something of myself on my own as well.

But at what cost? My mother spiraled away from love when it was given to her, and obsessed over her freedom. I didn't want to make the same mistakes my mother made. I always assumed that I could find the balance that my mother never could. I wanted to love someone the way she could never bring herself to love me. It may not have been a baby, but whatever was happening between Rhys and me was important.

A baby.

I touched my stomach and remembered the last time Rhys and I were together. We had no protection. He didn't want to feel that barrier between us. Until that very moment, I hadn't thought about a baby being a possibility. Did it cross Rhys' mind?

"Oh no." Tears immediately started coming down my eyes and I began shaking my head. Another panic attack was brewing as my thoughts started to jumble together. Being a dad was always on Rhys' mind, and it quickly raced through mine that he may have hoped that night would lead to a baby.

"No, Ash." I had just put all my faith in him and I was done making assumptions about anything else until we talked.

But what if I *was* pregnant?

Was it too soon to know? I pulled an app up on my phone that helped me track my cycle and I started to shake when I saw that I was due to start my period that day. If I didn't, I knew I could take a test and know for sure. I wasn't going to panic or worry.

Besides, the thought of being pregnant didn't scare me as much as it should have. Not nearly as much as the thought of Rhys deceiving me did. That would kill me, because I had just given him control of my heart, and he promised that not breaking it would be his new goal.

Chapter Thirty Six

Rhys

Ash was quiet, not talking much when I called her from my hotel. She told me she was tired, and distracted by school, but something felt off. One day into our relationship and I already had a bad feeling in my stomach.

This wasn't like when I was with Melanie. I wasn't angry or pissy, I was scared. Worried that she had come to her senses and realized she was too good for me. That I wasn't worth the distraction from her studies, and her job goals.

I didn't want to take any of that away from her, but everything happened so fast, and we succumbed to sleep, so we didn't get to hash out all the details of our feelings. Hell, there was still so much I needed to tell her, and had been trying to since the last time I was inside of her.

It was just never the right moment, or the right time, and I didn't know how she would react. Now that we were in a relationship, it had to be the first thing we talked about when I got home. I had to clear the air.

Barely bothering to check my phone, I went straight from my game to the airport, anxious to get back to Ash. She had told me she was going to study hard until I landed, so I still assumed she would be at my place like we had planned.

The car service I had hired to get me home wasn't fast enough, and I drummed my fingers on my leg while I sent a few texts to Ash.

Almost home.

You at my place?

No response and no little dots indicating she was typing something up.

The car dropped me off at the front of my building and I raced to the elevator. When the doors opened into my place, I could see Ash's silhouette standing in front of the huge windows that overlooked the bay and South Beach.

I sighed and tossed my phone and wallet into a bowl near the front door, then dropped my bag loud enough for her to hear that I was there. She didn't turn around, just bowed her head and waited on me as I approached.

"Ash? You okay baby?"

I got closer but stopped ten feet away, unsure how I should handle whatever was bothering her. She was wearing a long jacket, and her hair was up in a bun, but that was as much as I could see since the only light was from the moon coming through the window. The jacket wasn't her style though. She was always more casual, ready to play a soccer game if the opportunity arose.

"Ash, you're scaring me."

She shook her head and that was when I realized how wrong I was. The smell. She reeked of Roja, and the coat wasn't just a jacket, it was a Max Mara wool jacket that I had bought for a romantic trip up north a few months back.

"Melanie?" My voice was low and she jumped like she hadn't heard me speaking moments ago.

"Don't act angry, Rhys." She spoke with that hoity enunciation and proper grammar she always had. Like she was better than everyone else around her. Breaking her from the proper Miami doctor vibe was a mission of mine when we were together. I used to think, as our relationship went on, that I could break open her shell and loosen her up. Now I could see that it was all a ruse. She loved me, and I knew that was true, but not more than she loved herself.

"Why not act angry when I *am* angry?"

"I tried calling you for two weeks. You blocked me. You knew I would eventually come see you."

"No, I didn't, Mel. I figured you would give up and move on."

"If only it were that easy," she sighed. "Rhys, I..."

"No!" I yelled. I'm not interested in what you have to say. "Leave."

"If you didn't want me here, you would have changed your access code to the penthouse."

"That was an oversight. Get out."

I looked around for any signs that Ash was there. I could picture Mel coming and Ash choosing to hide until the wicked witch was gone, wanting to avoid being in the middle of our showdown. But there were no signs of her there and when I looked up at Melanie, she had a knowing smirk on her face.

"Expecting someone else?"

"Out!" I yelled again.

"No," she said louder than she had been speaking before. "We need to talk about this."

My only mission was to get to Ash and make sure she was okay. Melanie could stew in my apartment for days for all I cared, but I wasn't staying there with her.

"You know what?" I grabbed my keys and wallet, along with my phone and opened the elevator door. "I'll send security up to escort you out. I need to go."

"And find your girlfriend? She's too young for you, Rhys!" The doors closed as she spoke, and it took me until I was on the ground floor to even register what she had said.

She knew about Ash, she knew how old she was. Ash must have been there when Melanie showed up. Melanie was a snake, and I worried she somehow poisoned Ash's faith in me.

"No more," I vowed. "No more being scared. No more doubting me. No more Melanie."

Within minutes, I made it to Ash's and barely got the car in park before I jumped out and raced to her door.

"Ash!" I banged. "Open up."

A light clicked on and I heard her moving inside the room.

"Ash!"

The lock on the door clicked and she turned the handle slowly—the exact opposite of two nights before when I showed up to tell her how I was feeling. I leaned an arm on each side of the door jam and bowed my head, trying to be patient as the door slowly opened.

When I looked up and into her eyes, I could tell she had been crying. She had the same old blanket wrapped around her shoulders as she'd had before, and she pulled it tighter as if it was a safe barrier for her.

"Can I come in?"

She nodded and backed away, closing the door behind me, just as slowly as she opened it. Then she fell to her knees and the tears came hard. Her body was shaking, and she started to curl herself into the fetal position.

I scooped her up into my arms and sat down on the bed, holding her close. "I'm so sorry." I repeated those words over and over again, rocking her and kissing her hair. "Causing any of your tears is my biggest regret."

It took a few minutes, but once the tears subsided, she pushed back a little and looked up. "I've never been this insecure. I've never been this scared. I've questioned everything since I met you. My mind never stops questioning."

"She is all show. Fake. Troubled. I couldn't see it until I met you. But I promise I had no idea she would show up. I'm having her removed, and the codes changed, as we speak."

Ash's sadness turned to confusion and she tilted her head. "What?"

"My ex being at my place tonight."

"No," she whispered. "That isn't…"

"I was never in love with her. I thought I was, but fuck, until recently I don't think I even knew what love was. I always wondered why my love looked different than my brother's, but I just assumed it was because we were so different. Because love was what I sought while he spent his life trying to avoid it."

Was I admitting that I was in love with Ash? If I was, then it was only in that moment that I even realized I was. The need to get to her, make sure she was okay, and comfort her was something I had never felt before. And with Ash, it wasn't even the first time I felt that way.

Seeing the redness on her stomach the night I kicked the ball into her was when that feeling started. Then caring for her ankle, and overreacting every time Hunter turned in her direction. I was always wanting to be the reason she was okay, and never wanting to be the one that caused her pain.

Was that love?

"I never made it to your place," she cried. "I don't know what you're talking about."

Now I was the one confused, and I turned her to where she was straddling and facing me so I could look at her directly. "Then what's wrong? I don't want to fuck this up."

Her eyes closed tightly, fighting more tears. I had never seen her like that. My heart was breaking worse than it ever had. I needed her to tell me what I could do because all I wanted was to fix whatever it was.

"Ash," I whispered, encouraging her to talk.

"I took a pregnancy test." Her chest was heaving so hard as she tried to stop herself from crying. Meanwhile, my heart had moved to my throat and I froze, waiting for her to finish. "It was negative."

Relief helped me breathe again and my head leaned forward to touch hers. "You must have been so scared. I'm so sorry we took that risk, and I'm so sorry you've been alone today."

"I was scared that you may have considered that I might get pregnant that night. That you were hoping for it. But that thought didn't last long, I promise. And then once I had a chance to think about it reasonably, the idea of having a baby made me excited."

"Excited?" I didn't waste time being upset that she doubted me. She knew without me having to tell her that I would never do that to her.

She shrugged, and a few more tears fell down her face, so I reached up to wipe them away. "I had a shitty mom. I guess like you, I was excited at the thought of being able to prove I didn't become her. Because even though it's always been my plan to avoid becoming a mother, I would be a good one. I'd never choose anything over my baby."

"You're young. There is plenty of time for you to decide to have a baby. I'm glad it's not now. But there's something I've been meaning to tell you since that night together, and it's never been the right time, or you were gone, or we ended up talking about something else."

She was breathing harder, but the tears had stopped. Her hands wrapped around my neck the way mine had been on hers and she tilted my head up.

"After Mel disappeared, I decided that I could be a father

without her. Without anyone. I had the money, and the means. All I needed was a surrogate. My brother talked me out of it, reminding me that we had grown up with a single parent. We turned out okay, but being a single parent wasn't really what I wanted."

Her fingers moved on the back of my neck, caressing me.

"I ended up at the doctor though. In order to get started I had to be tested for all sorts of things. The doctor came back a week later and told me that my little swimmers could be retrieved, but I only had a five percent chance of reproducing the old fashioned way."

"Oh no," she whispered, knowing how much that devastated me.

"He couldn't tell me why. Nothing serious, I just had a low sperm count or something." I blushed, slightly embarrassed at admitting how inept I was. "No one knew. Levi was the only one that even knew what I was doing, and I had changed my mind before the doctor told me. It has always been something I kept to myself."

"So you knew that the odds of getting me pregnant that night were slim."

"I did, but we were so in the moment that I didn't tell you beforehand. I wanted to feel you so bad. In fact, I wasn't even thinking about my issues at that moment. Being inside of you was all I could think about."

"The next morning I was gone."

"Yeah," I laughed. "And halftime at your game seemed like a shitty time to tell you. Then when I came here, I was on a mission to beg you to be with me. Seemed like 'hey I can't get you pregnant without medical assistance' was a poor way to start off, so I didn't tell you then either."

"I'm hate that you've been dealing with that alone," she kissed my lips and rubbed her nose along mine. "And I am so sorry I didn't come to your place tonight. I was dealing with so many emotions. I lost track of time."

"You have all the time in the world to have kids. When *you* are ready."

"Right now," she sighed. "I'm just glad you always find me when I need you. And always know how to make me feel better. Complete."

"And I'm thankful you've shown—"

A pounding on her door cut me off and we both turned toward the manic screams that came through the thick wood. "Open up!"

Ash climbed from my lap and put her hand over her mouth. I stood up confused, not sure if I should open the door. I watched Ash, waiting for a cue to what she wanted.

"Open the door!"

Ash and I looked at each other at the same time. Our looks of confusion matched, and our eyes were locked in horror. Simultaneously, we said the only thing that came to mind.

"Oh fuck!"

Chapter Thirty Seven

Ash

"Rhys?" I put my hands up, attempting to stay calm, but knowing it was about to be a shit show. "Just give me a second to get rid of her."

"No, I'll get rid of her." He started toward the door, but I grabbed his arm and pulled him back.

"I need to do this."

"You don't, Ash. You never have to do anything alone."

I gave him a quick nod. We were trying to be a couple, and even though the timing was bad, we were going to have to face the devil eventually.

Rhys angled himself in front of the door, and I went to unlock the latches before easing it open.

"What do you want?"

"I need to talk to Rhys."

"Rhys?" I practically yelled. "I haven't talked to you in almost a year and you show up here wanting an autograph?"

"Ash?" Rhys' voice was dark, questioning, and gave me a chill down my spine. It was nothing I had heard from him before. There may have even been a hint of fear.

My mother laughed and took two steps into my apartment. I

shut the door to spare my neighbors but with all three of us standing at the foot of my bed, it was crowded.

"So I guess she doesn't know," she said to Rhys, still laughing in that smug way she always did.

"Know what?" Rhys and I both said at the same time.

"You mean you both have no idea? Rhys," she crooned, making the S on his name sound like a snake. "You knew."

"Mel," he got closer to her, "If you don't leave us the fuck alone, I will make sure—"

"Oh my God," I whispered, making Rhys turn to me as my mother started laughing again.

Not Melvin. Melanie. Even worse.

"Now we just need Lover Boy to figure it out."

"What the hell–?"

"Rhys, this is my mother." I said quickly. "And I am assuming she is also your ex."

"Your...? I thought..." Rhys was looking between the two of us, too stunned to speak.

My knees were close to giving out and I felt as though I was spiraling into a panic attack.

"Oh I am sure she made you think I was some drugged out skank. She likes to pretend I'm a huge disappointment in her life."

I stayed quiet, not yet finding my voice. Rhys was staring at me, and he started to get closer when he realized I was fading.

"Ash?"

I held a hand up to stop him, not wanting him to touch me until I knew I was strong enough to face them. My mother was laughing and rolling her eyes, but Rhys kept his focus on me. His concern was only about me, and he was completely ignoring Melanie. That alone gave me strength to speak.

"The only thing I ever told him was that you were absent in my life, and provided nothing for me, or my grandparents, since the day I was born. And how I want to be nothing like you."

"And yet here you are, stealing my fiancé. Momma has good taste, doesn't she?"

I wanted to vomit. I had to back away for a minute and regroup again. The fact that my mother was the one Rhys had been trying to get over hit me hard. A part of me felt I should have been angrier, but all I felt was confusion and heartache.

"Your names aren't even the same." Rhys was still looking between us, also confused and still trying to make sense of the fact that his ex was my mother. I guess in a way, I wasn't shocked at all. It would be just like her to date someone, and then disappear. She filled him with lies of her hopes and dreams about a family when all she really ever cared about was herself.

It made me feel guilty for being related to her in any way.

"She got married when she was eighteen to an old man who didn't want kids around him and his fancy things. The marriage lasted four months but it was long enough to get her name changed and her college paid for."

"You told me you had never been married. Never had kids."

"Rhys," she whined like he wasn't getting the point. "I love you so much, I was scared. Afraid you'd reject me if you knew I had trouble when I was younger."

"What about when you got older?" I yelled. "Even as you became a fucking doctor and started working at that fancy practice, you still never acted like I existed, unless you wanted something. Grandma and Grandpa had to sell their things just to feed me some days."

"Ashlynn, this is not the time. This is not about poor you." She put a hand to her temple, as if I was causing her great strife in her life. "I need to talk to Rhys alone."

"Fuck no!" Rhys yelled. He was finally done processing what was going on and stepped in front of me. "I already kicked you out of my apartment and you show up here? How the fuck did you even know I was here? That I was with Ash?"

"I saw a picture of you at my daughter's game. On the news. It made me wonder why. Didn't take much digging to figure out you were fucking her. I was actually moved that you would go as far as using her to get me back. Though, you definitely have my attention now."

My panic was twisting with my hatred and I started to come around Rhys, wanting to scratch her eyes out. Not just for me, but for Rhys. Melanie was a snake, she always had been.

"Wait, wait," Rhys held onto me, keeping me from committing a crime. He held me behind him, and turned his attention back to my mother. "Say what you need to say. Then get the hell out of our lives."

"Alone," she seethed, like he had missed the point.

"No. Ash can hear whatever you need to say."

"Ugh, Rhys, you're so hard headed. Fine. But don't say I didn't warn you."

"Spit it out," he yelled. His arms were shaking with anger and his body was stiff. I held on to his belt loops and pressed my head into his back to stay connected with him while we waited on Melanie to stop being dramatic.

"I'm pregnant!" Her voice sounded excited, like she had just yelled surprise at a party. "You're going to be a dad, Rhys-y. We are having a baby."

My head lifted from his back but I couldn't move, or risk looking at her. That sick feeling I had was returning and threatening to choke me.

"Please leave," he said calmly, taking me by surprise.

"I want to show you the sonogram."

"Leave. I will have my lawyer contact you tomorrow."

"Rhys!" She yelled. "This is what you wanted and I am making it happen for you!"

"I want Ash," he said evenly. "If you are pregnant with my child, I will be a good dad, but I won't be with you."

"Rhys!" She yelled again, this time higher. I wanted to roll my eyes and ask her what happened to "Rhys-y" but I stayed hidden behind him and continued to let him handle her, still in complete shock that he was asking her to leave.

"Ash? Pack a bag, baby. We're going to my place. The codes have been changed and security has been notified. We'll go there tonight to make sure we have privacy."

"You bastard! You were supposed to be happy. I have been calling you, texting you, and waiting for this moment. All of this is for you!"

I moved as Rhys instructed and packed a bag. Melanie would have access to my apartment as long as she wanted to, and could knock to her heart's content. But Rhys' place was where we could hide away and let this entire ordeal settle down.

Melanie opened the door and looked back at me while I shoved clothes into my soccer bag. "You were always the problem. I found him first, and you know damn well you stole him from me."

"Love you too, Mom."

She screamed again, and tightened her coat around her waist. I could hear her heels clicking as she made her way down the sidewalk to her car. Rhys closed the door softly and turned back looking haggard and exhausted. We stared at one another, so much more to be said, and both too exhausted to start.

"I'm ready," I whispered, slightly unsure if I should even go with him. He needed the chance to think things through. Melanie just left a bomb at his feet, and he hadn't had time to process the explosion that was bound to come from it all.

At the same time, I didn't want to run from him the way she had. I was stronger than her, and until we agreed that he had to focus on Melanie, I was going to stay by his side.

He licked his lips and looked around the room, nodding. Grabbing his keys and phone, then my bag, he opened the door and let me walk out first.

Melanie was still in her car, on her phone, and she watched as Rhys opened the passenger door for me. He leaned down and kissed me, then made his way around the front of the car. He didn't spare her a glance, but I knew he saw her as well.

The quiet drive to his apartment was intense, and by the time we got there, I was too tired to say anything at all.

Rhys helped me undress and slipped one of his shirts over my head. Then he lifted me into his arms and placed me gently into his bed.

"I need a minute," he whispered. His eyes were begging me to understand, and I did. I needed a minute as well. Being together, and talking when we were both so tired and overwhelmed, would lead to nothing but trouble.

"I know." I touched his cheek and let my hand fall to the pillow beside my head. He sat next to me for a minute, watching as I tried keeping my eyes open.

"Sleep."

I felt him lift from the bed and heard the door close. My eyes threatened to spill more tears, but I held off and begged the sandman to spare me.

Chapter Thirty Eight

Rhys

The prospect of me being a father came twice in one day, and it was nothing I expected it to be. Both times I was wracked with fear and denial, not wanting to face the fact that both times could have been true. Neither planned. Neither wanted.

I knew Melanie had less than a five percent chance of being pregnant. Not only because of everything the doctors told me, but because on top of that, we never had unprotected sex. It could still happen, of course, but unlikely.

What really bothered me was that Ash was in the middle of everything. Melanie was her freaking mother. Melanie was my ex. And I hated Melanie more for the way she treated Ash than the way she did me. I could move on, but Melanie was always going to be Ash's mother.

Did Colin know?

Doubtful, he never saw Melanie face to face. He couldn't have picked her out of a line up.

I was pacing along the window where I had first seen Melanie, thinking she was Ash. At first, I wondered how I could have made that mistake, but knowing they are mother and daughter explained a little bit. They were the same height with the same build.

When the lights were on, that all changed though. The only thing they had in common was their eyes, and it made me sick thinking of how many times I told Ash I loved her eyes, fearing that I was really seeing Melanie's at the time.

Pulling my shirt over my head, I growled and tossed it into the couch, just to release some anger. My hands ran through my hair and I pushed the urge to scream as deep as it could go.

My intention was to head to bed with Ash, but I was too wound up to sleep, and ended up spending hours pacing my floors. I was leaning on the railing of the balcony when I heard the sliding door open slowly. Turning my head, I saw Ash pad her bare feet across the tile toward me. I held onto my grip on the balcony, wishing I could change everything about meeting Melanie, and just have met Ash first.

"Hey." Her voice was quiet, unsure of my mood. My knuckles were white from my grip and my muscles were tense. I didn't want her to be scared to talk to me, so I softened my shoulders and turned to pull her into my arms.

"You having trouble falling asleep?"

"I slept for four hours. When I woke up, you still weren't there."

Four hours? I knew I had lost track of time but I had no idea that long had passed.

"I just can't stop thinking," I explained. "I don't know what to make of all this. How are you and Mel even related?"

"I'm having a hard time, too. Processing the fact that my mother is your ex. That she has been so close and intimate with you. That she shows up at my door..." Tears were coming down her face as she tried finishing her thought. Reaching out to her, I pulled her into a hug and held on tight against my chest.

"Being with you was never about her," I vowed. "Her being pregnant is not about us."

"I know it's not fair, but just the thought of her being loved by you, fucked by you...it makes me sick."

"I know." I kissed the top of her head and rubbed my hands down her back. I would feel the same way, probably worse, if she had been with someone I hated so much. Someone that had done me wrong and left me the way Mel left her.

Like my dad.

"Earlier tonight, I thought there was a chance I was having your baby. I spent hours in tears, alone, scared. Then she shows up and acts like...fuck I hate her."

My eyes squeezed shut and fear wracked my body.

"Please don't leave," I whispered, falling to my knees to beg her for the only thing that mattered. I'd spent most of my night scared that she would end things between us before they even got started because of the role her mothered played in my life. That she once thought of herself as my rebound and when it sunk in that it was Mel I had been pining over, she would hate me.

She pulled away from my hold and looked down into my eyes, more unshed tears that made my chest ache and my stomach turn. "She only wants you back because she found out I have you, Rhys. I know you loved her in some way, but Melanie has never loved anyone more than she loves herself. This is fucked up shit between us, but I won't let her win. Especially when I don't have to face her alone."

I reached up, my thumb skimming the dried tracks of tears on her cheek as I took in her words. So young, yet so strong. Ash amazed me with her backbone and determination. We were important to her, and worth not giving in to Mel's charade.

"We face this together." I nodded, agreeing with her. Mel had brought damage to both of us, but it was Ash that had taken the bigger blows in her life. Pregnant or not, Mel would never be able to hurt me the way she had her own daughter. And deep down, I knew we had been brought together so that she never had to face off with Mel alone, again.

"I'm not her," Ash whispered. "I'm not leaving. And I'm sorry, again, that I let her scare me away the night I saw that text. I had no idea it was her, I just thought I was imposing on something that you two were trying to fix."

"Don't." I shook my head and leaned in to touch my forehead to her stomach. "Don't go there."

I stayed on my knees, still with no shirt on and my jeans digging into the skin of my knees. I was willing and ready to continue to plead with her if needed. Not until she lifted my chin for me to look up at her did I considering getting up. "We got this," she reaffirmed.

I stood and wrapped her into a hug, feeling relief that she was so fucking strong.

"I never wanted you to wake up without me next to you again. Not after the last time."

"Last time it worked out well."

Smiling, I thought about that night and how we ended up making love. That was the night I knew deep down that I couldn't let her go without seeing where we went.

"Are you okay?"

She pulled from my hug and looked up into my eyes. "Are *you* okay? Seems you and I just keep taking blow after blow."

"Yeah, but I don't believe Mel is pregnant." I grabbed her hand and led her to the chaise, sitting down and pulling her between my legs. "I just hate that she spoke to you the way she did."

"She doesn't bother me. I'm more worried about how she made you feel. Wielding a baby as a tool to get you back."

"Well aren't we sweet?" I smiled and kissed her cheek.

The moon was on the other side of the building, making the balcony darker than it had been earlier. But I still knew that Ash was blushing. I knew her tanned skin turned a bright pink when she smiled like that.

"I have some questions," I started.

"Go."

"How old are you again?" I already knew but just in case, "because if Melanie is your mother…"

"Twenty-two. She had me when she was seventeen."

"That would make her thirty-nine. She told me she was thirty-three."

Ash laughed and rolled her eyes. "She can pass as that. All she has ever cared about is herself and her vanity."

"She was right though, I assumed your mom was some bitch that came to you for drug money."

"You have the bitch part right. But believe it or not, Melanie Keller slash Simpson always had goals of her own. Having a child just wasn't one of them. She wanted to be a doctor, but never a wife or mother. Even successful doctors can be completely shitty parents."

"You said she didn't know who your dad was?"

"She doesn't. That much I believe. I think she was sleeping around with whoever threw money at her. When she came up pregnant that ended for a while. My grandma once told me that the poor life they led had never been enough for her. She wanted to be something big and wanted to be respected, and they couldn't afford to send her to college. That is why keeping my scholarship is so important. They may not have been able to afford my college, but I promised them when I got the offer, and before they died, that I would play and let it help me with my education."

"She has money. She's at a very prestigious practice. A practice the team sent me to when I hurt my knee last year. She didn't offer to help pay for your college?"

"Oh please. I didn't even ask. Grandma asked her once but I

heard her yelling that I almost kept her from being someone special, and she wasn't going to help me either."

I felt sick, ashamed that I fell so hard for a woman so cold. In a way, I had been a victim of her act. She pretended to be everything I wanted and lied to me about things along the way. She was perfect, too perfect, and I should have seen through that. I should have been smarter.

"I guess I need to thank Colin for scaring her away then."

"Running was her only option that night, I guess."

"Were you at that game because she asked you to be?"

"No," she snorted. "I had no idea she was there. I really hadn't seen her in a year. Hell, I'm just connecting that night to all of this. Coach said he wasn't using his season tickets that night and told Erin and me we could use them. Erin didn't show up, but I went and then spoke to Coach after the game."

Pulling her hand to my mouth, I kissed her knuckles. "So I need to thank Colin for scaring her away *and* bringing you into my life."

"He has no idea who my mother is," she confirmed. "Not that I know of. Ya know, just to clear that up."

She laid down with her back to my chest and I wrapped my arms around her tightly. I thought we were done for the night. Too much at once seemed to be overwhelming and hard to process. Any other questions I had could wait.

"What happens if she's pregnant?" Ash asked with a strain in her voice.

"Then I become a father," I shrugged. "But other than being the best dad I can be, I will be nothing to Melanie."

"I'm scared."

"This is a crazy way to start a relationship, Ash, but I promise I don't want her."

"I'm not scared about us, I am scared that once she comprehends that she won't get you back, and if she really is pregnant, she will terminate the pregnancy, or use the baby as leverage with you. I don't want her doing to another baby what she did to me. I don't want her terminating the pregnancy either, especially if this is your shot at becoming a dad,."

I had never considered those options, but Ash knew Mel better than I apparently did. My head fell back against the chair, and my hold on Ash loosened. The stars were starting to fade as the first signs that the sun was coming up began.

"We need to sleep."

"Just one thing, though." She sat up and turned to face me with a smile on her face. "We have a tradition to uphold."

My eyes shot open and the heavy weight of our conversation faded away. "I have a feeling I'm going to end up staying up every night, just waiting for you to come find me."

Her hands went to the buckle of my jeans and then pulled the zipper down, freeing my cock. Her hand wrapped around my growing erection and she started stroking me. I got harder in her hand, watching her as she watched me. Her tongue kept wetting her lips and she looked fascinated with how hard my cock got for her.

"Slide your panties over and come sit on me," I urged.

"I'm not wearing panties," she purred.

"Then. Come. Sit. On. Me."

"Not before I taste you."

She got onto her knees on the chaise and bent down, taking me deep and pulling up tight. Her lips made a popping noise and I groaned, loving the sound of her sucking me off.

"Fuck Ash," I gritted between my teeth. "You make me forget everything else when your lips are wrapped around me."

"Good," she smiled with my tip against her mouth. "This is all I want you thinking about right now."

Her head lowered and she bounced up and down as her tongue swirled around me. Her hair was falling around us, making it hard for me to see, so I bunched it up into my grasp and held her tight.

Ash took me by surprise when she reached down between her legs and started touching herself. When she moaned, it vibrated around my cock and I had to pull her up by the hair to keep from coming down her throat.

"Ash?" I said with a deep scratchy voice that sounded more like the devil. "Get up here, now."

I pulled at her hair and she climbed up my body, straddling me. I held my cock up for her to find and she lowered herself down slowly. It felt like it had been forever since I had been inside of her body.

"Fuck me," I urged. "Fuck me as hard as you can. Use my cock to chase away everything that has happened."

She started bouncing and grinding. I pulled the shirt over her head and watched her tits bounce in my face. Her head fell back and she latched onto her tits, squeezing and pinching her nipples with her thumb and pointer finger.

"You know what I think?" I mused. "I think you love this. You have no problems using a cock to get yourself off *your* way."

Chapter Thirty Nine

Ash

I stopped moving and looked down into Rhys' eyes. He looked like he had discovered the game plan of every single one of his opponents—mischievous and proud. I was confused, tilting my head back and forth to analyze his meaning.

"Use me," he urged. "Let me see you fuck me your way."

I leaned down and put my nose to his then snarled. "Not with a man and a cock. Only with you and your cock."

"That's my girl," he smiled. "I want you to feel free and satisfied. Watching you pleasure yourself with my body is the sexiest thing I have ever seen."

I started moving again and instead of throwing my head back, I watched him. His mouth dropped open and his eyes closed as pleasure started pulsing throughout his body. He started moving his hips below me, and combined, I squealed as I lost control.

He came with me, grunting and mumbling my name as his head moved back and forth on the chaise. I rode his cock as long as I could, wanting to milk every last drop from him. Not until he held my hips still did I stop.

"You're going to kill me."

"You've had sex with my mother, Rhys. I need to make sure I am all you remember."

I was glad he could laugh as I teased the truth. He had sex with my mother. It wasn't the first thing I thought of when I realized they had been together, but it was definitely on my mind.

"She never fucked me the way you do, Ash. She never felt this good."

I kissed him to let him know I was teasing, but my heart was still twisted at the thought of him fucking anyone else but me—especially her.

He held me and stood, never letting our mouths separate, or his cock come out of me, while he walked us to the bedroom. By the time he laid me down on the bed, he was almost hard again and started moving inside of me.

"Never," he pushed into me, "Mention," he pushed again, "her name," a hard thrust, "while my dick" ... "is inside of you," ... "again."

I screamed, still so sensitive from my orgasm moments before. I started nodding, repeating the word, "*Promise*," over and over again until he pulled out of me and flipped me over. He pushed himself into me from behind and brought his hand down hard on my ass several times.

"Rhys!" I howled. It was too intense, to the point I started to sob, but Rhys never stopped moving. My body was jerking and I could hear him hiss as he started to come again. He snaked his fingers to where we were connected and pulled his cock out of me just enough to gather his cum before pushing back inside of me. Then he touched my clit and rubbed me, using his messy fingers to tease me until I came again as well.

"I never want to stop fucking you," he whispered.

When he laid down beside me, I felt the rest of his cum dripping down my leg. The sun was starting to peek through the curtains but I couldn't bring myself to care about responsibilities.

I stayed dirty, the way I knew Rhys liked it, and curled into his arms, finding safety in how honest I had been with him.

Unlike Melanie, I told Rhys everything I could think of, and never wanted to manipulate his decisions. It felt like we were our own team now, and in order to score the game winning goal, all we had to do was stick together and trust each other.

"She's definitely pregnant," Rhys' lawyer, Rick, confirmed. "These were signed by her doctor and sent to my office."

"What took so long?" Rhys sighed.

"Melanie had to sign a consent form for the documents to be sent, and she took her precious time."

I rolled my eyes and stood up from the couch. Rhys and I had been waiting for a week to hear confirmation on whether she was pregnant, or not. We both had traveled for out of town games, and gotten back, before she managed to uphold the request Rick had made on Rhys' behalf.

"What do you want me to do?" Rick sounded tired and pissed. I had just met him, but I could tell he hated dealing with the likes of Melanie Simpson.

"Nothing," Rhys shrugged. "I guess I am going to be a dad."

He sounded sad and regretful, making my eyes tear up. The one thing he always wanted, and he couldn't even enjoy it. I knew part of it was because I was in his life. On the phone while we were both out of town, he confessed that he felt guilty, like he had somehow betrayed me. But I assured him that we happened fast, and neither of us expected each other in our lives.

In fact, having Melanie in common had done nothing but bring us closer together, and made us stop questioning each other.

Having a common enemy did that to people, and even more so between people that already cared so much for one another. But our hatred was not what I wanted to base our relationship on moving forward.

"Ask for a paternity test," I suggested. "Once it's confirmed, we let this go, Rhys. I won't let you feel anything but thankful. Despite everything the doctor told you, and everything you have been through with Melanie, you may get to actually be a dad, and that is something to celebrate."

"I can see the apple fell very far from the tree," Rick sighed, making Rhys snort.

"Not even the same tree," Rhys winked. "Just the same seed."

Rhys and Rick started going over a few more things while I excused myself and went to lay down. Soccer and school didn't stop just because life gave me a boyfriend and a crazy mother. It was all a lot to balance and handle, especially while I tried keeping it away from the team and Coach.

After a while, Rhys woke me up just as the sun was setting, by rubbing my back.

"Can we finally go on our date?" he whispered.

"Tonight?"

"It's only seven thirty. I want to take you out in public."

"What happens when we end up in a picture on TMZ?"

"Are you telling me you want to hide?" He teased.

"I'm telling you that we start the College Cup tournament next week and Coach may have a coronary."

"Aww, Ash, you know I love making him crazy."

I laughed and sat up, wrapping my arms around his neck. "The only thing I have here to wear is jean shorts and flip flops."

"Miami's official uniform." He winked and stood, pulling me from the bed and onto my feet. "Perfect for the beach."

"I haven't been to the beach in probably a year. Not even for dinner."

"That should be illegal."

"Erin prefers the city, and she's been the only person dragging me into civilization."

"I want to take you everywhere." He held my neck and made sure I was looking into his eyes. "Thank you for taking a chance with me. On me. On us."

"Pretty sure I didn't have a choice. We were kidding ourselves when we said once would be enough."

"Speaking of which, I still have one question I can ask. I never cashed in on that." He rubbed his hands together like he was thinking of the most diabolical question. I laughed and started getting dressed while he tossed questions around in his head.

"What are you going to ask that you don't already know? My deepest, darkest secret ended up being your ex. How much deeper can you get?"

"Ohhh that is a good question. How much deeper can I get?" He licked his lips and ran his eyes up and down my body. "There are still places on, and in, your body I want to try reaching."

My face had never turned as red as it did with those words. I also had a shiver run through me at just the thought of him taking me in ways he hadn't before.

"Is that your question?" I asked, barely able to get the words out without catching my breath. I was fully dressed and walking toward the door, trying to act casual.

"No." He got behind me and ran his hands on my ass then around to the front and grabbed my breasts. "But maybe later."

Chapter Forty

Rhys

I took Ash to Havana Vieja, my favorite place on South Beach. There was always a crowd, but they cultivated an intimate environment, no matter where you sat. For me, they made sure we were in a corner booth, private enough I could make Ash come under the table if I wanted to.

And I considered it.

Our whole relationship had been surrounded with sex–and Melanie–though. For one night, I just wanted to *date* her. Toast to how amazing she was. Feed her dessert off my fork. Ask her about her goals in life. All those normal date things.

I already knew her goals, though. She wanted a safe job with a secure subsistence. Now that I knew who her mother was, it all made perfect sense. Going pro was too risky for her. Her grandparents were gone, she had no siblings, and she felt alone. Creating something safe had been her way of survival.

There was no way dating me was safe. I was twelve years older than her, could get traded to another city at any moment, and was apparently going to be a father to her half sibling. Being with me was a terrible idea. I didn't fit into her plans at all.

It was something I would never take for granted.

After dinner, we walked hand in hand along the ocean. The sidewalk went on for miles and the breeze was making me wish we could stay out there all night. Ash was looking at the ocean as the waves crashed onto the shore in the moonlight.

"What's on your mind?"

"Just thinking about how quickly things change. One day you're about to be benched because you couldn't care less about soccer. The next day you get beaned in the stomach with a soccer ball, and your whole life changes."

"I promised I would change your life, didn't I?"

"You did, indeed." She was laughing again. I loved making her laugh. I wanted her to laugh every day.

"Rhys Peyton?" I looked away from watching her, and toward the voices calling my name. Two ladies, about the same age as Ash, came running up to us. "Can we get a picture with you?"

Normally, I didn't mind at all. But I was on a date. Not just any date, a first date. I started panicking and shaking my head, torn between not wanting to be rude, and not wanting to turn my attention from Ash, for even a second.

"Calm down," she whispered. "It won't take long."

The girls had gotten within a few feet and were holding their phones, hoping for that picture. "Sure."

"Want me to take it?" Ash asked, holding her hand out for their phone.

"Oh my God, can you? That way we can both be in it."

"Exactly," Ash winked.

The girls got on either side of me, each touching one of my arms, and posing. Ash took a picture upright and then sideways. Then had them take another one because one of them had closed their eyes.

"Thank you!"

"No prob," she smiled at them, returning the phone.

I wrapped my arm around her and kissed the side of her head, hoping the other girls would read my body language as wanting to be alone with my girl. "Have a good night," I nodded to them.

"Rhys, you're amazing," one of them said. "We went to the game last week."

"Thank you."

"And we follow your brother on twitter. Well not him, just his team but, wait, is that him or someone else?"

"Levi definitely doesn't tweet," I laughed. "If you ladies would excuse us, I need to get back to my girl."

Their eyes widened, and then they gave Ash a proud look. Each of them was finally connecting the dots, and they gave Ash a thumbs up, along with a, "You go girl."

In all the times I had been approached by women, I had never blushed. This was the first time with a girl on my arm, though, and the way they gave Ash their support had me flustered.

I pulled her along, hiding my face in the darkness as they said their goodbyes. Ash was laughing next to me, knowing I didn't know what to do, or how to act.

"You always like that with fans?"

"No. I just didn't want to upset you or anything, and I didn't know what to do."

"Mmmm," she hummed, leaning onto my arm. "Always take pictures. I will always be waiting for you when you're done."

The mention of Melanie never got under Ash's skin. Every time we had to face issues with her, Ash handled it with as much grace as she did when we met the fans on our date.

Melanie had spent the week refusing to get a paternity test before the baby was born. She said it was too risky, and she wouldn't do anything to harm the baby. In the meantime, she wanted me to start going to her appointments with the doctor. She said, through our lawyers, that I would remember how much I loved her once I saw our baby on the monitor, and heard his, or her, heartbeat. She was even planning a gender reveal party, and said it would be an ugly look if I didn't attend.

She was delusional.

Somehow, I couldn't find it in me to give her the attention I probably should have. She spent too much time lying to me, and manipulating me. Not to mention the way she treated Ash. Having my baby, or not, I couldn't be around her.

And I still had a small nagging feeling that told me something wasn't right. I still knew something that she didn't—the low odds of me fathering a child.

After our date night, I told Ash I was going to confide in my coach. Sandy had a right to know of anything that may affect the team and our games. If I was distracted, he needed that heads up.

As far as Colin went, I was going to let Ash handle that. Although she told me there was nothing to say. He could find out organically as far as she was concerned.

Which was why when the Women's Cup started, I had shirts made, and flew to Atlanta for the tournament. Colin was about to *organically* find out what I thought about his left wing.

Cruz decided to come along, too, and we stayed at Levi's place for the first game. It was fun hanging with my brother, and the only guy on my team that knew about Ash and Melanie. I could say whatever I wanted, and it felt good being so upfront and real about where I was in my life.

"You don't even act the same as you did when you were with Melanie," Levi noted. "Ash has you flying back and forth, making shirts, and carrying pom poms."

I looked down at the pom poms in my hand. Maybe they were overkill, but it was my girl's last tournament, and probably the last games of her soccer career. She had been emotional, saying she had played all her life, and didn't know what it would be like walking away from the sport.

I reminded her she would always have soccer. Not necessarily a team, but I would go one on one with her every day if she wanted me to.

"Don't start," I pointed at him. "I used to fly back and forth for you too. James and I got super close when you were constantly fighting with Charleigh." James was the pilot we hired to go to and from Miami. He provided other charters for other people, but Levi and I had him on speed dial.

"Let's go," Cruz came in from the bedroom wearing his specially made shirt.

Levi laughed and grabbed his keys, leading us to the door. "I'm only staying till halftime. I have to meet Charleigh at the gym. Y'all better have a ride to the airport."

"Charleigh didn't want to come to the game?"

"Tell me when you're ready to introduce Ash to the family, and she will be here. Y'all are still kinda fresh. She wasn't sure she should come."

"This isn't like before," I told him seriously. "I want you both to meet Ash whenever you want. There is no pressure here. No agenda. No secrets."

Levi nodded and licked his lips, understanding where I was coming from, and seeming happy about it. He opened the door and walked ahead of us, down to the street level where he had his car parked along the curb, being watched by the attendant.

We climbed in and he drove us the short distance to the university where the tournament was being held.

"It's colder here," Cruz whined, not having spent a lot of time out of Miami.

"It's only sixty-five degrees," Levi laughed.

"Trust me," I backed Cruz up. "Your blood thins fast in the Miami heat. You're never down there long enough to adapt."

"Levi!!!!!" A girl screamed my brother's name and his eyes widened in horror. "Rhys!!! Cruz!!!!"

A hoard of fans heard the scream and flocked towards us before we could get to our seats. We spent several minutes posing for pictures and signing autographs before security came and broke up the crowd.

"Why did they ruin the fun?" Cruz asked, shaking his head. "Don't they know this guy is single and ready to mingle?"

"I think they were more worried about mob control, but I see your point," Levi laughed.

We were able to get to our seats in time to see some of the warmup, but Ash never saw me. She was so focused on the game, and I took pride in knowing the four orgasms I gave her the night before probably had something to do with that.

When she stood for the national anthem, and faced the crowd. she finally spotted me. I looked into those beautiful eyes of hers. Even far away I could tell how bright they shone. If Melanie did anything right, it was passing those eyes to my girl so that I could always look at them like that.

Chapter Forty One

Ash

"Why is Rhys Peyton in the stands wearing a shirt that says, 'Keller is Stellar?'"

Coach was slowly walking to the sideline after the anthem with a look of confusion. I hadn't noticed at first, but Rhys had shed his jacket and I could see what coach was referring to.

"He's, um..." "I tried to think of something to tell Coach, but I just kept smiling. Cruz was sitting next to him with a shirt that said, 'Erin ain't sharin'' and I could barely look that way with a straight face.

"He needed the distraction," Coach said plainly, finally answering himself. "The rest is not my business."

I held a hand up to stop him, not wanting him to explain the conclusions he had come to. It was obvious that Rhys was there for me, and based on how I was reacting, it would be hard to deny that we were way more than friends.

"I guess we needed each other," I shrugged and then ran off to take my position. It was the most accurate thing I could say. Rhys and I did need each other. We were both spiraling. With him it was his ex, with me it was life. I thought that the only thing that mattered were the goals I had, and reaching them, to set myself free.

In reality, like Rhys always said, goals were reckless. If all you ever did was try to reach those goals, you closed yourself off to the good things that came along the way.

"Remind me to kill Cruz," Erin laughed, catching up and jogging next to me.

"I'm glad you two have become good friends."

"He's a lot of fun. Way more bearable now that he's accepted that I won't sleep with him."

I laughed and took my spot on the field with a lightness I hadn't felt in a while. There were still so many questions with Melanie that needed to be answered, but for just one night, we were a normal soccer couple. He was a normal guy at his girl-friend's game, and it was surreal that I was that girl. It was also the first time in my entire college career that I had someone in the stands rooting for me.

The first two games he'd come to didn't count. Those were spent denying ourselves, and disguising it with him wanting to be sure I could focus. This time he was yelling my name and shaking the pom poms every time I kicked the ball. It wasn't a distraction either, it kept me focused because for every good play, I got to hear him call my name excitedly.

When I jogged in for halftime, he blew me a kiss, and I blushed before turning my head and making eye contact with Hunter. He had still been broody, but more bearable since that night at the club. Taking a chance, I smiled at him and he turned away, ignoring my attempt at being pleasant.

"He's going to take some time off after the tournament," Coach grumbled next to me after seeing Hunter turn away. "He has some things to work through. We've talked. They aren't team related, so let's cut him some slack."

"Of course," I nodded. If anyone knew about personal shit to work through, it was me. Hunter had shown me that he wasn't all bad, and had reasons for the things he did. We just didn't understand what those reasons were yet. But I couldn't help but smile at the rise he got out of Rhys; and how Rhys used that to stay closer to me.

After our win, Rhys was waiting outside of the locker room for me with his arms wide open. Rachel's jaw dropped as I ran toward him and jumped into his arms. His mouth was next to my ear and he started walking off as he whispered how proud he was.

Behind him, I saw Cruz grab Erin and they started laughing, walking side by side. Rachel was still standing there, completely dumbfounded at what she had just seen.

"Where are we going?" I pulled back, but Rhys didn't let me down. "Also you do realize I can walk, right? Carrying me everywhere isn't always necessary."

"The airport. And I don't care."

"I have to play again tomorrow!" I squealed. "We can't go to the airport."

"I'll have you back tomorrow afternoon."

"So we are flying all the way back to Miami just to sleep? Stay here in Atlanta with me. We can get a room away from my team, and spend time alone."

He set me down next to a black SUV that looked like a hired car service. Opening the door, he guided me to the third row and curled me into his arms as we waited on Erin and Cruz to take the middle seat.

"Tomorrow," Rhys whispered into my ear. "I have to meet face to face with Melanie about the paternity test and I need you there."

Looking up into his eyes, I could tell how serious he was. We didn't think Melanie was going to do the paternity test until the baby was born. "Did she do the test?"

"I hope so," he sighed. "I got the call before the game that she agreed to talk about it. but only face to face with me."

"Does she know I'll be there?"

"I honestly think she assumes you will be distracted in Atlanta, and it's the perfect time to talk to me alone. She has no idea you're coming."

I was glad he stole me away and was taking me home with him. If he had to face Melanie, I wanted to be there too. And not because I was his girlfriend and felt I had a right to be there. But because whatever the results were, he was going to need someone on his side to catch him if he fell.

"You played like a badass," Rhys smiled, changing the subject.

"I used that left footed fake you taught me."

"I saw that. Did you hear me saying, 'That's my girl?'"

"No," I giggled. "Dammit I missed that."

"I didn't," Cruz added, hearing what we were talking about. "I have tinsel from his pom-pom in my nose to prove it."

"Erin, you going home too?"

"Yeah, so she can fly back with you tomorrow."

"I just found this out," Erin added. "But flying in a private jet isn't a hardship, babe."

"We'll try to get back before the game, after our practice, but not sure we will make it in time."

"Rhys," I smiled. "You don't have to come to all the games."

"I know I don't have to, but these may be the last games of your career. I want to be there for them."

I rested my head on his shoulder until we got to the airport. The flight home was fun and quick, the four of us laughing like kids, and playing a card game on the table between our seats.

As we taxied down the runway, we all turned our phones back on, and Cruz's immediately started ringing. He silenced it, but the calls kept coming, so he held a finger up and took the call with a worried look on his face.

"Dad, I just landed and can't talk. Is everything okay?"

We stayed quiet and let Cruz listen to his call, watching as his face transformed from carefree, to a look of pure horror.

"No," he sighed. "Dad no!"

"Oh my God," I whispered, fearing the worst for him.

"Isn't there anywhere else? I will even pay!"

Rhys' eyes narrowed, intrigued. Erin, who was closest to Cruz, started smiling at whatever she could hear his dad saying. I settled back into my chair, relieved. If it made Erin smile, then whatever news Cruz's dad was telling him, wasn't life or death.

When the door to the jet started to open, Cruz said goodbye and stood up, grabbing his things.

"You gonna tell us what that was all about?" Rhys asked first.

"My freaking stepsister is coming to Miami next week and dad wants her to stay with me while she goes to a few job interviews."

"And you two don't get along?" I questioned.

"I haven't seen her since she was eighteen and even that was just for a minute. It's been years, I don't even know her."

"But she's family," I shrugged. "Take it from me. Family is important. Unless they suck."

"Her mom married my dad when she was twelve, and I was fourteen. I lived in Miami with my mom, so I only saw her every once in a while. I'm not really sure she counts as family."

"He said it was just a week or two," Erin sighed. "You have a big enough apartment. It'll be okay."

"I guess," he sighed and walked down the steps of the jet. "I just don't like sharing my space. It's sacred. And what if she wants me to talk to her?"

Rhys followed me down the steps and to another waiting car service. He and I were headed directly to his place where I had been staying since my mother reappeared in my life. I had stashed some clothes there, and for all intents and purposes, we had been living together.

Meanwhile, Cruz was pouting and mumbling in Spanish as he and Erin made their way to a different car that was heading to drop them off at their own places. Erin was about to get a hard core Spanish lesson on that drive.

"He's lucky he has a sister to be annoyed with," I mumbled to Rhys as we climbed in the backseat.

He started to speak, and then grimaced, unsure if he should say the words that were about to come out of his mouth. He stopped himself twice more before finally saying it.

"You will have one soon. Mine or not, this baby will be your sibling."

I smiled, the thought suddenly making me feel overwhelmed. A brother, or a sister, no matter how much older I was than them, was going to be a blessing.

"Wonder what Melanie will have to say tomorrow," I groaned, already anticipating her being a bitch.

Rhys pulled me into his lap and started kissing my neck. "Let's worry about that tomorrow. I want to celebrate your win tonight."

He squeezed my thigh and moved his fingers to the waistband of the team sweats I was wearing. I froze, worried the driver would see him dipping his hand down, and his fingers between the folds of my pussy. "Rhys," I whispered in warning.

"He knows not to look," he whispered back. "Just let me feel you. Let me see how wet my girl is tonight."

If I hadn't been soaked before, I was after he put his hand on me and spoke like that. My body was in tune with Rhys' voice and every time he wanted something from it, my body complied, whether my brain did, or not.

"This is such a rush," Rhys whispered again. "Touching the star of Miami University's soccer team."

"Rachel is the captain," I moaned, trying to distract us until we could get somewhere private.

"But you are the star, Ash. My star. My favorite player. My reason for even giving a shit."

I smiled and turned to kiss his lips. Other than the sound of our mouths molding together, the rest of the drive was quiet. When we arrived in front of Rhys' building, the driver had to cough to get our attention.

We raced to the elevator, and I jumped back into his arms when the doors closed. He spent the short ride up with me pressed to the mirrors on the walls and pushing his hard cock between my legs. I could see behind him, our reflection. A stark contrast to the first time I saw us in the mirror.

I pulled my phone out and held it up, taking a picture of our reflection. The way his hips moved looked erotic, even with his jeans on, it was sexy. Watching myself run my hands through his hair while he sucked on my neck made my stomach clench with excitement. I never wanted to forget us like that.

"You better text that to me," Rhys mumbled, knowing exactly what I did.

The doors opened, and he carried me straight to the bedroom. Together, we were all hands and lips as we shed each other's clothes, and kissed each other's bare skin.

Rhys ran one finger through my pussy and then straight to his mouth before pushing me back on the bed. "I needed one taste."

"Just one?" I teased. "Such a liar."

He smiled and climbed over me, covering my body with his. "Let me rephrase that. Just one for now. I need inside of you even more."

Pushing into me, we moaned together, loving how we felt when we were connected. He stayed still, giving us both a minute to adjust before his hips started moving again. Then it was as if he had been possessed by lust, and pushed us both close to a quick orgasm.

As he started to slow down and get control of himself, I

pushed up from my waist and begged for more. "We have all night, Rhys. Come with me this time, please."

"Dammit," he growled, giving into me. He found his rhythm again, and when I started coming and squeezing him, he came as well, losing his breath as he let himself go.

Our foreheads were pressed together and our lips were inches apart. We were both still catching our breath and holding on to one another as the high started to settle.

"Forever," he whispered quietly, almost to himself. I didn't answer, because I wasn't even sure he meant to say it out loud. But I smiled and silently agreed that together, we were looking like forever.

Chapter Forty Two

Rhys

Ash and I were up and dressed bright and early. We were meeting Melanie at her lawyer's office, but Rick would be there too, just in case he was needed. He didn't know the specs of the meeting, or what all they wanted to talk about, but he was assured it would be professional and cordial.

Melanie was already there when Ash and I walked in, hand in hand. Her eyes narrowed when she saw Ash, making me want to strangle her for looking at her daughter that way. But to her credit, she stayed quiet.

"Did you agree on the paternity test?" I asked without beating around the bush with niceties.

"I have," she sighed. "My office doesn't like the poor publicity this may cause since you are in the spotlight. I agreed, but only to keep my spot at the practice. If something happens to our baby, I am suing them for everything they're worth."

The human side of me wanted to tell her they were a piece of shit and couldn't force her to do anything. The other part of me was glad she cared about that prestigious job so much that she was willing to do the test.

"When are you having it done?"

"My client went yesterday, and with your DNA on file, we were able to get a rush on the results. They were just delivered a few minutes ago." Her lawyer spoke eloquently and held up a manilla envelope.

"Wait," Melanie held her hand up, stopping the lawyer from opening the results. I felt like I was on an old episode of Maury, and my baby momma was a drama queen. Other than Maury being there and cameras filming, it wasn't a stretch from the truth. "I have some conditions."

"Are you in any position to make demands?" Rick asked her, shaking his head with disdain.

"After the results," she said anyway, "I want you to start coming to my appointments with me. I want you to be a part of this with me. I was alone when I was pregnant with Ashlynn. It shaped me in a way that I'm not proud of. I want to make sure this baby has a father."

I was holding Ash's hand under the table and she tensed when Melanie spoke. I squeezed her hand, knowing what I was going to tell Melanie was something we would both agree on.

"If the baby is mine, Mel, I will be the best dad there ever was. But I'm going to tell you again that I am with Ash, not you. There will not be a happy ever after between us."

She started to roll her eyes, but stopped and pretended she had something in her eye. She nodded and waved towards the results, letting her lawyer open them up.

"Okay," he sighed. Reading the paper, he shook his head, and then set one paper in front of me and one in front of Melanie. "You are not the father."

His Maury impression didn't make me feel the relief I thought I would feel. Unlike on the show, I didn't jump around and cheer like those guys. Nor did I feel the need to tell Melanie that I told her so. I just nodded and bowed my head as Melanie stood up to run from the room.

"Wait!" I yelled, making Melanie stop in the doorway and turn around. She had a small glimmer of hope in her eye, but hope was not something I could give her. I just had one thing to say to her.

"Thank you," I said sincerely. "I know you were young when you had Ash, and I know it was scary and hard. But you brought her into the world, and I'll be forever thankful for that. Now you're getting a second chance and I hope you make the most of it."

She didn't answer me, just huffed and continued her dramatic exit from the room. Her lawyer left behind her, and Rick stood to leave as well. "I'll let you two have a minute to process this. I'll be in the hallway."

"Thank you," Ash answered for me and waited until Rick was out of the door. "Rhys?" Her fingers were still entwined with mine. She turned her chair to face me and took her other hand to my cheek.

"I'm sorry." Clearing my throat, I tried to show her I was fine.

"This was a chance you didn't think you would get, Rhys. I wanted this for you, even if it was with Melanie because I know you would be an amazing dad. And what you just said to her was more than she deserved."

"Let's go," I stood, not wanting to talk about it anymore. She had two hours before she had to be on a flight back to Atlanta and I didn't want to spend that time sitting there.

We opened the door and Rick was standing in the hallway, his eyes going between me and the closed door down the hall. "Hey, I need to tell you something."

He led us to the elevator, and when we were alone inside the small space, he sighed. "I just overheard Melanie yelling at her lawyer that the results were supposed to be changed. She knew all along it wasn't yours. Of course, that is a conversation I wasn't supposed to hear, but her voice carries."

"Why would she do this to him?" Ash wailed. "I just never understood how she could be so selfish and cold."

"Based on what I've learned and what I've dug up, I think she wanted her freedom and her career. But when she came up pregnant, being with Rhys was better than being alone." He turned to me, finishing his thought. "She didn't anticipate you having moved on, and not interested in rekindling your relationship. Especially if she was able to give you a child. She seems like the kind of woman that gets her way and doesn't accept anything else."

"She is," Ash and I both answered together.

When we exited the elevator and walked outside, I took a deep breath, wanting to leave all my feelings about Melanie there on that sidewalk. Ash rubbed my back gently and Rick turned to shake my hand goodbye.

"Rick?" Ash asked. "What happens to the baby if Melanie doesn't keep it? Does she know who the father is?"

"I don't know," he shrugged. "But I will keep my ears to the ground, and keep an eye on what happens."

"I am blood related to that baby. That is my sibling no matter who the father is. If Melanie decides she doesn't want to be a mother like she did when she had me, then I want to step in."

I nodded at Rick, telling him that I agreed. It was important to Ash, and therefore it was important to me. And regardless of how things turned out for the two of us, I would help her and pay for Rick to help her. He would keep us posted, and if we needed to, we would step in and file whatever we had to in order to ensure Ash was given the chance to give Melanie's baby the same love her grandparents gave her.

When we returned to my apartment, Ash took a call from Erin and I waved, telling her quietly that I would be in the bathroom. I shut myself in for a minute, just needing to be alone and process everything.

I must have taken longer than I thought, because Ash started tapping on the door and easing it open to peek in. "You okay?"

I lifted my head and smiled at her as I sat on the edge of my tub. "Yeah, of course."

She had taken her shoes off and walked across the tile quietly, kneeing between my legs on the floor. Taking her hands to my chest, she looked up at me and gave me a sad smile. "This hurts, and I know it hurts you more. I'm here, though. Okay?"

Smiling, I grabbed her neck and leaned down to kiss her. "I'm thankful for Melanie. She gave you those eyes."

"I just hope you never look at them and wish they were hers. Or worse, look at them and resent them because of her."

My stomach twisted, scared she actually believed that would ever happen. "Melanie was nothing more than a lesson in my life. A hint at what I should have been looking for all along instead of focusing on one goal. Her eyes were just an arrow to make sure I found you. It was always supposed to be you, Ash."

"You will still reach that goal, Rhys. I know you will."

"But it no longer controls me. I just want to enjoy being in love with you. I want to be glad you entered my life when I needed someone, and allowed me the chance to be more than a fling."

Her eyes widened when I said the L-word. It didn't slip off my tongue, nor was it unintentional. I knew I loved her and it finally felt like the right time to tell her.

"I love you," I said clearly, so she knew I was serious. "I thought we were on different paths in our lives, and maybe that's true. But I think our paths will always merge back to one another."

"I think so too." A tear fell from her eyes. "Because I can do anything while loving you."

I pulled her off her knees and into my lap so she was straddling me, the way I always did. "You love me too?"

"More than math," she giggled.

"Oh shit." I stood and her legs fell to the floor, catching her as I started running out of the bathroom. "You have to be on a plane."

"So about my phone call…. Erin told Cruz who told Colin who told Levi that we needed a delay. Your brother texted the pilot and we have a little bit longer. The details are yours to tell, but they all trusted us enough to make the call."

"I just have to make my own call, really quick." I pulled my phone out and dialed my coach, smiling when Sandy's gruff voice answered.

"What?"

"Hey Coach," I smiled at Ash as she watched me curiously. "I'm gonna miss practice today and maybe tomorrow."

"What?" he yelled. I had never missed a practice, he probably assumed I was dying.

"No worries, I'll be back before our next game." I pulled Ash closer and kissed her lips before I finished explaining myself to Sandy. "It's just… My girl has a game tonight in Atlanta and I love her more than soccer."

Epilogue

1 year later

Ash

Glancing at the clock, I closed my laptop and turned the lamp off on my desk. I gathered my things and shoved them into my bag, knowing I had to hurry if I was going to make it to the game by kick off.

After falling short the year before, Rhys and the Miami Inferno were chasing a championship, and the whole city was buzzing with excitement. Including my new boss, Jeffery, who popped his head out of his office and gave me a panicked smile.

"Go," he pleaded. "Leave all that. Just go."

I laughed and shook my head, still packing my bag. "It'll be fine."

"It is a documented fact that Peyton plays better when you're in the crowd. Even the sports networks know to keep an eye on your arrival status."

"Well, thanks to you implementing the casual game day rule, I save time by not having to change my clothes. And, Rhys had a car sent to pick me up, so I don't even have to bother finding a parking spot."

Jeff had no idea I was dating Rhys Peyton when he hired me. But when Rhys dropped in to bring me lunch one day, I had to pull Jeff off the floor and threaten to call 911 if he didn't calm down. Luckily, there was no one in the office to witness that but me.

I found Jeff when he placed an ad at the university looking for "cheap help" during the tax season. He had a new start up business doing taxes and accounting from a small office, and had bitten off more than he could chew. Soccer had ended and I was close to graduating, so in hopes of gaining experience and knowledge in my field, I applied for the job.

Right after I graduated, Jeff offered me a full time position as his assistant. The pay was more than the part time work, but less than I had hoped. Jeff was honest and excited, though. He made me want to be a part of his journey, and help him build up his business. So I accepted, knowing that one day, I may be in his shoes.

"Take tomorrow off," he urged. "Just go be a good luck charm and stop making me crazy."

"Tomorrow is Saturday, but thank you for the offer. I will cash that in another day."

I zipped my bag closed and glanced at the picture of Rhys and me on my desk. It was taken right after we won the Women's College Cup last year. Confetti was stuck to our faces, Rhys had his arm around my shoulders, and his shirt read, "Two is my Boo."

As I left the building and got into the car service, my mind kept drifting back to that night we beat Texas for the win. The way it felt when Rhys ran onto the field and twirled me in the air before kissing me in front of everyone. The secret of our relationship had been out amongst our friends and teammates, but it was his first intentional public display of affection and we turned quite a few heads.

My phone chimed with a text, bringing me back, as the car pulled up to the stadium. I smiled when I saw it was from Charleigh.

Please tell me you are almost here.

Just pulled up, why?

Because Rhys keeps looking for you and it's getting on my nerves. These field level suite seats he has us in puts us too close to his face while he warms up.

I sent her a quick laughing emoji and jumped out of the car. It still amazed me that I was friends with her. Just like with Rhys, despite our age difference, she and I clicked right away. We met at the College Cup when she and Levi came to the finale to cheer me on alongside Rhys, Cruz, and a few other teammates of theirs. It was like having my own family there when I was almost the only one that didn't have parents or siblings in the crowd.

"Dang it," I wiped my eyes at the memory of how special Rhys made that night for me. It always made me tear up and as I pushed through the door to the field level suites, I had to stop getting mushy. There were too many people at the game tonight who had no interest in seeing me cry.

"There she is!" Erin shouted, running up to hug me like I hadn't just seen her a few nights ago for dinner. She was still working her way to a pro team, and had been assigned to train with the Fort Lauderdale USL league. It kept her close to me, and it put her one step closer to the pros.

I hugged everyone that had come to watch Rhys play, including Coach, who insisted I call him Colin now. That wasn't going to happen, he would always be Coach to me. He was sitting next to Rhys' mother, who I had also met soon after my Cup finale. She didn't come to the game, but had flown from California to meet me a few weeks later. I loved her so much. She had been nothing but warm and loving toward me.

After all of my hellos, I took a seat in the front row of the suite. We were right next to the bench and level with the playing field, so I waved to Sandy as he walked by toward the locker rooms.

The rest of the team started to trickle in from their warmups and when Rhys finally locked eyes with me, his entire face lit up. He jogged to the short wall that separated us and I jumped up into his arms.

"How's my girl?"

"Ready for my man to kick some butt tonight," I teased, then lowered my voice and spoke into his ear, "And then celebrate afterward."

"You get my cock hard in these loose shorts," he growled so low only I could hear him, "And I'll have to drag you to the locker room to help me get my focus back."

I laughed and pulled back so that I could give him a quick kiss. But just like every other time, once wasn't enough so I leaned in again, trying not to shove my tongue into his mouth with everyone there watching us.

"Okay, Okay," Cruz came running up and pulled at Rhys. "Say bye to Lover Boy."

I let Rhys go, laughing as the two of them got ready to take the field for the start of the game. "Good luck to you too, Cruz," I hollered through my cupped hands.

He turned back and winked, raising his arms in the air. "Gonna be another scoreless night for Atlanta," he announced, making our entire suite cheer for him.

And it was.

Miami beat Atlanta and took the number one seed in the Eastern Conference for the playoffs. Rhys celebrated with his team for a minute, then ran back to our suite and scooped me into his arms. Our kiss was on the screen for the whole stadium to see and I blushed when I realized the camera was following us.

As the celebration continued, I watched everyone taking turns hugging Rhys and I couldn't believe how lucky I was to find all of them. They were my family. It may not have been my original goal, but now, all I cared about was keeping them in my life forever.

Rhys and I got to the penthouse and I immediately jumped in his arms again, only that time, we were alone. We clawed at each other's clothes and he stumbled toward the couch, anxious to celebrate the way we always did.

Instead of laying me down, he set me on my feet and pulled my jeans down while I took my, "Had a Fling with the Left Wing," shirt over my head and tossed it somewhere in the dark room. Then I went to work on Rhys, pulling his jeans down and making sure his shirt was nowhere to be found. I scratched my fingers down his bare chest, and tried lowering to my knees. But Rhys stopped me, and lifted me back into his arms.

"You never let me use my legs," I laughed followed by a hiss when my back was pressed against the cold glass of the huge windows.

"You never need them," he groaned as he pushed his cock against my stomach.

His mouth moved to my neck and then my cheeks, then back down again as he lined himself up to my core. With the window holding me up, he used one of his hands to finger the tight hole of my ass and teased me while his cock pushed into my pussy.

"Mine," he growled. His movements inside of me got hard and rough, just the way I liked it when we were so desperate for each other. We had spent the rest of the evening having dinner with everyone after the game, and the entire time, Rhys traced the slit over my jeans from under the table. I was more than ready by the time we got home, and I didn't want him to take it slow and easy.

"Harder," I begged, making his chest rumble with appreciation. His strong thighs were working our bodies, grinding and fucking in such a base way that I couldn't hold back any longer.

My breathing got uneven and as my orgasm started to crest, Rhys bit my earlobe and whispered, "Milk my cock, baby. Take everything."

His words always intensified my orgasms and I screamed as I felt him jerking inside of me. By the time he pushed us both to the end, my legs were useless and he had to carry me to the couch and set me down.

He took a quick moment to clean me up and then slid his oversized shirt over my head. "Stay here."

When he came back, he was wearing Miami Inferno shorts with no shirt and held two glasses of water in his hands. We curled into each other on the couch and made small talk as we got our bearings back from our intense fuck.

"You picking Mia up tomorrow?" He asked, referring to my little sister.

"Yeah, Melanie and Jim have a date planned so I am going to keep her for the afternoon."

"Poor Jim," Rhys laughed.

Jim was Melanie's lawyer, and surprisingly ended up being the father of her baby as well. It was why he refused to change the paternity test, because he knew there was a chance that the baby Mel was having was his.

I guess it worked out, because he pursued Melanie and gave her everything she wanted. Rhys and I felt bad for him at first, but it seemed to have worked since they were still together and raising Mia together.

Melanie and I still didn't speak much, and she and Rhys never spoke at all, but through Jim and Rick, she agreed to let me be a part of Mia's life. In fact, she had gotten pretty cordial with me as her feelings for Jim got stronger and her life seemed to be settling into place. I would never fully forgive her for being absent in my life, but I was thankful she was making different decisions with Mia.

Jealousy was her ultimate motivation when it came to Rhys. She left him heartbroken and it gave her a sense of power. But seeing that I was the one that found him was too much for her, and the main reason she tried getting him back. I hated her for that, but I also felt sorry for her. She never knew how to love anyone more than herself, and in return, she had never been on the receiving end of unconditional love.

Rhys lifted from the couch and grabbed a remote from the coffee table, turning the music on. I thought he would lay back down with me and relax but he stood and put his hand out for me just as the first cords of the song started.

Unchained Melody filled the room and Rhys smiled as I took his hand. "Dance with me."

Just like my grandpa used to do, those memories were always one of my favorites and my first display of what real love looked like. I blushed a little as Rhys pulled me into his arms and swayed back and forth with me around the living room.

As the song ended, he pulled back and looked down at me, caressing my face and smiling. "I finally thought of what I want my big question to be."

I tilted my head, almost confused at first because I had nearly forgotten about our one big question. It had been over a year since we met and there were no more questions he could have asked. He knew me better than anyone.

Then he dropped to his knee, and I gasped, realizing instantly what his one question was.

"I saved this one," he smirked. "I knew one day I would want to ask you this big question and would need to cash in. I fucking love you, Ashlynn Keller. From the moment those gorgeous green eyes locked with mine, I knew I had spent my life looking in the wrong direction. It was like I was finally being given the green light, and a fucking arrow to help point me where I needed to be all along. Not to mention, I had to wait on you to get old enough."

I laughed and shrugged, letting him take my hand in his. We always joked that when he started playing soccer professionally, I had just started playing recreationally in the youth leagues.

"Ash, baby. Will you marry me?"

"You know it's never been my goal in life to be married, Rhys." His smile faltered for a minute so I hurried up to make my point. "But goals change, and ever since I met you, I think it's been my goal to have this moment with you. So yes," tears started pouring down my cheeks as I nodded my head. "I can't wait to marry you."

Rhys pulled a ring from his pocket and as he slid the emerald–the color of my eyes–onto my finger, he whispered, "Making you happy is the only goal I have left."

2 years later

Rhys

Ash and I didn't waste a lot of time before we got married. Everything about our relationship had been sped up by our inability to keep our hands off one another and with the promise of a week-long honeymoon, secluded on a yacht, we practically ran down the aisle.

We decided on something simple, and ended up saying our 'I do's' in the center of the Inferno field, surrounded by our family, close friends, and teammates. Colin even got ordained so he could be the one that named us husband and wife.

Then we spent a week on a yacht, but other than leaving the pier, I couldn't even tell you where we went. Ash and I spent most of our time in the bedroom and when we weren't in there, we christened every part of that boat that wasn't inhabited by a crew member.

Since then, we'd moved out of the penthouse and bought a place near the beach. We still had the penthouse when we needed it, but Ash wanted to start fresh–and somewhere her mother hadn't had sex with me. She never let mine and Mel's relationship affect us, but even I agreed that the penthouse had been tainted.

Plus, Ash deserved whatever she wanted.

She worked hard, for less pay than she deserved, and did so with integrity and morals that were hard to find when it came to money management. Proud couldn't even begin to sum up what I thought about her. Not just in her career, but in her relationship with Mel as well.

Mia brought them together in a small way, and even if they were never meant to have a normal mother and daughter rela-tionship, Ash still found peace through her love for Mia. And Mel, to her credit, was raising Mia and allowing Ash to see her as much as she wanted.

I hung a swing in our new backyard and that was where Ash was, pushing Mia in the baby swing, making Mia laugh. With her father being a lawyer, and her mother being a doctor, Mia spent the night with us at least once a week.

Jim and Mel had a weird relationship, and I wasn't

completely sure there was a whole lot of love between them, but for Mia, they were making the best of it. Not that I spent any time with them. Even when Mia turned one, I declined my invite to her party and let Ash go alone. It wasn't out of resentment, but out of respect to Jim. Mel tried using him, and their daughter, to get me back and I couldn't imagine how seeing me would make him feel.

I was just thankful he agreed that Ash was important to Mia, and he never minded her coming to our house. He knew when it came down to it, I would risk my life to save Mia's. Without question.

"Hey pretty girls," I hollered, walking toward them under the tree that shaded the swing.

Ash turned around and smiled, while Mia made noises as she started to slow down. I reached for her and flew her through the air, soaking in her smile. Then I leaned over and kissed Ash, while I settled Mia onto my hip.

"How was practice?" Ash asked.

"Off season practice is hard. I'm getting too old for this."

"My poor old man," she teased, rubbing the small of my back. I cut my eyes to her and she laughed, then took Mia from my arms and started walking inside. "Come in, I'll make some dinner. You and Mia can share mashed potatoes and smashed peas."

"Ha, ha," I grumbled, then grabbed her by the waist and pulled her into me. "You weren't teasing me about how old I am last night. I believe you were begging me to ease up."

She covered Mia's ears even though Mia had no idea what we were talking about and laughed again. "Your cock was like having a steel rod splitting me open, and you spanked me like you were my daddy."

"Mmm, I can't help myself. I love seeing your skin turn pink and flush."

I nuzzled my nose into her neck and started to kiss her before

Mia took her hand to my hair and pulled, reminding me she was there.

"Reeree," Mia called me, holding her arms for me to take her. Ash handed her back to me and we walked inside to play while Ash cooked. It was moments like that, with Mia and Ash, when I felt like I was a part of the family I'd always dreamt of. I never regretted how my life turned and fell into place, but I was thankful for those glimpses Mia provided.

We sat together at the dinner table and ate, while Ash recounted her day at work before picking Mia up. Then I filled her in on practice and how Sandy was thinking of retiring. If he did, Colin was up for the job and we both got excited at the prospect of him coaching in the pros.

"Let me lay Mia down. Don't move," Ash said after dinner. Mia's head was nodding, sleep trying to take over, and Ash made quick work of cleaning her up. She took her to the bath and then laid her down in the temporary crib we put up when Mia was with us.

Meanwhile, I moved and cleaned up the kitchen, then sat in the living room. I was staring at a framed picture on the mantle, the one Cruz took of us that day on the field. He had it framed for our wedding gift as a joke, but joke was on him because I could look at that picture all day, secretly knowing what I was saying to her that made her cheeks so red.

"I told you not to move!" Ash said as her feet hurried down the stairs.

"You wanted me to fuck you on the kitchen table? That's fine," I teased, and started to stand from the couch.

"Just sit," Ash laughed. "I got you a present."

My brain started scanning the dates, worried I had forgotten our anniversary, but since it was last week, I knew that couldn't have been it. My birthday wasn't close either. Yet, Ash pulled a large box from a cabinet near the fireplace and handed it to me.

"I'm going to assume you like it when I spank you." I licked my lips and nodded toward the gift, making her flush pink again.

"Oh," she moaned and sat close to me, rubbing her tits on my arm. "I love it when you're rude and mean, you know that."

"Do I get a present every time? Because we may go broke."

She laughed and swatted at my shoulder, then touched the gift. "Just open it."

I lifted the lid and sifted through the paper until I pulled out a t shirt. Making custom shirts had become our thing, I knew it was for the new season coming up.

"Rhys got a piece." I read the shirt out loud and laughed, the placement of the words being lower than normal. "A piece of what?"

"Everything. You got a piece of everything. My heart, my body, my ass. But there is another one," she urged.

I pulled up the smaller shirt and read it out loud, "My daddy is a baddie."

It took me a minute, because we had just joked about me spanking Ash like I was her daddy. But then I realized the shirt was way too small, tiny. When I lifted it from the box completely, I saw that it wasn't even a shirt. It was a onesie, like the kind Mia wore when she crawled around the house.

"Not much else that rhymes with daddy," she shrugged. "But I figured he or she will always think you are a badass."

"Are you...?" I couldn't even comprehend the possibility that Ash was pregnant. We had talked about seeing a doctor and trying one day, but in the meantime, we weren't taking precautions, just leaving it up to fate.

"There is a new Peyton that will be kicking me in the stomach."

"How? When?" Fuck my brain was all over the place.

"I found out yesterday and had Ms. Hilda, down the road, make these shirts real quick. The words on mine will hit right at my stomach. I was going to wait until we didn't have Mia to tell you, but I couldn't wait that long. And as far as how...we will sign you up for a seventh grade science class. It will be okay."

I smirked and shook my head at her. "I mean how is this possible?"

"Maybe you're no longer recklessly trying to force it and all those goals you strived for are just happening at their own pace."

"Are you okay? Are you ready?"

"I'm so ready. Rhys." She climbed into my lap, the way I loved her to do, and ran her nose against mine. "We are going to be the best parents in the world."

"Fuck, I hope so," I sighed, suddenly nervous.

Ash kissed me, sweet and soft at first, but our kisses always turned hot and heavy. I stood up with her still in my arms and twirled her around, finally letting the excitement hit me. I was going to be a dad and there was only one thing I could think about beside how much I loved Ash.

"How small do they make cleats?"

Acknowledgments

Starting a new series after three years has been TERRIFYING. I feel like I have been working hard and applying everything I have learned over the years into this series, finding my voice, and building the trust of my readers to give ALL THE FEELS while staying true to Katie Rae.

This is not the same process it used to be. I have an entire team of people behind me and I don't want to let any of them down! This may be a long one, but there are so many people that I need to thank!

As aways, my family has been my number one support system! **TJ and the girls** always help me find time to write and achieve the goals I have set in place for myself. But just like Rhys and Ash learned, I also learned that having goals can sometimes be reckless, and this book took turns I was not expecting. There were times I was not sure I would finish but my family pulled me through.

I also want to make sure I thank my friends: **Gail, Ashton, Lori, Sara, Rachel, Autumn, and Tits.** You all have played a role in this book. From helping me with my blurb to helping me decide on the formatting to checking in on me as I wrote to make sure I was hitting my word counts. You all mean the world to me and I love you babes!!

Next, I want to send a **HUGE thank you to Amanda.** You helped me plan and brand this entire series, and you didn't even have to. The amount of late night texts I sent with questions, time on zoom, and hyping me up has been nothing short of unbelievable. I am so lucky to have you in my life.

My cover designer KB Barrett: You... put up with me. Haha. I know I drive you crazy but I hope you know how much I adore you and am amazed by your talent. THANK YOU for being there when I need to talk it out, making adjustments gracefully, and being able to see inside my brain.

Brenda, my editor: You have become a staple for me. Finding an editor you vibe with is hard, but you know me and how I like to write. You allow me to fuss and make changes as you go and you deserve ALL THE LOVE for being a part of this one. Haha.

To my beta readers, Michelle and Meg. Thank you for your honesty, your feedback, your suggestions, and your willingness to squeeze this book in when I needed it.

Kandace and Issa. Kandace, you took over my content creation right when I needed you most and I KNOW for a FACT this book would not have been completed if it wasn't for your help.

To my admins, Jenn, Elizabeth, Caitlin, and Katie. My lifelines! The ones who keep Katie Rae relevant when she just can't even (yes I said that in third person because I cannot always be Katie Rae lol). I don't thank you all enough for how much you do in Katie Rae Reader Group. But I hope you all I know it means everything to me.

My street team and ARC team: Thank you all for your belief in me! The shares and reviews make me weepy, and my heart is so full.

Also a special thank you to **The Author Agency** for tackling the promotions for this one! You ladies are amazing!

TO MY READERS! Y'all...*takes a deep breath and tries not to cry* Thank you for "getting me" and letting me write what my heart wants to write. It's hard sometimes, battling between what is trending and what the story is inside my head. I fight myself with being *more* and keeping things even (ie: No third act break up lol). But you all show me time and time again that you will love whatever my heart gives you and I love y'all so much for giving me that freedom and trusting me.

About the Author

Katie Rae is a wife and mother, first and foremost. She and her husband, TJ, have been married twenty years and have two girls who she homeschools. They live in South Florida and enjoy boat days, sunshine, and family time.

Visit www.katieraebooks.com for signed paperbacks, march, events, and extras.

Join Katie Rae Reader Group to chat all things books.

Also by Katie Rae

Miami Inferno FC Series (Interconnected Standalones)

Reckless Goals

Scoreless Nights

Twisted Assist

The GAMES Series (Interconnected Standalones)

The Games We Play

The Lies We Tell

The Love We Make

The Way We Dance

The Way We Fight

Men of the Military (Complete Standalones)

Ranger (Army)

Raptor (Air Force)

RECON (Marines)

Rogue (Navy)

The Boys of Summer Novella

Pretty Boy

Man of the Month Club Novella

Love Bites

Another One Bites the Dust

Silverbell Shores

Now and Then

Co-Write with Zoey Drake

Dirty Monsters

Christmas Freebie

Manny Christmas